In the Shadow of a Truth

A Collection of Fareview Fairytale Novellas

Book 4

By Maci Aurora

In the Shadow of a Wish, book 1

In the Shadow of a Hoax, book 2

In the Shadow of a Dream, book 3

In the Shadow of the Truth—the Novellas, Book 4

In the Shadow of a Vow, book 4.1

In the Shadow of an Obsession, Book 5

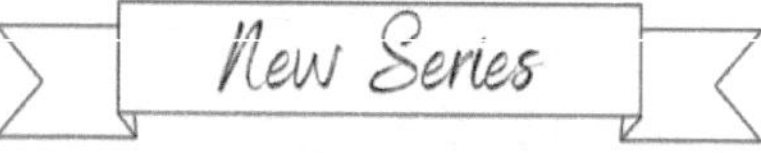

The Accidental Seraph, Carran Hollow Fated-Mates book 1

The Ring Academy: The Trials of Imogene Sol

The Messy Truth About Love

The Stories Stars Tell

In the Echo of this Ghost Town

When the Echo Answers

The Letters She Left Behind

In the Shadow of the Shadow of the Truth

A Collection of
Fareview Fairytale Novellas
Book 4

By Maci Aurora

Mixed Plate Press
Honolulu, Hawaii

In the Shadow of the Truth
Fareview Fairytale Book 4
©2024 Maci Aurora w/ Mixed Plate Press
Honolulu, Hawaii

cover art: Sara Oliver Designs

ISBN: 979-8-9891543-2-6 (paperback)
ISBN:979-8-9891543-3-3 (eBook)
Vow ISBN: 979-8-9891543-4-0 (eBook)

About this book: *In the Shadow of the Truth* was inspired by a mash up of Grimm's Fairytales, "The Princess in Disguise," "Tom Thumb," "The Robber Bridegroom," and "Maid Maleen.". It contains explicit sexual situations and is intended for mature audiences (18+).

DEDICATED TO

My husband.

In the Shadow of a Vow

A Fareview Fairytale Novella

Book 4.1

By Maci Aurora

Scarlett

Scarlett Fareview, mother to Jessamine, Tarley, Brinna, Aurielle, and Mattias, wife to Tomas, and runaway daughter to the Mad King Zollah Cumbria and Queen Alea Cumbria of Echo Landing, had failed. Sitting near the fire with a blanket wrapped around her shoulders, she watched as others in the cottage spoke, could hear their voices, but nothing coherent penetrated the haze that consumed her.

Her second born, Tarley, wrapped up in her husband Lachlan's embrace, stared unseeing. Brinna, third in the order of her children, had her hand in Auri's, her fourth. The youngest, Mattias, stood, his arms across his chest, looking like the man he'd become while they'd been sleeping, talking to the gods, Nixus and his brother, Lucian a few paces away.

And Jessamine, her first born was missing.

A sob ripped through Scarlett's throat, and she caught the sound with her hand pressed against her mouth.

She'd failed.

She looked for her constant companion—the love of her life—and found him staring unseeing into the fire across from her. Tears filled her eyes, and his form blurred. She shouldn't cry, knew she didn't deserve the pity rising in her heart like a raging sea, but the flood came anyway.

"I'm sorry," she whispered. "I thought–"

Tomas turned his head, his forest eyes finding hers—but for the first time since she'd know him, they were empty, as if his soul had been scooped out and discarded. He didn't smile. He'd always been the one to smile, no matter the circumstances. He was the one who saw the world in rose, painted any situation with positivity.

Now, he looked at her with hollow eyes, opening his mouth to say something but didn't, turning back to the fire once more.

Her heart cracked open, leaking out the substance that made her who she was.

A commotion at the door grabbed her attention, along with everyone else in the cottage.

"Your highness." A soldier stood in the doorway. He was tall and lean, his face pressed from granite. His features were sharp, his green eyes bright and his wheat hair short.

On his chest, he wore the leather breastplate stamped with the tree of Jast, a short sword strapped to his back.

Tarley's husband, the Crown Prince of Jast, stepped forward. "Jude."

The man ducked his head in deference.

It reminded Scarlett of a life before. Before her mother had died. The irony wasn't lost to Scarlett. No one knew her children were of royal blood, and they were also godblood descended from gods on her mother's side. She'd concealed those facts to hide them, but now that was over.

Jessamine was missing.

Scarlett knew who had her daughter, but how to find him was another matter. She didn't even know where to begin. The witch in the woods, perhaps, but the last time they had met, when Scarlett had insisted on the sleeping spell in spite of the witch's wisdom to forge a different path, the witch had said it was the last time they would speak.

"Where?" Lachlan said, his tone loud enough to capture Scarlett's attention once more.

"He left," the soldier named Jude said, looking over his shoulder, then back.

"Johesha left? His post?"

"He handed me this" –Jude handed whatever it was to Lachlan– "and said he'd be back."

Lachlan frowned. "I don't understand."

"There was someone in the hedge when it...

disappeared," Jude said.

Scarlett stood, her heart thumping painfully.

"The stranger was carrying... someone, and Johesha said he was going after her."

"Jessamine," Scarlett said and every face in the room swiveled to her. "He has Jessamine."

Emotions flashed across their faces: anger, frustration, hurt, dismissal. She couldn't blame them. She'd known this would be the case, even if her intentions had been to protect them.

She'd failed.

Baba told you it was a house built of cards.

"*He* who?" Mattias shouted. "Tell the truth. I'm fucking sick of your lies."

He was seething, shocking Scarlett. Her son, who'd always been like his father, was genial and slow to anger, but the rage in his eyes was like a living creature, breathing fire.

Scarlett looked down at the floor.

"Mattias," Tomas said, his voice a warning.

"She drugged us," Auri snapped. "She deserves our anger, Father."

Tomas didn't argue. Frankly, neither could Scarlett.

"Who is *he*?" Mattias asked.

The layers of spells had been broken. There were no ribbons, no hedge, no sleeping spell. Scarlett stood before her family and their loved ones completely exposed for the first time in the 28 years since she and Tomas had disappeared behind the hedge.

Now, with nothing to hide behind, no spell to determine what she shared, there was no reason to conceal the truth any longer but for the pain it would cause her to relive it.

"I don't know his true name," she said, turning back to her children.

Jessamine was missing.

"True name?"

"Your given name. Like mine–" But her throat closed around the words, and she wished Tomas was standing beside her, giving her strength.

But he had been, hadn't he. The entire time. He'd been the strong one all along and she'd failed to listen to him, failed to honor his strength and belief in her. Failed to trust his wisdom.

She tried again to say her true name, but she hadn't uttered those sounds for a lifetime, had tried to forget they existed. Her true name was attached to a promise stripped away by pain and prevarication.

"Wait. It's not–" Tarley frowned.

"Your name is Scarlett," Auri said.

Brinna—her dreamer—was silent, but Scarlett noticed when her daughter's gaze sought the golden god's.

Swallowing the sounds that cut like glass, she sighed,

dug deeper for her own strength, and finally uttered the curse. "Azleah. My real name."

Brinna, sweet Brinna, burst into tears and turned into the golden god's—Lucian's—arms.

Scarlett didn't understand Brianna's reaction.

Lucian's gaze rose to meet Scarlett's. She wasn't sure how to decipher his look, but she felt supported somehow.

"But why?" Auri sank to the bench near the table. Alone.

Scarlett's eyes jumped to Nixus, the dark god, waiting for him to move to Auri's side. They'd expressed their intention to exchange vows with one another, but he remained where he was, his eyes on her daughter, but changed, somehow removed. This wasn't how they'd been, before...

Something was wrong.

Scarlett sank back into her chair. "It's time I tell you the story." She paused as the words stuck like broken glass in her throat once more. "But it isn't an easy story to hear," she said, spitting them out as her chin quivered. "I know it's past time you knew it."

Then she began...

Once upon a time . . .

Azleah Cumbria, first and only daughter of Zollah Cumbria, king of Echo Landing, and his late wife, Alea, knelt at the death mound of her mother. She'd visited nearly every day for the last three years, since her mother's untimely passing, if only to find comfort in what once was rather than what it had become since her mother had returned to the stars.

The steep peaks of the mountains tipped with snow rose around them in the valley of the dead. Mounds much like her mother's, a testament to the royal Cumbria line, dotted the landscape, though her mother's was the most recent. The white blossoms of the lox heather covered the mound, and for that Azleah was grateful. Something beautiful to give her a moment of peace and hope. Moisture seeped through the fabric of her wool dress as a stiff wind whipped at her braid, grabbing hold of her red tresses and pulling them from the plait. Both reminded her that peace was temporary.

"Mistress?" her companion said quietly from behind her, though Azleah could hear the distress in Nettle's tone.

Azleah didn't answer, offering a prayer instead to the gods that they might take mercy on her. "Please," she whispered. "Mother. He's not himself anymore. I don't know what to do."

But the gods remained silent.

"They're coming!" Nettle's fear rang out in her whispered warning.

Nettle's hand slid into Azleah's, her grip tight, but still Azleah didn't move. She held her friend's hand, head bowed, and continued to beg the gods for their mercy, hoping that at her mother's graveside somehow, she would be saved. That maybe her estranged grandparents—gods of fabled Elysian—might even hear her prayer.

Still she prayed, even as the sound of heavy footsteps in the sod surrounded them. It wasn't until she heard Hale Commander Arn's "Princess" that she looked up.

She'd considered running, but there wasn't anywhere to go. There wasn't a soul in this godsforsaken kingdom that would harbor her from the mad king. The palace guard—seven of them—surrounded her and Nettle, an enclosed circle around the girls and the mound of her mother's bones. Each man stood at attention in their royal regalia—leather and buckles, bracers and breastplates, swords and daggers—waiting for the order to seize her. It wouldn't matter where she ran. They would find her.

Azleah stood, Nettle's hand still in hers. She straightened her spine and lifted her chin, looking at Hale Commander Arn. "You know this is wrong," she said, feeling so much older than her sixteen years.

"He's my king."

"And he is not right. Not since–" Her eyes slid to the grave. Nothing had been right since her mother had died. "You know this."

"I made a vow." Hale Arn's eyes slid away, dragging guilt with them.

"To uphold the honor of the throne," she said. "There's no honor in this."

He didn't respond, didn't look at her, his gaze elsewhere.

Nettle's grip tightened. "He's coming," she whispered.

Azleah looked from the Hale Commander's pale face and followed Nettle's gaze to watch her father walk through the swaying grass toward her, framed by the massive stone castle behind him. He was dressed strangely in the thick, full-length fur robes layered with chains of gold he'd taken to wearing, uncharacteristic of the man she'd once known. His hair, which had been a dark brown threaded with copper, had turned white over the last three years. It was too long over his shoulders and in need of washing. His beard was scraggly and drooped down his chest. The worst change, she knew, would be the moment she met his gaze. His once deep gray eyes had changed color, now a disconcerting blue blasted with striations of red and rimmed with a ring of bright copper. He had the manic twitch of a man invested in too many mind-altering petals.

Nettle dropped to her knees, and the soldiers of the guard dropped their gazes.

Azleah remained where she was, the wind whipping her dark blue dress around her legs.

"Lord Father," she greeted him, dipping her chin to her chest in acknowledgement of his place as king for just a moment before looking up, hopeful he'd changed his mind.

That something, anything, a miracle had intervened on her behalf. That the crazed look would suddenly be cleared from his vision.

The Mad King stopped an arm's length away, his awful witch—the horrible reason for his dabbling in necromancy—several steps behind him. Her father had once been called Zollah the Benevolent with Azleah's mother at his side. While Azleah understood the stripping effects of grief, it had broken and torn away who he'd once been and had formed him into what he'd become: a man succumbed to the darkness of malignant magic, leaching anything that was once good from him.

"Alea." He dipped his head, the crown of bones looking like spikes in his white hair.

"I'm Azleah," she said. "Your daughter." Her hand drifted out, gesturing to the grave mound. "Mother is there."

He didn't look, his awful eyes fixed on her, and instead took another step closer. "You're returning to me," he said and smiled. He reached out and slid a finger over her cheek.

Tears filled Azleah's eyes. Memories of the father she loved stayed with her. When she was little, when Mother had still been alive, he'd been everything a father should be: kind, protective, patient. He'd held her hand as they'd walked through the gardens. He'd taught her to swim when they'd visited the sea. He'd read her stories and patiently waited with a smile on his handsome face while she told him her own stories. He'd offered wisdom when she'd been frustrated and hugs when she'd been hurt. He'd loved her and her mother with absolute conviction.

This man, filled with grief and rage and dark magic, wasn't the man she'd known. Not anymore.

Not only had she lost her mother, but her father as well.

She couldn't contain her sob, stifling it with her hand

before pleading, "Father. Please. I'm not Mother." She turned her head and looked at the guards. "Please," she begged. "Help me."

But instead of intervening, their gazes drifted away.

Her father's worshipful gaze jumped from her to look at each of the guards with accusation and mistrust. "They want you for themselves." The words dripped from his tongue with malice. "They want to steal you away from me." He snatched her hand and yanked her after him as he stalked back over the grassy plateau of Remembrance Valley toward the castle. "This is for the best."

"No." She pulled, but he adjusted his grip, reeling her closer.

Nettle kept hold of Azleah's other hand and jerked to her feet, following behind.

"Alea, your reincarnation isn't complete," he rambled. "The witch says I must keep you safe until then. Keep you from someone who might want to steal you away from me."

"Father!" she screamed. "Stop!"

"Then we'll marry. And everything will return to how it was."

"Stop, Father. Stop!"

But he didn't listen, dragging her through the wooden door of the palace. He drew her through the hallways, servants dropping to their knees as they passed. Their eyes lifted to watch the procession, to listen to his ramblings and her begging through her tears, their heads following as they passed. No one intervened. The guards had fallen in behind them, their quick steps smacking against the stone.

"The tower is the safest," the king was saying. "Witch and I have made it safe. You'll see. And then when we marry—when your change is complete—all will be well. I promise."

"Father!" She fought his hold, but his physical strength was uncompromising even if his mental capacity had faded. "I'm not her. She's gone. Dead. Mother hasn't come back."

Her pleas fell on uncompromising ears.

When they reached the new tower door, Azleah fought, jerking backward.

Her father's grip tightened. "Witch said you would fight, but it is only because you don't understand what's happening to you. You're lost in the remaking," he said. "Trust me."

Nettle's grip slipped from Azleah's.

Azleah turned her head, frantically searching for her companion. "Nettle? Nettle! Don't leave me!"

But the guards restrained her best friend, her only companion. Though Nettle fought through tears and protests, she wasn't a match.

The king forced Azleah, fighting and screaming, through the arched doorway into an alcove at the base of a set of spiral stairs. Still, she fought, her nails breaking against the stone, the wood, but it was useless.

"Two more years," her father said. "Then you'll be yourself, and we can be together."

He shut the door between them, and the sound of a key sliding into the mechanism clicked. Final.

A dark gold light flashed over the wooden door before blinking out and trapping Azleah inside.

From beyond, she could hear Nettle's cries matching her own, fading as she was taken away.

Pressing her palms to the door, the warmth of its magic leaching into her skin, Azleah leaned her forehead against the wood, then drew back and pounded it with her fists. "Let me out," she cried, then shrieked. "Let me out!"

Over and over she called until she was hoarse from screaming, until there was no sound on the other side of the door but the echo of her cries matching the echo in her heart.

Time passed, and Azleah was alone. The days stretched into weeks, into months, toward a year, broken only by the rising and setting sun. Though her father, in his madness, had constructed the tower room to offer comfort and diversions, Azleah struggled between the bed and a single chair that faced the small window barely bigger than her head, too small to crawl out and face a death she would have welcomed over her proposed future as the bride of her own father. She'd considered it but didn't have the means. The tower's enchantments prevented it.

She was permitted two visitors: a single lady's maid, who came each morning, and her father's trusted witch, who visited in the evening. Azleah trusted neither woman and so spoke little, sure that whatever she might say would be reported to her father.

The maid, whose name Azleah hadn't even been given, said nothing and took great care never to meet Azleah's eyes. Every morning, she climbed the stairs with Azleah's breakfast and announced like clockwork, "Your bath has been drawn, Princess." Azleah would descend the stairs for the bath awaiting her in the alcove by the locked door, and while she bathed the maid replaced her soiled clothing and bedding with clean linens. Then Azleah would climb the spiral stairs back up into the tower, and once back in her prison, the maid left.

The witch would arrive every evening, bringing Azleah dinner, but unlike the maid, the witch lingered, talking and telling her about the kingdom. "The festival in the village burned your father in effigy," she'd said one day, or "I can empathize with your plight, my dear." While Azleah was curious about what was happening in her kingdom, she had very little inclination to engage with her father's witch and only spoke to her once that first year.

"How is Nettle?" she'd asked early in her confinement. She'd been staring out that single window as the sun set casting the landscape beyond in golden relief.

"What is a Nettle?" the witch had asked.

At that, Azleah had turned her head and truly looked at

the witch for the first time. The woman was tall and thin, and while she wouldn't be called beautiful, her appearance wasn't hideous as Azleah had assumed, her features sharp and angular. Her dark hair was thick and full, reaching down her back and drawn away from her face by a sparkling fastener. She wore a dark robe over her clothes and sat in one of the chairs at the table where she set Azleah's dinner each evening.

Azleah turned back to the window. "My best friend."

The witch made a noise that stretched out from her nose, and that was all that had been said.

The next evening, the witch returned with Azleah's meal. "Hale Crue—your guard—says your Nettle has fled the palace. Not much of a best friend."

Azleah, staring out the window, didn't flinch at the news, hopeful it was true rather than a lie hiding that Nettle was dead.

More time passed, and Azleah was alone. The days continued to march on, broken only by the rising and setting sun. When Azleah opened her eyes the first morning of her seventeenth year, she cried. She was one year closer to the impending doom of her eighteenth, when she would walk from the tower dressed as a bride to marry her father.

Days passed, and Azleah stopped eating.

The witch became more insistent.

"Why aren't you eating? Your breakfast tray is full when

I retrieve it, and the maid has reported removing your dinner with most of the food still on the tray."

Azleah ignored her, as usual.

"You won't be able to fight."

It was a ludicrous statement. Azleah scoffed, wondering what it was the witch suggested she fight. Her father? His guards? Her? The damn witch was his agent.

"So you do hear me," the witch said. "What do you lose by speaking with me?"

When Azleah remained silent, the witch sighed, stood, and walked across the room to where Azleah sat. Standing next to her, the witch slid a rolled bit of parchment into Azleah's line of sight. The small roll stood out against the dark stone of the tower. It was tied together with a tiny thread of twine.

Azleah refused to give anything to the witch. Not a look, not a flinch, not a word or a sound, even though the tap of the witch's sharp, dark nails against the roll seemed to suggest she wanted one.

When Azleah didn't move, the witch finally said, "Eating will keep your strength up."

"Have you poisoned it?"

"Why would I do that? I need you alive."

"Maybe it would be a mercy," Azleah said and looked up into the witch's shrewd face.

"But that wouldn't serve the right purpose," the witch

said and leaned down to meet Azleah's gaze. Her eyes were as dark as the rest of her. "It's your kingdom, too." Then the witch left the room.

Azleah listened to the witch's steps retreat down the spiral stairs, waited for the sound of the door, then reached for the parchment. She pulled off the string, unrolled it, and read the handwritten words:

His mind is lost. It's time to get you out.

She didn't want the hope that unfurled in her chest and looked over her shoulder at the empty doorway to the stairwell.

Still, hope fluttered with curiosity and possibility. Was the witch offering her help? Azleah stood and walked to the table where her dinner waited. She looked at it, smelled it, then sat and ate.

The next day passed the same but brought with it a new note:

The people are with you.

Azleah ate her dinner and walked the stairs an extra time. She stood at the doorway, listening. "Hello?" she said.

Silence answered, but then there was a shuffle of feet beyond the door.

The next day brought another note:

Nettle is in Mercy Row, serving the House Bicus. She's safe.

Azleah ate her food and walked the stairs, stopping at

the door once more. "Hello?" she said.

This time, someone on the other side knocked. Azleah went to sleep with hope hot and bright inside her.

When the witch arrived the next day, Azleah wasn't sitting at the window, she was facing the door, waiting. She watched the witch hesitate upon entering the room, then walk to the table with Azleah's dinner. Instead of sitting as she usually did, the witch faced her. "You look better."

"Who is writing the notes you're delivering?"

The witch looked over her shoulder, a hesitation, then turned back to Azleah. "I shouldn't say, princess."

"Why would you deliver them, then?"

The witch stepped around the table. "Because you are our hope."

"From what?"

"Him."

"Yet I've been left locked in this tower."

"There's a spell," the witch started, "on the castle. Few know, those that do aren't... able to defy your father... and the rest forget. Nettle forgot the moment she left the castle."

"You cast it."

The witch nodded.

"You can undo it."

"Not without consequences. It's better to make a way forward than attempt to remake the past."

"And why should I trust anything you tell me, Witch?

It's your fault we've descended this far into hell. It was you who took him on the dark path of necromancy."

"I only wished to ease his grief, but the path he's forged is of his own doing."

"But you've aided him."

The witch hesitated, then nodded, lowering her eyes. "I cannot change what has already been done, but I can choose a different path to modify the future. I wish to help you, and I'm the only one who can."

"Convenient. And why should I believe you?"

"Because I'm not offering out of kindness." Her dark eyes met Azleah's, and they were filled with hunger. "You have something I want."

Incredulous, Azleah looked around her prison room. "What could I possibly have that you want?"

The witch took a step away and dipped her head. "I promise to reveal it, Princess, but my divination informs me it isn't time."

"And when is it time?" Azleah shouted. "The last I checked, I have less than a year before I'm forced to be a bride for... for my father." She nearly gagged on the words. "He thinks I'm my reincarnated mother. And *that* is your fault."

The witch didn't look up, remaining where she was with her head bowed. "Allow me to prove my worth, Your

Highness, and after I do, then, and only then, will I make my request."

"And how much time do you need?"

"For you, it will feel like an eternity," the witch hedged.

Azleah laughed, but there was no joy in it. "Of course. Convenient."

"I promise you, I will prove my worth."

Azleah studied the witch. She'd waited over a year and had nothing to lose by waiting another day, a week, a month. She could only hang onto the hope coursing through her veins. And if the witch failed, freedom would mean either her death or her father's. Either way, only one of them could remain alive. So she agreed.

The witch looked up and smiled as she backed away. "First" –she looked at the food– "regain your strength." Then she turned and left the tower.

Azleah ate and did her turns on the stairs, stopping at the door each time to call out, "Hello?" On the third turn, she asked, "Hello? Is anyone there?"

"Princess?" a man's voice asked from the other side of the door.

"Who are you?"

"Hale Crue," the voice replied, and Azleah recalled the name of the guard the witch had mentioned. "Your Highness, are you unwell? Do you need help? I cannot open the door."

"I am as good as can be expected, I suppose, and that is alright. Hearing another voice is nice," she said.

"Would you like to... talk?"

"I would."

"I can do that."

Azleah smiled from her side of the door. She wondered what he looked like and imagined him with dark hair and green eyes. Was he tall?

"Did the witch give you my message?" he asked.

Azleah tilted her head, looking at the grain of the door with the sheen of the spell cast over it. "You gave me a message?"

"Yes, Your Highness. I found Lady Nettle for you. She is safe."

"Oh. That was you?" She smiled and pressed her finger to a knot in the wooden door. "Yes. I received it. Thank you for giving me that peace."

"It is my duty."

She wanted to tell him to let her out—that was his duty—but knew it was futile. Between the spells and the magic lock, she wasn't sure why he needed to be out there anyway. "How do you remember it's me? The witch said–"

"I am one of the few who remember."

"Is there no way to get me out?"

"I'm afraid not, but should there ever be a moment when I can storm the tower and bring you to safety, you have my word, Princess, I will do it."

Azleah's heart trembled in her chest at his words and the vehemence with which he conveyed them. "Thank you, Hale Crue." She pressed a hand to the door.

"Don't thank me. I was there the day you were locked in," he said quietly, then fell silent on the other side of the door.

Silence descended on her side as well, shocked as she was by his admission.

"Are you still there?" he asked.

She reached for indignation and anger, but it didn't surge. Instead, she sighed, resigned to the circumstances that had victimized them all. "Yes. And there wasn't anything you could have done. Not alone."

"I wish that wasn't so, but I carry this guilt because I didn't do anything." He was silent, then, before asking, "Would you still like to talk?"

"Yes," she answered. "I would like that very much."

She slid down to the stone floor and sat with her back against the door as she and Hale Crue spoke well into the night. She learned he'd been in the palace guard since he turned sixteen, and now he was twenty-one. That to join, he'd had to leave his family and forsake them for the crown. That he wasn't allowed to marry as a palace guard, but when he was ready, he could be reassigned to the city guard ranks.

"Is there a special someone?" she'd asked.

"No, Your Highness," he'd answered. "There is no one."

All the next day, Azleah replayed the conversation in her head. When the witch arrived with her dinner, she delivered another note with her meal. The witch didn't speak but offered Azleah a slight smile and a nod before leaving.

As soon as the witch was done, Azleah tore open the message:

Dear Princess,

Thank you for speaking with me last night. I know it is too forward to speak of such things, especially considering the vast chasm between our circumstances, but I found myself hopeful and my mind replaying our conversation. Is it too much to look forward to speaking with you again?

Hale Crue

Azleah's heart kicked up the strongest rhythm she'd felt in her breast in a long time, and she was unable to keep the smile from her face.

That night, she knocked on the door. "Hale Crue?"

"Your Highness," he answered.

She could hear his smile.

There was timidity between them initially, but eventually, as midnight approached, they fell into a familiar rhythm of conversation.

And so it went, night after night. Day after day. The maid. The Witch and her messages. Conversations with her guard, Crue.

"What would you do?" Crue asked after weeks of speaking with one another. "If you could get out?"

"Claim my kingdom," she said.

"And your father?"

She didn't say she would kill him—couldn't bring herself to admit it, for some reason—so she said, "He would be treated justly. But I can't do it without supporters."

Crue was quiet for some time.

"Are you still there?" she asked.

"I will get them." His voice was barely perceptible from the other side of the door. "Supporters."

"How?" she asked. "The witch said there's a spell."

"We need to break it, then."

"It can't be done. Not without the witch."

"Then you need to do everything you can to get her to do your bidding, Your Highness."

Azleah knew he was right. It was time to demand answers.

"I want answers, Witch," Azleah demanded the following night. After speaking with Crue, she'd spent the day ruminating on her circumstances. Despite everything stacked against her, she needed to take charge somehow. She refused to wait for the Mad King to determine her fate.

The witch hesitated at the opening to the stairwell, obviously surprised by Azleah's greeting, then regained her composure. "What sorts of answers?" She slid the tray across the round table. "There are many questions."

Azleah descended from the dais where her bed was located to where the witch stood at the tableside. "You are playing a game, somehow–"

"No game." The witch set down a rolled parchment message.

Azleah's gaze jumped to the message, greedy for it. The witch noticed, her eyes glittering with an unfamiliar gleam. Azleah didn't trust the witch, but she also knew the witch was her only way out. "What is it you want?"

The witch pulled a chair and sat. "The bones determined today isn't the day to tell you. You don't trust me yet."

"I will never trust you."

"And that will never modify the future." The witch plucked at something on the sleeve of her dark dress. "Allow me to offer a gesture of goodwill and intention."

Azleah narrowed her eyes. "Goodwill? Let me out."

The witch sighed. "As I have previously said, Princess, there are spells already cast that are unable to be broken without sacrifice. Hence consulting the bones." She gestured to emphasize her words.

"Sacrifice? What kind?"

"The death kind."

"So kill him."

"You assume whose death would be required. Perhaps if you knew, you wouldn't wish it."

"The king's?"

"No. Not his, or mine." The witch's eyes revealed the truth, a look leveled upon Azleah that she couldn't hide from.

"Mine."

The witch gave a single nod. "Timing is everything. Ask for something else."

Besides being released, there was only one thing she could think to want that was within the witch's power. "Allow Hale Crue into the tower."

The witch's eyebrows rose over her dark eyes.

"It's not what you're thinking," Azleah said quickly.

The witch smirked. "My thoughts are irrelevant. What is relevant is your father finding out."

"Don't call him that," Azleah said, spinning away from the witch and stalking to the window. "My true father is dead, and you've left a monster in his skin." She turned her head and studied the witch. "If you want to offer a gesture to gain my trust, this is the compromise. Only you and the Mad King can open the door, but you can open it for the guard to enter."

The witch stood looking down at the parchment, then looked back at Azleah and nodded. "Fine. Ten minutes."

"Tonight?"

The witch nodded. "Look for Hale Crue in an hour." Then she left.

Once again waiting till she was gone, Azleah rushed to the table and unrolled the parchment with impatience.

Dear Princess,

You asked me weeks ago if there was someone who'd captured my attention. I truthfully replied, no. Now, however, I find my concentration wanes during the day. I recall our conversations, the sounds, the words, pondering the nuance of what you've said and wondering if I might be making more meaning than I should. I imagine your smile. Then I chastise myself for it, because I'm but a palace guard and you are a princess. And perhaps I could earn your favor by freeing you, but I am unable to do even that. I imagine finding a way to rescue you. As I dream up possibilities, I find myself scolded by my superiors. So I renew my focus to not be removed from my detail, which would end my favorite time of the day and my ability to speak with you. You, dear princess, have captured my attention. I am filled with presumption—sharing this with you—but I find I cannot fulfill my duty with the unanswered question hanging over me. I know not your feelings, which I should think are not reciprocated, but if they are, you will make me the happiest of men.
Yours,
Crue

Azleah pressed the parchment to her heart and smiled. Then she spun in place, feeling the hope that had been born inside her weeks ago finally take flight. Too excited to eat, she moved restlessly about the confining room, putting things in order, brushing and re-plaiting her hair, then leaving it loose. Unsure where to wait, she paced, trying several different locations, testing what to do with her hands, her nerves fluttering in her stomach and heart.

In the end, she miscalculated the hour, because suddenly he was clearing his throat, and she was whirling in place to face him.

Crue stood in the doorway.

Her breath caught. "It's you." The words came out with the breath she'd momentarily lost.

He was beautiful. Tall, muscular in his uniform. Instead of brown hair, as she'd imagined, his was raven black, the tips of which brushed the top of his shoulders, though he'd tied the top back to keep it out of his eyes. And his eyes weren't green but intensely brown, so dark they appeared black, framed with thick brows. His jaw was square and clean-shaven, highlighting the beauty of the contours of his face. Her eyes dipped to his even mouth, his full lips curving up as he smiled.

"You are..." His words faded, then he dipped his head. "Your Highness."

"Not Your Highness, please. Not with you," she said. "Just Azleah."

He tipped his head slightly, his eyes lifting to her face.

Her heart raced in her chest. "Where's the witch?" she asked, trying to find something they could speak about to chase away the awkwardness between them.

He cleared his throat and straightened. "Waiting. We only have a few minutes." His eyes scanned her face, then her body before he met her gaze again. "Gods, you're beautiful." He clamped his mouth shut and shook his head. "Forgive my impertinence."

His words fluttered her heartbeat and, combined with the weeks upon weeks of speaking with him through the door, she could hardly speak. She wrung her hands together at her waist and blurted, "I got your message," holding up the parchment.

His cheeks darkened before his eyes fell, and he swiped a hand over his face. Then he moved, his leathers creaking, the ceremonial sword tapping against his thigh. "You think I'm a fool."

She took a step closer, shaking her head. "No."

He didn't lift his head, but his eyes met hers once more. Then he straightened and stepped toward her.

"I..." She paused, nervous and afraid, for she'd never felt the riot of sensations driving through her just then and wasn't sure how to interpret them, how to communicate them. If she even should. Only Crue had shared how he was feeling, so she sought that bravery. "I feel... so much. I feel... the same." Her cheeks heated at the admission, afraid that somehow, she'd been mistaken.

He took another step forward, his eyebrows arching high over his beautiful eyes. "You do?" His shocked grin filled her lungs.

She took another step toward him. "I can't sleep. Can't eat."

He moved closer. "Can't think. Can't concentrate."

"For thinking of you."

And suddenly he was there, standing in front of her, close enough to touch. His head tipped down to look at her, while hers tilted up.

"What are we to do?" she asked.

Crue reached out as if to touch her, but then stopped, awaiting her permission.

Azleah leaned toward his outstretched hand and closed her eyes when his calloused skin touched her cheek. It had been so long since anyone had chosen to touch her, and even longer since it had been someone she cared for, though this was the first time anyone had touched her for whom she felt attraction.

When she opened her eyes, she saw he was studying her.

"This," he whispered.

Her heart expanded, making room for this person who'd been the first in so long to show her anything akin to affection, to love. She was starving for it.

Crue smiled, then pulled away, looking over his shoulder at a sound coming from the bottom of the stairs. When he turned back around, he retreated, but grabbed hold of her hand. "I have to go." With a squeeze, he backed toward the stairwell.

"I'll follow you," she said, "and then we can speak through the door."

He nodded and released her hand. "Wait. For the witch to leave." Then he disappeared around the stone curve. She listened to his steps growing fainter the further he descended the spiral stairs. That short time would never be enough with him.

By the time Azleah followed and pressed her palms to the door, feeling that familiar magic with its strange bite through her skin, she felt out of breath. It wasn't from her rush down the stairs but rather all the feelings she'd stored up for Crue.

"Are you there?"

"I am," he answered.

Azleah smiled and made herself comfortable on the floor as she had so many nights before, her body filled with more joy than she'd felt in as long as she could remember.

The next evening, and the next, and the next, the witch gave them time to be together. On the fifth, Crue asked to kiss her. Azleah allowed it, her heart beating like a drum inside her chest. When the witch gave them more time, they didn't waste it talking, since that could be done between the doors. Rather, there was more kissing, touching, and not enough connection.

The fourteenth evening after first meeting Crue face-to-face, the witch arrived and left dinner as usual—along with a small pouch.

"What is that?" Azleah asked, picking it up between two fingers.

The witch watched her. "Herbs. You need to drink it with your tea."

"Why?"

The witch leveled her dark gaze on Azleah. "To prevent pregnancy, Your Highness."

Shocked, Azleah sucked in a breath, though it would have been a lie to say she and Crue hadn't crossed several lines. "Oh."

"Should you require it." The witch turned to leave.

"How do you know?" It was strange to ask this of one of the parties responsible for her imprisonment, only Azleah didn't have anyone else to confide in.

The witch stopped and looked at Azleah over her shoulder.

Azleah took a step. "How do you know if you're ready for... that?" She had given it some thought—it was difficult not to think about the ways Crue made her feel when she was with him.

"Only you can answer that question," the witch replied and disappeared into the stairwell.

Azleah weighed the possibilities in her mind, unsure of herself but feeling in her heart of hearts that what she felt for Crue was real. Despite that feeling, by the time he appeared, she hesitated, though their last several meetings had been an instant meeting of hands and mouths.

"What is it?" he asked.

"What are we doing?"

Crue stepped closer and gathered her in his arms. She loved how safe she felt surrounded by his strength. "Being together—any way we can."

"I don't feel like this is me getting out of here." She stepped from his embrace.

"Why am I here?" he asked.

"Because I asked it of her."

"Why?"

"This allowance is a gesture of her goodwill on her part, so that I will trust her."

"Do you?"

Azleah's gaze slipped to the pouch and the tea she'd finished. When she looked at Crue, her heart expanded inside her chest. "I think I am beginning to."

He smiled. "That's a start."

She walked back to him and reached to unbuckle his sword belt.

Crue grasped her face between his calloused palms and kissed her as his sword fell to the floor, followed by another belt.

"Is this what we're doing?" he asked.

"Yes," she whispered into his mouth. "This is what I want. With you."

The appearance of the witch at midday was out of the ordinary. Azleah started from the book she was reading, jumping to her feet. "What are you doing here?"

The witch glanced over her shoulder; her dark eyes harried as she entered the room. The Mad King arrived on her heels.

"Oh," he breathed. The stairs had clearly exhausted him. A smile broke out on his unfamiliar face. "Alea."

"Azleah," she replied, shocked at the changes in him. Before, he had looked worn. Now he looked like a shade of himself. His skin was nearly transparent and loose as it hung from his bones. His hair was a shock of white, unkept and long like his beard, which had grown even longer. He frightened her.

He either didn't hear her or ignored her. "The witch has assured me you are well, but I wouldn't be deterred. I needed to see you for myself. It has been much too long."

Azleah's gaze jumped to the witch, who wasn't looking at her. She'd kept the Mad King away?

"I could forgo seeing you forever," Azleah replied.

His disconcerting eyes narrowed. "Witch?"

"My king?"

"My Alea doesn't speak to me so." His gaze shifted from Azleah to the witch. "What magic is this?"

"I have suggested you refrain from visiting, sire. The magic requires time," she explained, and though Azleah didn't know the witch well, she could see the annoyance in her countenance, in the taut way she said the words.

The Mad King's eyes flicked from the witch back to Azleah. "Is it working?"

"No," Azleah said.

"Yes," the witch said at the same time, narrowing her eyes at Azleah—a warning, it seemed, to play along. "Yes, Your Majesty. And it will take the remaining time to mature." The witch silenced Azleah's protest with a look. "But your visitation slows things–"

Azleah couldn't believe what she was hearing.

The witch was helping her. Just like she'd said.

"Then for what purpose is there to wait?" The king asked, stepping further into the tower room.

Azleah shrank back.

The witch shifted, moving to stand between Azleah and the king. "Sire. You want your true Alea, yes?"

A stranger's eyes—horrifying orbs of unnatural color—sought Azleah's, then cut back to the witch between them.

"Sire?" the witch prompted.

"Yes." He nodded. "Yes."

"Then you must allow the magic to work."

As one would with a small child, the witch turned him, grabbing hold of his arm and steering him back to the doorway and down the stairs. Azleah listened to them speak, though it was the hum of indecipherable sound rather than discernible conversation.

Her heart racing in her chest, she couldn't return to reading. Instead, she took the stairs and knocked on the door.

"Crue?"

"Who's there?" a stranger's voice asked.

Azleah fled up the stairs and crawled into her bed, filled with terror that exploded from her in sobs and tears. When a light touch landed on her back, she flinched and turned.

"Shhh." The witch sat on the side of the bed, her hands now in her lap. "I've calmed him and consulted the bones. It isn't time to go, but I think we need some added precautions to protect you. I'd like to give you some magic to wield."

Azleah sat up. "What kind of magic?"

"Prophecy Augur," she said. "To prevent something like today. You will see him coming before he comes to you. It will protect you from him."

"You can't do that already?"

She shook her head. "I can use my smooth tongue to soothe him—as you saw—but he's getting more erratic."

"And why don't we just do what we need to do to get me out, then?"

"Because the bones suggest that if we do it before the designated time, we fail."

"And I will not become like... him? By taking this magic?"

The witch shook her head.

"Fine. I will accept this gift."

"I will touch you," the witch said and lifted her hand, waiting.

When Azleah bent her head, the witch's hands— startingly soft—slid along the skin of her cheek, her fingers smoothing a lock of her hair from her face and tucking it behind Azleah's ear. Chills danced over her flesh— confusing—because she had felt it only once before with Crue. When Azleah raised her eyes to the witch, the woman's face hadn't changed but for her dark eyes, somehow darker.

The witch spoke words Azleah didn't recognize, and that chill on her head changed into a spike of brilliant heat settling deep into her body. Then it was gone as quickly as it had come.

"There," the witch said and drew back.

"How will I know if it worked?" Azleah asked.

"It will work. Concentrate on what you want to know, the magic should reveal those truths to you." The witch stood and retreated to the doorway.

"Will Crue come?"

The witch looked over her shoulder and nodded. "Same time."

Later, Azleah and Crue lay in her bed having just found comfort in one another's bodies. She was settled in the crook of his arm, her head tucked under his. His fingers drifted back and forth over her arm and shoulder blade as Azleah told him of her father's appearance.

"And on the day you had leave," she finished.

"I missed the excitement." Crue's fingers trailed her bare skin. "Were you frightened?"

"Yes, but..."

He adjusted so he could see her face. "What?"

"The witch helped me. I think, maybe, she's been trying to help me this whole time."

His eyebrows shifted over his eyes before he moved once

more, tucking her in closer against him, making a humming sound.

"And was your family well?" she asked.

"Yes. They asked me to return home."

Her heart constricted with both jealousy and sadness. She knew she couldn't ask him to remain for her sake, even if she longed for it. "And what did you tell them?"

"That I was beholden to my vow," he said, his voice lowered to a timbre that sent shivers down her spine as he maneuvered his thigh between hers. She made room for him as he settled in between her legs. "A very important vow," he added, placing a kiss on each cheeks.

"And what is that?"

"That I have vowed to protect the princess." He kissed her nose.

"What else does this vow entail?" she asked, smiling, for she could feel the length of him hardening.

He hummed and placed a kiss at the corner of her lips. "Lots of things."

"Like?"

Crue reached between them, taking himself in hand to slide through her slick heat. "Like pleasing her."

She sucked in a breath and tilted her hips to offer him more room.

He accepted the invitation, slowly sinking into her. "To make her feel... good."

"You do," she breathed, grabbing hold of his shoulder blades. "You do."

He kissed down her neck, moving slowly. "Azleah...This..."

Suddenly, a bright heat sliced through her vision. She sucked in a breath as an image of the Mad King darted through her mind. He was stalking through the corridor. She started, drawing away from Crue.

"What is it? Azleah?" The concern in Crue's voice pulled her back.

"The king. He's coming."

Crue pulled out of her body and jumped from the bed.

"The witch is at the door?" she asked, looking about to where she might hide him, but her room had no such place.

Crue stumbled across the room, a foot in a pant leg, stammering about needing to get to the door. "Where is he?" He buttoned his pants and shoved his head into his tunic.

"Somewhere in the corridor."

He slid the breastplate on, and Azleah helped him buckle it as he fastened his many weapons. Then he was running out the door, and Azleah stood, naked, watching him go. But he came back to press a needy kiss to her lips, before disappearing down the stairs one more.

Azleah waited, her heart slamming against her chest, her breath shallow and fearful, but seconds, then minutes, then an hour passed and nothing happened.

The king never appeared.

Crue didn't return, either, so she was left to worry until the witch appeared, announcing she'd appeased the king.

Crue did return the next night, and the night after that. And so it went for weeks, Azleah losing herself in Crue, giving herself to him and taking what he offered, falling deeper and deeper into love.

Then one day, when the witch brought her dinner, rather than offer Azleah a story about the kingdom, she said, "The bones have decided I must offer you another gift. Prophecy has saved you—and Hale Crue—from discovery, but I wonder if you might be able to use a different gift to sway the king."

"Like your words?"

"Somewhat," the witch said. "Perhaps the power to influence his thoughts?"

Liking the sound of that, Azleah nodded. "How?"

The witch stepped up on the dais in front of Azleah and said, "Dream walking. The power to infiltrate his dreams and speak with him. Influence him."

This sounded like something manageable. "This won't make me like him?"

The witch shook her head. "But it is... darker magic."

"As long as I won't lose myself, I will accept it."

"Lie down on the bed," the witch said.

So Azleah did, her heart's rhythm turning tinny in her chest with anticipation. The witch touched her once more, this time in the center of throat, then running a finger down her body in a straight line as she spoke her strange words. The same heat infiltrated Azleah's body as before, slithering through her until it settled around her spine. The witch's finger stopped at Azleah's heart, just between her breasts.

When the witch was done, she stepped away. "Have you been taking the herb?"

"Yes. Every night with dinner."

The witch nodded. "Good." She stood, turned, then left the room without another word.

Azleah fell into a routine, with the maid, the witch, and now with Crue, her gift of prophecy keeping them from discovery. One night, after Crue had returned to his post, Azleah—so very tired—closed her eyes, only to drift into a dream that took her deep within the confines of the castle to a place she had never seen, where she found the Mad King sleeping restlessly atop a bed.

The sensation of being drawn into something grabbed hold of her, and when she looked around, she stood in a garden, with her father—not yet the Mad King, but the father she remembered holding her hand. He was staring at her, a sly smile upon his lips. "Are you sure, Alea?" he asked. "This could change everything."

"I'm not Alea," Azleah said inside the dream. "I'm Azleah."

Her father's smile faded, and the brilliant garden withered and wilted around them, turning black. He shook his head. "Alea. Why would you say such a thing?"

"Because it is the truth. Have you not told me to always tell you true?" Azleah asked.

"But–" The king looked around then, at the garden landscape ugly and decrepit. His face began to age. "That can't be." He glanced at his hands. Startled, he yelled as they withered before his eyes like the garden.

"Know me, Father," she said.

And suddenly she was torn from the dream, racing across the seam of reality before starting awake in her own bed. She sat up, clutching her chest, her body coated in sheen of sweat as nausea overtook her. Bolting for the pot, she eliminated everything, then crawled back into bed, unable to move as morning overtook the room. The maid came and went.

Minutes or hours later, she had no notion, there was a strange noise at the doorway.

Azleah raised her head from her pillow.

The Mad King stood there watching, then he shuffled across the room.

"Where is the witch?" Azleah asked, unable to move, her body weak.

The king said nothing, the deep lines in his face somehow deeper with his frown. He stopped at her bedside and looked down at her.

Azleah raised the covers to her chin. "I'm not my mother. Know me, Father."

He sighed, a great heaving of... Azleah couldn't name it... then turned and left the room in great haste, leaving Azleah's heart racing and hope blooming in her chest.

When the witch came later with dinner, Azleah was bursting with it. "Then he left," she finished. "I think... I think the dreaming worked."

"Perhaps for a moment," the witch said, pushing a dish toward her. "His purpose was unchanged when I saw him today."

Azleah picked up the bowl of steamed carrots and ate. "Is there magic that might be more lasting?"

The witch settled her hands in her lap. "Magic is a fickle servant," she said. "You might think it is the answer, but are we not in this predicament because of magic?"

"Yes," Azleah said slowly and took another bite. "But you said to yourself we will need magic to get out of it. We're just waiting for the right time."

The witch sat forward. "I did."

"What did the bones say?" Azleah asked, setting down

the dish and standing. Unable to stay still, she paced, awaiting the witch's wisdom.

"That you would seek another gift, and I can give it, but I find myself... wary."

Azleah stopped. "Why?"

"I have been careless with your father. I don't wish to harm you. Come. Eat."

For the first time, Azleah looked upon the witch not as the object of her torment but as a trusted friend. She sat once more and picked up her fork. "I appreciate that, and this is my choice. I need to protect myself."

The witch measured Azleah with her gaze before her shoulders fell, as if resigned to the inevitable. "As you wish," she said. "But after you eat."

So Azleah ate, and when she was done, the witch stood. "A warning, princess, this magic—a third gift—can be heavy to carry."

"What will it be this time?" Azleah asked, excited.

"Wisdom Oracle," she said. "To rule words and to harness knowing."

Azleah stood. "That might make it last?"

"It is the gift that I have used on your father. I am gifting it to you. I will lose it as you gain it, just as I have all the others."

"Wait." Azleah tilted her head to study the witch. "You've been giving me your own magical gifts."

The witch nodded. "It is the least I can do for the pain I have caused." She extended a hand. "Come."

Azleah took the witch's hand, letting the witch turn her so they both faced the same direction. Then the witch stepped in closer, fitting her body into the spaces made by Azleah's back and curves. Azleah's breath caught in her lungs at the nearness of the witch, at the way those warm chills of her touch danced across her skin.

"What…"

"Hush," the witch said, her breath near Azleah's ear. The woman slid her hands around Azleah's waist and pressed her palms against Azleah's belly. As she said her words, the bright, hot warmth built inside Azleah, flowing through the witch's touch. The witch's hands shifted a touch lower, spanning the space just above Azleah's pelvis, and the heat radiated, until the witch made a sound.

Suddenly, her touch was gone, leaving Azleah so cold she shivered.

"How will I know if it worked?" Azleah asked, and turned, but the witch was gone.

Later, Crue visited, nearly out of breath when he burst through her doorway. Azleah waited for him, wrapped only in a blanket.

He stopped abruptly. "Oh. Gods, you're beautiful. I missed you," he breathed and started with his buckles.

A vision danced across her mind of Crue removing the

witch's clothes. She blinked and watched him take off his breastplate.

"Is the witch waiting?" Azleah asked.

Crue's eyes flitted up, then quickly away. There was a breath of hesitation, then he smiled. "Yes." The thud of his breastplate on the floor cut the word short.

He was lying. She wasn't sure how she knew and wondered if perhaps it was the new magic inside her. "What aren't you telling me?"

Crue stopped, his pants unfastened, his shirt untucked. "What?"

Azleah walked toward him, the blanket dragging behind her as she did. "You just lied."

"I didn't. The witch is watching."

Azleah shook her head. "I asked if she was waiting."

Crue took a deep breath. "What's this?"

"What aren't you telling me?"

Crue straightened, his arms at his sides. He curled his hands into fists, then hung his head. "I knew giving you these gifts would change things."

And then his form changed.

His black hair grew, his body leaned and lengthened, and his face morphed until the witch stood before Azleah, dark, knowing eyes and all.

"Oh," Azleah gasped. She fell backward onto the bed. "You?"

"Am I?" the witch asked, and the change began again. Her face transformed into Crue again, then aged, his dark hair sleeker and threaded with bits of silver. The masculine body filled back in until a man stood before her, a different Crue, but older with the same dark eyes filled with knowing like the witch.

"Who are you?" Azleah whispered.

"One and the same."

"Crue?"

"And the witch. This" –the man waved a hand in front of him– "is my true form."

"But–" Azleah stammered. "I don't understand."

The man, no longer clothed in Crue's uniform but head to toe in black, walked across the room and pulled a chair away from the table. He waved a hand at the dinner tray, and it was refilled with fresh fruit, cheese, and bread. "Come. Sit." He lifted a goblet of wine to his lips.

Azleah did, frightened but curious, her breath coming in shallow pants.

The man set a goblet in front of her. "It will be fine for the baby."

"Baby?"

"It would seem the herbs weren't as effective as we'd hoped." His eyes dropped to her belly.

"What?" Azleah pressed her palms to her stomach, her gaze following her hands.

"I'd like to tell you a story." The man smiled—Crue's smile—and pushed the tray closer to her.

"A story?" she asked, slowly. She suddenly couldn't find her bearings and felt as though she might be floating outside her body.

"I came to your father because he summoned me after the death of your mother. My magic is unparalleled," the man said, "and I relish the opportunity to demonstrate my prowess. As I traveled, I was regaled with stories of your parents' great love. My magic, of course, cannot summon this, and while I am content in most things, I should like a great love story. I found myself jealous but curious about this great love, so I agreed."

Azleah watched him pop a grape into his mouth.

"When I arrived and found your father's bereaved state, I decided it was only fair to support his desire to speak once more with your mother. Who am I to stand in the way to true love, after all? We dabbled in the darkest of magics to find a tether, and I eventually found a way for them to speak across time and space. But when your father returned, he wasn't the same. His grief had taken on a manic shine, no longer content to just speak with her. He asked for her resurrection."

"And you said 'yes.'"

"I said no," the man said. "This is a kind of magic that can't be done. And I was set to leave, only I saw... you." His eyes connected to Azleah, and the depth of feeling in them raced down her spine.

"Me?"

He nodded. "At the sight of you, I felt strange. It was as if the world had suddenly begun spinning properly but sent me careening in the opposite direction. A feeling with which I was wholly unfamiliar, and I wondered if this was what was meant by being lovestruck. So I lied to your father and told him that I might know of a witch who could help him."

"You are the witch."

He nodded. "I stayed, to remain close to you. To see and learn about love."

"And you drove him mad."

"No. No." The man shook his head. "What has become of your father is a result of his own choices. I offered him magic, told him the consequences–"

"Like you've done with me?"

"Yes. Only..."

Azleah stood and turned away from him, moving to the window. "You tricked me. You pretended this whole time."

"Would you have listened had I revealed myself from the beginning?"

Azleah didn't look at him. She knew she wouldn't have, but she didn't say it. She felt... angry. Hurt. Foolish. She had fallen in love with Crue. Had given her heart, her body, her soul to a figment. Tears filled her eyes, but she wouldn't let them fall.

She folded her hands over her belly. A baby.

"And what is it you want of me?" She turned back to him. "Because that is what this is all about, yes? You want my kingdom? My riches?"

He offered her a patient but short grin. "Oh, Azleah, use the wisdom I have given you. I can acquire these things without you." He stood and crossed the room to stand before her. "Search your body... your heart, your mind, your instinct, and know me."

"I loved Crue. Not you."

"I am Crue." He reached out and pressed his palm to her heart.

It fluttered with feeling, and the rest of her came alive just as she had with each touch of the witch—with Crue— with each of his touches. Her feelings for Crue overshadowed her bitterness, and her mind opened.

"I want you," he said, then slid his hand to cover her belly. "I want our child."

She staggered away from him. "I don't know you."

"You do." He sighed. "Search your heart and consider all I've told you. The bones say it is time to go. I would like to free you from your tower. I promised this... as Crue. This I will do, either way, but I hope you will choose me." He paused as if allowing that to sink in. Then he said, "I'll return tomorrow and seek your answer."

She watched the man disappear down the stairs. Then, and only then, did she finally let herself cry.

The next morning, instead of the maid, the man—older Crue, as she'd begun thinking of him—appeared in her doorway, only he was more frantic than she'd ever witnessed the witch or her Crue. Dressed all in black like the night before, he hurried to Azleah's bedside and fell to his knees. Her Crue was in his face, and her heart pinched, leaning toward him, but she was still hurt and angry by his duplicity.

"Your answer?"

"You'll get me out of here?"

"You'll get yourself out of here. I will give you the magic to do it, and I would like to care for you and our baby. I mean... if you'll let me." His head fell forward, his dark hair obscuring his eyes.

Azalea had spent the night crying and knew she was out of options.

"What do I call you?"

"Crue."

She sat up and swung her legs over the side of the bed next to where he knelt. As much as she wanted to be stubborn, there wasn't room for it. She needed to get out of this tower room, and she needed to be away from her father. And this magician—this Crue—was willing to help her. "You are promising to help me leave my father?" It was the thing she most wanted to hear.

He looked up at her, hope softening the severity of his face.

He was her Crue once more.

"Yes."

"Then I will go with you."

He breathed a sigh of relief. "We're out of time."

And so they made a plan.

"The king is coming for you tonight," Crue said, "and I won't be able to intervene, because I will need to restructure the spell. Which is why I need to give you one more gift."

"What is it?"

"Time Runner."

"And what will that do?"

"You'll be able to skip through time, but it is very important that you keep in mind where you need to be and when. Time running is dangerous." Crue put his hands on her once more and said words she didn't know. The heat of the magic seeped through her, joining with her body.

"And where should I think to go?" Azleah asked.

"I have a cabin in the Eppers."

"The Haunted Bog?"

"You've been there?"

"Yes."

"There. That's where you'll go. And it isn't haunted." Grabbing a piece of their old parchment, he conjured a writing implement, then sketched a map, wrote out directions, and pointed to a spot. "This is where you need to go. I will meet you there."

"I have to go by myself?"

He took her face between his palms. "I have every faith you can do this. But you must wait for your father. It will give me time to work on the spell."

She could have said no, but that version still left her trapped. This seemed the best means to get what she needed.

Out.

She could only think about that, especially now with a child. Her trust, her worries didn't matter, so she nodded.

He pressed a soft kiss to her cheek.

Her Crue—at least, that was what she told herself.

Beyond escaping from the tower, the palace, her father, she would take things with him one moment at a time. Crue would have to regain her trust, and this would go a long way. He had always promised to help her escape, and now he was, even if his methods left something to be desired.

"I'll see you at the cabin." Then he turned and left Azleah to wait.

Her father arrived just as the sun kissed the horizon. "Alea."

Azleah turned to face him. "I am not Alea."

Anger marred his features as red flushed his face. "Enough of this!" He started across the tower room. "I shall not wait any longer. The witch is a liar!"

Azleah had run out of time. She shut her eyes, thought of the Eppers, of the spot that Crue had pointed out. "Right now," she whispered. "Right now."

With the sound of a shutting door, a whirl of air swept up and blocked her father's yell. When she opened her eyes, she stood next to the river that fed the Epper Marsh.

The Marsh, which looked more like a waterless mish mash of tufts of green grass and muddy bog, stretched on and on. The river didn't run through the marsh but veered off, bordering it as it flowed to the farmlands of Echo. On the horizon, she could see the shadow of the Narrow Mountains.

Azleah turned in a circle and shivered at the chill in the

air. Her mouth opened with noiseless awe, then she whispered, "It worked." She squeaked with joy and added a little dance, then remembered the map, which she dug from her pocket. The sun was falling quickly, and she needed the light. She followed Crue's directions, turning toward the cluster of trees that eventually turned into the woods. It was there she'd find the house.

"Look for the craggy lone tree" he'd said. *"You'll turn toward the hills there."*

So she did, following his directions until a quaint house materialized in the woods. Though it was small, it looked as if it belonged nestled between giant trees, a part of them, the wood slick with a mossy sheen, its roof hidden in the bowers of the branches. Lamps were lit in the two windows, and smoke drifted from the chimney.

She followed the stone path to the door painted a vibrant shade of red and knocked.

It cracked open to a wrinkled eye, then swung wide, revealing an old woman. Her silver hair was threaded with black, her shoulders hunched, a cane in her hand. "Who are you?" she demanded, her voice coarse.

Azleah's heart thudded in her chest, wondering if she'd come to the wrong house, but there didn't seem to be another. "Azleah. Crue told me to meet him here."

"Who the hell is Crue?"

Azleah's mouth opened, then shut. "Um." She

swallowed and looked back over her shoulder at the darkened woods, knowing she didn't have anywhere else to go. "He... works at the castle. In Echo Landing."

The woman laughed. "Work? Is this a joke?"

"No." Azleah bristled.

The woman's eyes narrowed, and she shuffled a few steps to look out the door, glanced around, then shuffled back inside. "Come on then." She waited for Azleah to enter, then shut the door. "Crue, huh? Is that the name he's using now? He get you pregnant?"

Azleah's cheeks reddened, but she didn't answer. "He said to meet him here. That he would help..."

The old woman clicked her tongue. "That's what he tells them all. He has no intention of helping you raise your... issue."

"But–"

"He said he loves you?"

It wasn't until the old woman asked that Azleah had ever thought about it, but upon mention, she realized neither of them had ever said those words, even if she'd felt them. Though she wasn't sure she still felt them, considering his trick.

"He won't," the old woman said with authority. "He can't. He's sold his soul and gave up his heart."

"What?"

At a sound beyond the doorway, Azleah jumped.

"Hide," the old woman hissed, pushing Azleah into a small alcove of the hearth behind the potbelly woodstove. "Hush and listen. You will see," she said, then disappeared from Azleah's sight.

Though Azleah couldn't see, she heard the door open and steps start over the wooden floor, stilling suddenly.

"Aunt Mercy." It was Crue's voice—older Crue, of course—filled with a sound Azleah couldn't identify. She suppressed the urge to jump from her hiding place and rush into his arms, and instead forced herself to listen, just as the old woman had suggested. It was a knowing of some kind, a hesitation, and the hint of a voice inside her telling her to wait.

"As you see," Mercy said. "No thanks to you."

He scoffed. "I thought–"

"What? That I wasn't coming back?"

"You left for the sea." Crue's steps sounded on the floor once more. "I set you up nicely there. You didn't like the cottage?"

"It was a dump. So I have returned. Besides, it was too cold and too wet."

"Joyous occasion, then," he answered, but his voice didn't sound joyful. "I'm expecting... someone."

"A girl."

"Is she here?"

"No. She came and left. I saved you from having to

break the news. Or should I say, I saved her."

"What news is that?" Crue asked. A creaking sounded, hinting that he might have taken a seat.

"That you won't raise the bastard." The old woman's cane hit the floor as she said each word. "How many more will you hunt?"

Hunt?

The air changed as if all the oxygen was being deprived from the room, compressing Azleah's lungs. The light dimmed, slipping toward a gray twilight as if the sun shone through a thick cloudbank.

The old woman coughed.

"You," Crue's voice took on a horrifying edge, "have meddled for the last time, Aunt."

"I am your kin!" She wheezed. "I raised you."

"The sea cottage was a kindness, and you have trounced on my goodwill for the last time."

More coughing. "I cannot see you kill another. I cannot," she choked.

Azleah covered her mouth with her hand and squeezed her eyes shut. *Kill?*

"I have saved her from a horrible existence as her father's bride!" Crue yelled.

"Only to die by yours?" the old woman squeaked.

There was movement, a slide, a lurch, a step. The old woman coughed, then there was a thud, as if something had fallen. A gasp for breath.

Azleah held hers.

"Where is she?" Crue demanded.

"Or will you finally come to? Raise your child. I can't," Mercy's voice broke.

"Can't what?" Crue's voice was nearly unrecognizable. Azleah knew it had to be him only because she knew he was the only other person in the cabin. "I will do what I always do. I have given her gifts she must return, and she is godblood. I will be a god."

"You will consume them? Like the others?"

"Where did she go?"

"You are an abomination," the old woman spat.

"A very powerful one." He paused. "Where is she?" he shouted.

Tears sprang to Azleah's eyes, and she squeezed them shut. With her hands pressed to her belly, she thought of her mother, of her mother's burial mound, of Remembrance Valley.

"Mother," she whispered, and just as had happened earlier, a door shut on the sound of Crue—the wizard—and the old woman yelling and struggling. Azleah opened her eyes and crouched in the darkness before the shadowy swell of an earthen mound. Then she buried her face in her hands and cried.

"I have nowhere to go," she sobbed, and after her tears

had subsided, she wiped her eyes. She glanced at the shadow of the castle, at the tower where she'd been held captive. "But I am out," she whispered and ran her hand over her still flat belly. "And I have magic. I will do everything in my power to protect you," she vowed.

"Azleah?"

Her head whirled at the voice. It was too dark to see anything, but she knew it was him.

"Azleah? Are you here? This is where you always went... before."

She held her breath.

"My aunt Mercy said she sent you away. She's..." He paused.

She could make out his footsteps in the loam.

"Look, she probably said some things that sounded crazy. The old woman is senile. I took her to the coast, where I thought the sea air would help her, but... Azleah?"

She squeezed her eyes shut and lay down, her back against her mother's burial mound. "Not here," she whispered and imagined leaving, imagined anywhere else. It started with the color green and sunshine before fear grabbed hold.

The door shut once more.

When she opened her eyes this time, she was sitting in a dense, green wood unlike anything she'd ever seen before. She stood and turned in a circle, looking up at the sun shining through the green leaves.

"Hello!" a kind voice called.

Azleah whirled, afraid that Crue had followed her somehow, but it wasn't his voice, and the forest around her was empty.

"Down here," the voice said.

Azleah looked down at her feet and there—no bigger than her thumb—was a man. Startled, she fell backward.

"Oh! I didn't mean to startle you, woman! Apologies," he said, and climbed up onto her ankle using the holes in her boot and laces to help himself. Then he traversed the length of her dress to her knee, where he stopped.

"You're... what are you?" she stammered. "A sprite?"

"Not a sprite," he said. "Just a man." He grinned, and his eyes—as green as the spring leaves around them— twinkled. Brown hair stuck out from beneath his tiny blue hat, with a brown beard to match.

"But you're so..."

"Small?"

She nodded.

"I might say the same of you, though the opposite. You are rather large, yes?" He sat, settling into a groove made by the fabric of her skirt. "It's a matter of perspective."

"I suppose you're right. Is everyone in this land like you?"

"You're not from around here, then?"

She shook her head.

"Unfortunately not. I am rather small." He laughed.

She couldn't help but giggle even as tears stung her eyes. "But why?"

"Why am I small? My parents wished this on me. They had me when they were older, you see, and they never expected to have a child, so when I was born, they wished for me to remain small. Instead of growing bigger, I began to grow smaller as I aged, and here I am."

"Magic."

"Which is probably why you can hear me at all. Someday, I will grow so small I will cease to be at all." Despite the implication of the words, he offered that easy smile once more and held out a tiny hand. "I'm Tomas."

Azleah held out a finger. Despite everything careening through her, his touch brought joy. "It's nice to meet you, Tomas. I'm..." She paused, knowing she had to leave her past behind. Glancing around, her gaze settled on a bush filled with bright red berries, and she thought of the red door of the cabin. "I'm Scarlett, and I'm afraid I'm lost."

"Well, good thing you nearly fell on me." He stood on her knee once more, dusting himself off. "Despite my size, I am a big help. Put me on your shoulder, and let's be off. We have some lunch to look after. Then maybe I can help you find which way to go."

Scarlett

"Are you well?" Tomas asked her from his perch on her shoulder hidden in her hair.

They had been traveling together for months, and Tomas, despite his diminutive size, used his wiles to find them what they needed. They always had a place to sleep and food for their bellies. They'd slept in barns, inns, and offered bedrooms. They'd been given coins and livestock to trade. They'd had traveling companions who'd offered places: caravans, performers, farmers off to market. Scarlett had wanted for nothing.

Tomas's craftiness made it easy to trick people into offering necessities to keep them alive. It wasn't a life she'd grown up living, but she was free, and she'd never felt more cared for. Though they were always moving, and the wear and tear was beginning to tax her growing frame, she had made a friend in Tomas. They laughed together, told stories, shared insecurities and vulnerabilities. Somewhere along the path between meeting Tomas and the six months since, her heart had shifted from friendship toward something deeper. Six months of running from Crue. Six months with Tomas as her guide. Six months to grow to love him more than she'd ever loved anyone.

"Scarlett?" he asked once more.

With her heart thumping a powerful awareness, the baby inside her moved as if in agreement with her choice. She smiled, placing her hand on her belly.

"The baby?" Tomas asked, concerned.

"She's okay."

"She?"

"Yes. The witch from the woods told me. From my dreams. Remember?"

He hummed a sound. "Right. The witch." She could hear his skepticism, and that made her smile even more. He was a man no bigger than her thumb.

She continued walking. "It isn't as if I have much of a choice when a sorcerer is after me. After the baby." She grabbed hold of her protruding stomach protectively. She'd calculated she had a couple more months to go. "We need to find a place where we can stop. Settle," she said. "This baby will be here before we know it. We have to prepare."

"We?" Tomas asked, a smile in his tone.

She blushed. "I–"

"Stop," he said. "Of course I'll be there. There is nowhere I would rather be."

Suddenly a vision sliced through her mind, and she stumbled, grabbing hold of a tree trunk to keep her upright. She hissed in pain.

"What is it? Scar?" Tomas asked, but his voice receded as a thick impenetrable darkness spread around them, exactly where they stood on a trail in the heart of a wood somewhere she didn't know. She had used her gifts so frequently she'd lost track. Prophecy, time running, dreaming. They'd become second nature even if she didn't know how to control them. It was as if the magic itself was trying to keep her safe from Crue.

Heart pounding, she labored to straighten, turning toward the forest, her back against the tree.

"What is it?" Tomas repeated.

"He's here. He found us."

"Milady?" one of the two men traveling with them asked. Tomas had used his smallness to convince the farmers Scarlett was a good-luck fairy by pretending to make one of their oxen talk. She glanced at him and at the other young man, his son, suddenly worried for them.

As if she had summoned him, Crue stepped from the shadows. Young Crue. He looked as she remembered him, dressed in the soldier's regalia of her kingdom. Every choice the sorcerer made was a manipulation of her emotions.

One of the farmers made a sound of surprise, pulling his hat from his head. "Sir," he said. "We have papers."

Crue ignored the farmer. "My love. I've found you. Are you happy to see me?"

The second of the two farmers, holding onto the harness of the oxen looked between Scarlett and Crue. "Is this your babe's father?"

"Yes." Crue's eyes measured her form greedily, looking at her pregnant belly. "You look well."

"This is him?" Tomas asked, his voice determined in her ear.

She nodded.

Frowning, Crue tilted his head. "Whose voice is that?" His eyes jumped to the two farmers, then back to Scarlett. "Who is speaking?"

"Me!" Tomas boomed, surprising Scarlett, his voice so imposing it startled the birds in the trees around them that they took flight.

The farmers fell to their knees. "The ox is speaking!"

Crue looked from the oxen to Scarlett. "That is no ox." He crossed the woods toward her and the men. "And who are you?" He bent, turned, adjusted as he looked for Tomas.

"A touch of magic, it would seem."

"One who sees what's true."

"And what truth do you see?" Crue asked, lifting the tarpaulin tied over the farmers' wagon.

"One who is noble, and one who isn't."

"I think we know which one I am." Crue chuckled, then twirled in place, arms outstretched, and laughed louder. He reached out and touched the man closest to him—the older of the two—and Scarlett watched the farmer crumple to the ground. Dead.

The second man yelped, dropped to his knees, and bowed his head, his mouth moving silently in prayer. "Father," he cried, grabbing hold of the older man and dragging him into his lap.

Scarlett's eyes rose to Crue's. "You are cruel."

"A death-touch spell." He wiped his hands together and grinned before turning his head to gaze at Scarlett once more. "Rather simple, actually. Perhaps, faceless voice, you should show yourself."

"No," Scarlett said, her mind drifting toward the witch she'd been dreaming of the last several weeks, the witch she'd told Tomas about. She knew they couldn't use magic against Crue, he was much too adept and powerful. Her only choice was as it had been for the last six months, run as far as she could and hide, but this time there would be help waiting.

"I insist." Crue took a step toward her, his hand out. "Or you and the babe will face the same fate, my love."

"No. We won't," she replied, lifting her chin, calling Crue's bluff. "You need us." She covered her belly with her hand and glanced at the young farmer cowering in anguish over his dead father.

Tomas stepped out from under her hair. "Here I am."

"No!" Scarlett said at the same time.

Surprised, Crue took a step back, a grin bursting on his face along with a surprised laugh of delight, as if Tomas were a prank being played upon him. "What is this magic?"

"A gift," Tomas replied.

"For me?" Crue asked.

"For her."

Crue's amusement grew dark, his eyes flying from Tomas's face to Scarlett's. "After all we've shared together, this is why you stay away. I loved you."

"You have no love for me."

Crue's brows collapsed together, then softened. "You carry our child. And yes, I was angry you ran," he confessed, moving slowly toward her. His lips puffed together in a pout, but then he grinned and clapped his hands together. "But let us not focus on the past, and instead the present and future. I'm overjoyed that I have found you. That I get to be a father. We can be a happy family."

Scarlett hummed a noise and took a step back. "Except

for the fact you would consume us upon the babe's birth. You want my godblood and the babe's."

Crue stilled, his brows furrowing over his dark eyes. Then they smoothed out. "Your gifts?" He scoffed. "Gifts I've given you."

She didn't move, wary and unsure how the wizard might react. But she knew what to do now, had practiced with the dream witch how to use the time run to take her, the baby, and Tomas where they could insulate themselves from the wizard's sight. She just had to do it before he acted, had to wait for the right moment.

"And what do your gifts tell you now?" he asked, taking another step toward her.

"That you are darkness, consuming everything in your path."

"And you and our baby are a part of that power," he replied.

"I'll create a diversion," Tomas whispered. "Then you run."

"No, Tom," Scarlett said. "I can do this."

"Tom?" Crue's head snapped around, looking at Tomas. He laughed. "A small name for a small man."

"And yet, so much more of a man than you," Scarlett replied, and just as she'd done over and over, she closed her eyes and slid through the seam of the realm in between worlds, a door snapping shut behind her, cutting off Crue's enraged bellow as she and Tomas disappeared.

But this time she didn't stop, hopscotching through various realms toward the woods where she would find Baba, the witch in the woods, losing Crue in a trail of time. She envisioned the gnarled tree with the woman's face from her dream and whispered, "There."

When she stopped, Tomas still clinging to her, she collapsed into the loam at the foot of the gnarled tree.

"Tomas," she cried when she felt him fall from her shoulder.

"I'm here," he reassured her.

Then, just in case Crue's powers had let him follow, she crawled into a thicket of brush to hide, and there she cried with Tomas to comfort her.

It wasn't until her belly grumbled with the need to eat that she and Tomas emerged from their hiding place. The forest had been silent, but the tree with the woman's face stood sentinel, a great hulking beast of a tree, gnarled with an unnatural grace.

Scarlett struggled to her feet and called out, "Baba. I'm here. I have come."

The face in the tree moved, shifting as if made of clay, the wood groaning under the strain.

Startled, Scarlett gasped.

"Scarlett," Tomas warned, pulling at her skirt with all his might.

The wood of the tree crackled and fractured open, spewing bright light. From the light, an old woman materialized, old in a way that made Scarlett think of the beginning of time, and the tree stood whole behind the witch once more. She was hunched in her clothes, rags hanging from her body as if they were layers of her rather than a fabric covering. Her hair was a bright silver, nearly white, obscuring her face. Though Scarlett couldn't make out her features, she had the impression Baba's eyes were glowing orbs of darkness.

"Scarlett. It's still Scarlett, is it not?"

"Yes, Baba."

"Your baby has reached the nearing," the old witch said. "Just in time."

Scarlett spread a palm over her belly. "Yes. It's time to hide," she'd said. "I have to keep her safe."

Tomas scurried up a tree to a branch where he could see Scarlett's face. "Why are you doing this? With her? Nothing is free."

Of course Scarlett knew this, but she'd had to take measure of the lesser of two evils.

"I need to keep her safe," she replied. "Please, Tomas. I have trusted you, and you have kept us safe. Now I need you to trust me."

"And what is it you require?" Tomas asked the witch.

The old woman looked at him, tilted her head, and

waited as if her body remained but her mind traveled. Then she said, "I have seen. And in the end, I will be rewarded."

"I don't–" Tomas started, his tiny hand pointing at the witch.

"Trust me?" She cackled, her head tipping back as she did. "That is a good thing, small man," the witch told Tomas. "It will be necessary for her and the babies."

"Babies?" both Scarlett and Tomas asked.

"But" –the witch tapped her chin– "you cannot stay this small. Time to reverse the wish." She wiggled her fingers.

"Wait!" Scarlett cried.

The witch looked at her, her hands frozen in front of her, violet threads of light intertwined between her fingers.

"But I love him just this way," Scarlett admitted quietly.

Tomas straightened on his tree branch. "Love me?"

Scarlett lifted her head to meet his gaze, her cheeks hot. "I'd wished to tell you," she said, embarrassed, "but not by blurting it out so."

The witch interrupted. "He must. If you are to hide, he must be able to blend in at your side."

"Yes," Tomas agreed, nodding, his eyes never wavering from Scarlett's. "I should like that."

Scarlett's heart picked up its wayward beat as her cheeks grew hotter.

With a muttered spell, the violet lightning burst from

the witch's hands and Tomas began to grow, and grow, and grow, his clothes tearing from his body, leaving him naked and exposed. The branch on which he was perched broke, and he fell to the ground, into the brush. He grew and grew, his body expanding.

He yelled out with pain.

Scarlett cried, "Tomas!" and surged forward, but the witch stopped her with a hand, her power creating an invisible wall between them.

"Let it happen," Baba said.

And still he grew.

Eventually Baba's lightning ceased, and the forest was quiet—no birds, no breeze, nothing.

"Tomas?" Scarlett whimpered, suddenly afraid she'd made a terrible mistake.

"I'm here," he groaned, reassuring her as he always did. He moved in the brush, getting to his feet.

Scarlett tilted her head up to look at him—at least a foot taller than her—the size of a tree, it seemed. She swallowed. She'd thought him handsome for so long, only now it was difficult to take in the beauty of his face in such visible relief. Her body heated as she looked at him, and then she realized she was staring too long and removed her cloak, handing it to him.

Baba laughed, her cackle an unnerving sound. "Babies."

But Scarlett barely noticed it, unable to look away from Tomas, her heart a rapid beat in her throat. Despite the heavy burden of the baby inside her body, her heart beat for the man standing before her.

He took her offered cloak, his skin pinkening with a blush as he wrapped the fabric around his hips. Then he stepped forward, grabbed hold of Scarlett, and pulled her into his embrace, pressing his face into the space between her neck and shoulder. "This," he whispered. "I've wanted to do this."

Scarlett melted into the rightness of his embrace, her hands grasping hold of the strong muscles of his back.

"There's more work to do," Baba said. "There's a village at the edge of the woods called Sevens." She pulled a small, glass bottle from inside her cloak, still talking. "You'll go there so that you aren't far from me." Her eyes had jumped between them, and she'd grinned once more. "Yes, you will need me, it seems." She nodded, her gaze clouding. "Yes. You will need me."

Then she shook herself back to the moment and held out the bottle.

Scarlett took the small vial, not much bigger than her palm. "And then?"

"Build a life," the witch said. "It is what you have wanted, yes?"

"Yes, Baba." Scarlett looked at Tomas and when he

smiled, she grinned but struggled to keep connected, suddenly nervous.

"That potion is for the wards." Baba rustled through a rucksack that had suddenly materialized against her hip.

"Wards?" Tomas asked.

"A protective spell to hide your home, the power she carries, the babies." The witch stopped, pulling out a red ribbon woven with a second ribbon shimmering pink, with violet and golden threads as she leveled a stern look at Scarlett. "But beware, if you tell the truth, the ward will fail."

Scarlett nodded.

"This is for the baby," the witch continued, holding out the ribbon. "It will hide her from the wizard's sight."

Scarlett spread the silky trinket across her palm.

"The same applies to this," the witch said. "Should you ever reveal the truth fueling the spells, they will fail and expose everything."

"To remain hidden, I must conceal it?"

"Yes. There is one other thing that will break the ribbon's spell," the witch warned. "True love. Do you understand?"

"Yes, Baba," Scarlett replied.

So she and Tomas did as the old witch instructed—they built a life. They built a cottage in the woods outside of Sevens, set the wards around it, and watched the hedge grow overnight. When her daughter was born filled with the magic of her father and mother, she and Tomas named her Jessamine. They tied her tiny wrist with the magical ribbon. They learned what it meant to love one another and lived as man and wife. Just as Baba predicted, she had been needed.

When Tarley was born, she took Scarlett's gift as a Prophet Augur, and Scarlett tied a red ribbon around her wrist. Then Brinna was born, taking Dream Walking and receiving her ribbon. Auri, Wisdom Oracle. Mattias, Time Runner.

Nearly twenty-eight years later, Scarlett now sat in the cottage where she'd made a life, her grown children—all but Jessamine—with their true loves, listening to the story.

Scarlett's secrets were revealed. Though the weight of carrying the burden of the truth should have lifted, it hadn't. Rather, the weight of shame and guilt came crashing down.

Tomas

Tomas Fareview, only son of Remison and Ginnet Fareview, husband of Scarlett and father of their children, watched the fire move in the hearth like a dancer. While he might have appreciated that at one time, at the moment he couldn't seem to feel anything but all-consuming hurt. It was a gloom that swallowed up everything inside him, a beast feeding on everything that had once made him feel whole. Now, he was just parts, and those parts were scattered and haphazardly existing without any semblance of being cohesive again.

He felt eviscerated.

He wished he had been. It might be easier to be lying out under the open sky with his guts dripping around him as he bled to death. Less painful.

Only as Scarlett—the object of his pain—finished telling her story to their children, that pain increased.

It wasn't as if he hadn't known her story. He had. She'd already been pregnant with Jessamine when they met. He'd been the tiny man traveling about the woods coercing people with his cleverness into helping him—a novelty, a joke, a trickster. He'd been whatever he needed to be. But the moment he'd met Scarlett, his purpose had shifted. He hadn't looked to serve himself, to coerce or trick for his own selfish needs, but rather to take care of her.

When she'd trusted him, she'd told him her story. Though she'd been named Azleah in another life, Scarlett was the only name he'd ever known. That was her true name to him. Scarlett, who'd looked at him like he was a giant rather than the tiny man no bigger than her thumb. Scarlett who'd loved him before the witch in the woods had reversed the spell making him a full-sized man he was now. Scarlett, who'd owned his heart long before then, but he hadn't ever considered that she would one day be his.

He'd never entertained the idea that a woman would ever love him. And even after meeting Scarlett certainly not a woman as lovely as her. He was content to be her friend, her helper. Being small had ensured his loneliness. Only

Scarlett made sure he wasn't alone. She had stayed. As time passed, he'd fallen in love with her, accepting it would be unrequited. Content to love her in secret, for who could ever love such a small man.

But then she'd confessed her feelings: *"I love him as he is."* That moment became his entire reason for his existence.

His love wasn't unrequited.

Scarlett loved him.

Of course he'd agreed to the witch-of-the-wood's plan to make him a full-sized man. To hide with his family. To love them. To protect them. To carry Scarlett's secrets to keep them all safe.

And he'd loved her with every fiber that made him whole. He loved her like a giant.

But she'd lied to him, and that, he wasn't sure he could forgive.

"What?" Auri breathed the question. "Jessamine's father?"

Tomas looked away from the blaze at Scarlett, who was staring at him once more with a pleading look in her eyes. He loved her eyes, those windows to her soul that reflected a stormy sky. But it hurt to look into them just then. She'd made a promise to tell the truth. Instead, she'd tricked them with the sleeping potion. She'd been willing to let them all sleep their lives away lost to the nightmares rather than tell them the truth.

"Crue. Yes," she said, telling the truth now when telling it risked nothing.

"Father?" Mattias's voice, then his hand on Tomas's shoulder grabbed his attention.

"What?" He tilted his head up to look at his son.

"Is this true?"

"Yes," he answered Mattias.

"And you knew?"

"Yes." He had. Every bit of it. Perhaps he was no better than Scarlett, keeping it from them, but he hadn't felt it was his story to tell. He'd known the consequences of telling it. He'd promised to help her keep them safe. And now Jessamine was gone.

He stood, turning to face his family. Mattias stood next to him, nearly even with his gaze now. Tarley and Lachlan, Auri, Brinna, the gods, and the soldier. "I knew. And I remained silent. And Jessamine may be… someone else's blood, but she is my daughter as much as each of you. I love her like I love each of you."

"You've been lying to us our whole lives." Tarley's anger was fair.

They weren't wrong. He knew he could have come up with a million excuses, but none exonerated him from holding onto Scarlett's lies.

Rather than say anything, he nodded.

Dropping the blanket from around his shoulders into the chair where he'd been sitting, he moved away from the fire, unable to keep the floating parts of himself contained. He wondered if he was on the verge of shrinking back down to the size of a thumb now that the spells had been broken. Perhaps becoming what he once was had always been his fate. He wasn't sure if it would be a sad relief to become as small physically as what he felt on the inside. Perhaps it would relieve the massive ache in his heart.

Grabbing his ax from next to the door, he walked from the cottage out into the woods, because at least there, his smallness felt right against the size of the trees.

Scarlett

Watching Tomas's broad shoulders disappear through the doorway crushed her. She stood, wanting to go after him but knowing she couldn't. Not yet. He needed his space, and she needed to finish what she'd started here. She'd finally revealed the truth, and they needed to find Jessamine.

"Don't blame him," she said. "I asked him to hold onto my secrets. And the secrets—not that I'm offering it as an excuse—were tied to the spells. Had I revealed any of them, the ribbons, the hedge would have failed."

"So you didn't trust us," Tarley snapped.

"I didn't trust Crue not to find us."

"Well, he found us anyway. Spells and all," Auri replied. "And now he has Jessamine."

Scarlett nodded. "He did. But your father… he asked me to tell you the truth for years."

"And you didn't," Brinna said.

"I didn't. I was afraid." She paused, wanting to explain herself but knowing that perhaps there was no way to appeal to them. The witch had warned her, and Scarlett hadn't listened. "I was afraid of Crue. His power. I was afraid of him hurting any of you, because of the magic–"

"What magic?" Mattias asked.

Scarlett pointed at Tarley, "Prophet Augur," then at Brinna, "Dream Walker," then to Auri, "Wisdom Oracle," and to Mattias, "Time Runner."

"You knew?" Brinna asked.

"Suspected. When you started dreaming, I realized the gifts had been transferred to each of you. It was just a matter of time to figure out who'd developed which gift."

"And Jessamine?"

"Healer," Lucian said, his hands on Brinna's shoulders. "She carries the godlight gift."

Scarlett nodded.

"Like you," Auri said.

"Yes. Like my mother before me." She paused, looking at the fire, wishing it were warming her. She just felt cold. "We have to find Jessamine. I don't know what he plans to do with her." Scarlett's heart stopped up in her chest, and tears flooded her eyes. "He once said he would consume her—us—for the magic."

"That's disgusting," Nixus said with a grimace.

Scarlett glanced from the god to Auri, whose head was tilted down. With one hand she clung to Brinna, and with the other she swiped her own tears.

"I don't know if it was literal," Scarlett said, "but I didn't have any reason to believe it wasn't."

"How do we find her?" Mattias asked.

"We wait," Lachlan said.

"What? We can't–" Scarlett started, tripping out of the blanket as she stood.

"We have to. We don't know where he took her, and Johesha—the captain of my guard—has gone after her. He'll be back when he has information. He'll also have a plan," Lachlan said. He turned to Jude and took the trinket the soldier had handed him. "In the meantime, you're promoted to captain in Johesha's absence."

"But, Your Highness–"

"No," Lachlan held up his hand to silence Jude. "Johesha handed the duty to you. I trust him—and you—completely. I need you to round up the camp and get them prepped to leave. Pick three soldiers you trust to leave behind."

Jude nodded and left.

"That's it?" Scarlett asked. "All we're going to do is wait?"

"Technically, we aren't waiting," Nixus said. "There's a man on it. He's a little cranky for my taste, but he seems pretty good at his job." He was leaning against the wall near the door where the soldier disappeared, then smirked at Lachlan, before his eyes flitted to Auri as if hoping for a reaction. He didn't get one.

"And what do you suggest we do while your soldier is on the job," Scarlett snapped.

"Prepare ourselves," Lucian suggested. "You've said his man is a powerful sorcerer. We'll need to have a handle on our own power."

"His name," Nixus said. "We'll need his true name."

Lucian spun to face his brother. "You remember?"

"I told you, I don't forget things."

"You have," Auri said, without looking at him.

Scarlett swallowed. "Why doesn't he remember?"

Nixus made a disgusted sound and stomped from the house, a trail of shadow following even as they stretched to reach for Auri.

"The god-yoke."

"What is that?" Scarlett asked.

Brinna stood. "It's when two godlights are bound. A recognition of their matched souls." She glanced at Lucian.

"But when those godlights are stretched thin with distance, it affects the pair," Lucian explained.

"Because of the spell?" Scarlett asked.

"I had to make a choice," Lucian said. "It was to lock away his memories or let him and Aurielle die. I chose the memories."

Scarlett's stomach rolled. "Die?" Her hand covered her mouth. She swallowed. "I didn't know–" She paused, turning away from Auri and another way she'd caused her children pain. "Will he remember?"

"I hope so," Lucian said. "With time. Maybe."

A house of cards.

Scarlett needed to see the witch.

She turned back to her family, resolved. "I think you're right," she told Lucian. "They need to be far from here. And they need to learn how to use the gifts. But I never learned, not truly. I tore through time and space with Mattias's gift just trying to get away. I never learned how to use it."

"Then how are we supposed to learn?" Mattias asked.

She didn't have an answer. She couldn't be sure she'd find the witch.

"You'll come to Sol," Lucian said. He looked at Brinna, who smiled at him shyly.

Scarlett's breath caught at the look in their exchange, at the bright light that swirled around them. "You too?"

Brinna's head whirled to look at her, her cheeks stained with a blush. She glanced at Auri, then down at her own lap. "Yes. We dreamed together."

"And how you were able to break the spell," Scarlett

finished.

"What's Sol?" Mattias asked.

"Sol is my godseat in Elcadia," Lucian said. "We should take everyone." He paused, measuring Brinna's reaction, then glancing around at everyone else. "It will be safe there, and we'll find someone to teach you how to use your magic."

"We're supposed to be in New Taras," Lachlan said, glancing at Tarley. "Supporting Queen Keyanna with her transition of power."

"We can transport Tarley in and out of Sol and New Taras," Luc offered. "There's room at Sol for everyone. Aurielle, you'll have to come. The god-yoke."

Auri nodded.

"And Elsewhere Doors," Brinna said. "They're these doors that lead to…"

Scarlett's attention drifted to observing the group, disconnected from it. Though a pall hung in the cottage, everyone began talking about new possibilities, about the magic, about how to use it to go after Jessamine. There was hope. Scarlett was confronted with the realization that the burden she'd been carrying for so long hadn't needed to be hers alone. The witch had said as much.

Then it hit her like a punch to her heart: she hadn't been alone. Tomas had carried the burden with her the whole time. She just hadn't seen it.

Tomas

With the cart unloaded and replaced in the barn, Tomas stood at the entrance to the cottage, unsure. His time in the woods, the physical exertion of chopping down trees in his path, of swinging the ax and sinking it into the wood, had been helpful in releasing some of his hurt and anger. He'd cut more wood than necessary, however, and couldn't waste it. So he'd returned for the cart, collected the wood, then stacked it under the lean-to outside the cottage, as it glowed from inside with a welcoming light. They wouldn't need wood for a while.

The thought stopped him.

It felt like the acceptance of a future.

And now he stood at the door, unsure about what to expect upon entering the home he'd shared with his family. Unsure about what he wanted, and if there was a future at all.

With a deep breath, he turned the doorknob and walked in. His boots stamped against the wooden floor, making a comforting noise he'd always liked. It reminded him of home. There weren't many places where his boots made that sound. He associated it with returning to Scarlett, because that's what he'd always done.

He hung his hat on the hook and set his ax next to the door, fortifying himself. When he turned, Scarlett waited in front of the table. She looked as beautiful as she always did. Her auburn hair was braided, the end of it draped over her shoulder and tied with a strip of fabric. She wore a dark blue dress. He'd always liked when she wore blue, and he was sure she knew it. The cottage was clean. Any vestiges of that last night before their sleep was cleared away. The table was set with two place settings. The fire was warm, candles glowed, and the scent of food cooking made his mouth water.

"Where is everyone?" he asked, afraid to know the answer.

"Gone," she answered.

His breath caught in his chest at the realization, a harsh

reality of the lies. He looked down at his feet, then sat to remove his boots like Scarlett liked. He paused, thinking maybe he wanted to stomp around in them, scatter dirt, but then discarded the thought just as quickly. He didn't want that at all. He just didn't want to hurt.

"Not forever," she added, quickly ascertaining the pain in his breath. "They'll return."

A breath of relief filled his lungs as he finished removing his boots. "They don't hate–"

"No!" She cut him off, and he looked up at her. She had that look of desperation he remembered from when they'd first met, her large eyes wide with fear, her features tense with uncertainty.

"They don't blame you," she said with a shake of her head. "The blame is where it should be."

"On Crue? Your father?" They'd been over that for years. He'd never blamed her for what had happened to her. Even now, he didn't begrudge her the truth of what brought her to him. It had brought her to him. His anger now was because she'd lied. She'd tricked them into consuming the sleeping potion rather than tell the truth, which he understood was related to her fear, but it highlighted a lack of trust in him, in their love, in their family. That was why it hurt so much.

She looked down at her hands clutched tightly in front of her, but didn't add anything. "Tarley and Lachlan are going to New Taras as planned."

"Is that why there's a flurry outside of the campsite across the way?"

"I assume. They'll return when we have news of Jessamine."

"We'll look then? For her?" Tomas walked across the room, passing Scarlett and the table to wash his hands at the sink. He pumped the water.

"We? Us?"

He heard the hope in her voice and picked up the bar of soap. "How else will we find her?"

"Lachlan's man. He thinks he'll return here–"

"To the cottage?"

"Yes. So he's leaving soldiers for when he does." She paused. "Mattias is going to go with Tarley."

Tomas swallowed the lump in his throat. "He always wanted to go to New Taras." He lathered the soap in his hands. Scarlett made it layered with citrus and lavender, and the scent made him think of her, always. Of that space on her neck just below her ear.

Scarlett hummed an affirmation.

He liked that sound. It made him think of when they kissed, when he touched her, tasted her. Annoyed with the direction of his thoughts, he smacked the bar of soap into the little dish near the sink and pumped clean water onto his hands, rinsing away the soap. Then he dried them with a clean cloth she'd left near the sink for that purpose. When he was done, he turned and leaned against the counter, his hands framing his hips. "Where's Mattias now?"

"With the girls. They've gone with the gods to Elcadia."

He harrumphed a sound. "That was always Auri's plan. Brinna too?" He couldn't bring himself to look at Scarlett, hesitant because he knew that the moment he did, staying angry would be difficult. He wanted to be angry. He wanted to rage and throw things. Then realized he had, with his ax. He'd burned a lot of his anger away, and now what he had left was unresolved hurt caused by the woman he adored.

He wasn't sure what to do with it.

It wasn't as if they never fought. They did. A lot. Scarlett was too stubborn for her own good most of the time. Usually when it came to their kids, hiding things, being unreasonably controlling, and Tomas trying to get her to be reasonable.

But now the truth was out.

And the cottage was empty for the first time in over twenty-seven years.

He finally raised his eyes to hers.

"I'm sorry," she whispered.

"Sorry for what?"

She took a deep breath. "For a lot of things, but mostly for not trusting you. I shouldn't have done this. I shouldn't have lied."

Tomas didn't move, frozen in place at her admission, though he shouldn't have been surprised. While she was extremely stubborn, she wasn't characteristically dishonest. Their squabbles were never around those kinds of things. They were always around her need to control.

The thought caught Tomas's breath.

Nearly twenty-eight years with this woman, he knew her. She hadn't lied to hurt him, not intentionally. She'd lied to keep control of a situation that was slipping out of her control. Tarley had married and planned to move away. Auri had announced she was leaving. Mattias was ready to venture out. For Brinna and Jessamine it was only a matter of time for the same. Without them contained, she couldn't keep them safe. And that—keeping them safe—had always been at the heart of their quarrels, the heart of Scarlett's motive: her needing to control things to keep them safe, and him wanting to loosen the reins.

But he was tired of begging her to let go. To let him take the lead.

"It's quiet," he said, suddenly unsure where they stood with one another. Everything that had once defined them was now stripped away. Though there was a new crisis—finding Jessamine—who they'd been together had been about averting it.

"I made dinner," she said, darting across the space. "It's ready."

"I'm not sure if I'm hungry," he said, though he was famished. He wasn't sure what he wanted. Wasn't sure if he could sit at a table worrying about Jessamine.

She stopped short. "Oh." Her face fell and Tomas hated that he'd done that.

It wasn't in his nature to hurt her. He'd spent his life trying to support her, so much so that this felt strange and unfamiliar. His first impulse was to backtrack, to appease, but he knew he couldn't, not for her, but for him.

"Okay." She was back to wringing her hands.

"I'm going to wash up. Since the girls don't need their room—I'll sleep there."

She nodded but didn't reply.

Tomas supposed there wasn't anything she could say. For the first time in their relationship, it felt as if he held the power, and it felt wrong somehow. He'd always thought of them as a team, until now. "I need some time," he added.

Scarlett swallowed but punctuated it with another nod. "I understand."

He pushed away from the sink and walked away, through the room they usually shared, though the doorway that led to a small vestibule where they often put the bathtub. Tomas didn't fill the tub. He pumped cold water and used it to wash away his dirt. Then, just like he said he would, he retreated up the stairs to the room his daughters had shared all these years and lay on his back staring up at the ceiling. It was the first time he could remember sleeping apart from Scarlett. Even when he'd been small, he'd curled up in the fabric of her clothes or in the softness of her hair.

What he knew was that he still loved her. He would always love that woman. The question was, would that love be enough for a future that felt so uncertain?

Scarlett

Without news and only her imagination to feed her worry, Scarlett was a mess. Not only was Jessamine missing, but the rest of her children were gone, and Tomas was distant, speaking in short, clipped sentences about nothing of substance. The next day passed in a blur of stops and starts, trying to find projects to keep her mind and hands occupied.

She'd started in the girls' room to make their beds, but the thought of what she'd done, of what they'd gone through, what they now faced, that she'd failed them, that they were gone, pulled her regret out in broken, unfettered sobs until she'd been unable to stay in the room.

She'd taken the sheets she'd stripped to wash and hang,

but as she pressed them into the water along the washboard, she found herself sinking into the memories of her youth until she felt like she was drowning.

She'd left the washing for the garden, where the soil and plants usually brought her balance. But as she'd sat amongst the herbs, the glaring absence of her daughters brought forth the fresh anguish of the truth.

Her children were gone. Jessamine was missing. She'd failed.

So she'd left for the kitchen.

When Tomas returned from the barn that afternoon, the sound of his boots on the floor captured her attention as she stood at the kitchen counter he'd made for her. His form in the doorway—wide and encompassing—was at first a buoying relief then a crushing disappointment.

She'd failed him.

He stalled, assessing, his eyes dragging along the countertop where she stood amidst a haphazard wreck of herbs—her supplies for making tinctures and medicines she took on calls and sold at the market.

"Did you mean to leave all your tools in the garden?" he asked. There wasn't any accusation in his tone, only curiosity. "And the laundry undone in the wash basin?"

When she didn't answer—because she couldn't seem to align the words with meaning—he asked, "What's going on here?"

Scarlett looked down at the mess she'd made, opened her mouth to tell him what she was doing, but her mind went blank. She couldn't remember what she'd been doing. She didn't know what she was doing anymore. The longer she looked at the greens, the pestle and mortar, the boiling pot, the less sense any of the disarray made.

"It's chaos, Scar," he said quietly next to her. "Unlike you."

She looked up from the mess to his face, to his kind eyes shaped with concern.

Scar. She'd always loved the way he shortened her name, the only one who ever did.

Then without warning, she burst into tears, pressing the towel in her hands against her face as her grief, pain, worry, regret, disappointment wrenched out of her with horrific gasp. She'd ruined everything.

Tomas gathered her into his arms with soothing sounds. "Hush," he whispered, his wide, heavy hand on the back of her head.

"I'm so sorry," she sobbed, grasping hold of his shirt, her face pressed into the strength of his chest.

He held her.

"They're gone," she sobbed. "I failed."

His arms squeezed her a touch tighter, and when his face pressed into the place between her neck and shoulder, Scarlett wrapped her arms around his neck, drawing up onto her toes, needing to be closer to his comfort.

"I failed too," he whispered, his lips against her skin. "We both have."

She shook her head. "Not you, Tomas." She drew back to look at him.

Raising his head, his eyes connected with hers, the sadness a deep, evergreen forest swirling inside them where he was lost. And it was her fault. She knew this. Had pushed him to go against his nature by keeping her secrets, securing the spells.

Unsure about anything but the tumult of emotions she couldn't seem to harness, Scarlett reached for comfort she knew he provided, a comfort she could reciprocate.

She kissed him, her hands framing his face, his beard soft against her palms.

He froze, tension tightening his shoulders.

And she thought he might pull away, but suddenly he was kissing her back, capitulating, needing, seeking. His tongue sought entrance, and she granted it. It was hungry, two souls on the periphery of starvation, finding one another in the darkness.

Groaning into that connection, Tomas growled and lifted her.

He was hard, and Scarlett tugged at her skirts between them, needing to feel him pressed against her core. "Please," she begged against his mouth. "I need you."

Tomas—still kissing her with relentless and punishing abandon—carried her across the space and put her on the cleared table, nipping at her lips with his teeth. She shoved forward with her own fiery answer to his angry kiss, needing, wanting the pain he might inflict. His discipline.

He growled and pushed her down onto her back.

Scarlett fought against the submission, coming back to tug at his suspenders, then fumbling with the buttons at his waist. "In need you in me, Tomas."

He shoved her skirt up, sliding his calloused palms up the thighs. When he reached her undergarment, he tugged them aside, and dipped his fingers inside her.

Crying out at the invasion, she grasped his shoulders.

"Already wet," he said, and circled her clit with his thumb.

Scarlett convulsed at the sensation tearing up her spine, mewling and moving her hips against the pressure. "Please."

With a roughness she'd never known from Tomas, he growled as he pulled his cock from his pants and gripped her hips, tugging her to the edge of the table, before pushing into her. She cried out, but he didn't check on her to see if he had hurt her like he might have in the past. Scarlett appreciated this taking. She ached. She wanted to hurt everywhere.

But Tomas didn't hurt her.

He never had. As Scarlett wrapped her legs around his

thrusting hips and dug her heels into his backside, she didn't feel hurt, she felt paradise, and didn't deserve this pleasure. She cried out with pleasure as Tomas pounded into her, but it turned to a sob that she tried to hide from him.

But Tomas never missed a thing.

He stilled, his chest heaving with exertion and need. With a frown, he grabbed her face and made her look at him. She knew what he'd see: tears streaming down her face. She knew that he'd misinterpret.

"I hurt you?"

She shook her head. "No. No."

But he was already withdrawing.

She scrambled off the table to her feet, grasping at his arms to keep him from buttoning up. To finish what they'd started. "Don't go."

His tortured eyes searched her face, emotions he'd never been able to hide playing out on his. "This was a bad idea. I shouldn't have–"

"Please. Tomas. No."

He shrugged back into his suspenders as he backed away. "I shouldn't have–"

"I asked you. I begged–"

But he held up a hand and shook his head. "I should be stronger when it comes to you," he said, and his throat bobbed. "This doesn't fix what's broken between us." Then he turned and left the cottage.

Scarlett watched him go, unsure how long she stood looking at the empty doorway before she burst into tears. She didn't know how to find a way forward.

Tomas

Inside the barn, Tomas ducked into Wilhemina's stall, his chest heaving with anguish at the thought he'd hurt his wife. The mare snuffed at him, looking for treats in his pockets, and Ferdie, the gelding, knickered on the other side of the stable wall as if he was missing out. Tomas wrapped his arms around the horse's neck and breathed deeply, drawing in her earthy scent to clear his head of Scarlett.

But he couldn't release what had happened between them, seeing it over and over in his mind. The frantic way he'd felt. The frenetic way she'd responded.

I hurt you?

She'd said no, but the tears...

His breath caught at what he'd done.

Never, in all his years as Scarlett's husband, had he ever been rough with her. He was so aware of his size, his strength. But just then, he'd found pleasure in dominating her. He'd never felt the need before, and it frightened him.

He'd learned to be a good lover to Scarlett. He'd asked her to teach him what she liked early on, and she had. She'd reciprocated, learning with him what he liked. They shared enjoyable intimacy and four of their own children to show for it, though in a small cottage filled with people, time together had been stolen and rarely exploratory. Never once, had he ever been so... forceful. Even now, in the aftermath, he felt the rush of it as if heated his cheeks and zipped down his spine with... longing. He swallowed and doused it with guilt.

She'd been crying.

And you left.

He'd never once left her. Not like that. The accusation and self-recrimination burned his chest. With his forehead against Wilhemina's neck, he pressed his hand against the ache. Even in spite of his hurt, he still loved Scarlett, and if what happened a few moments ago was any indication, still wanted her, needed her. Finding comfort in her body amidst the chaos of the rest of the emotions had felt... right.

He sighed, straightened, and dragged a hand over his face.

Wilhemina pushed up against his chest, huffing her frustration at his inattention.

"I didn't bring anything, girl," he whispered, running a hand down her neck.

She nuzzled him, switching her weight from one side to the other.

"Fine," he said and offered her and Ferdie some grain. Then he went back to work on repairing a bit of leather he used for hitching the horses to the cart.

When he'd worked through his chaotic thoughts, he knew he needed to find a way forward with Scarlett. He spent some time figuring out how to articulate it all, then returned to the cottage to talk to her. But as he walked in just before the sun sank below the horizon, Scarlett was tying on her cloak.

"What are you doing?" he asked.

"Going to the woods. There's some stew on the stove."

"At this time? That's not a good idea. Crue is still out there. The darkling."

"I can't wait. Sundown is the best time to find her."

"Who? Jessamine?"

She slipped on gloves. "Baba."

Frustration bubbled up inside him. "For fuck's sake, Scar. Haven't we had enough of magic," he snapped. "Look at where it's gotten us." He flew out a hand, indicating nothing, really, just the empty space of the cottage that felt like it was smothering them.

Her eyes narrowed. "I want to find Jessamine."

Stubborn woman.

"And I don't?" he retorted.

"That's not what I said."

He heaved a sigh, trying to reclaim that calm that usually ruled him. But since waking from the spell, it wasn't as easy. The dreams haunted him, so much so that even now, closing his eyes to sleep made his chest tighten with fear and despondency. But he gripped the feeling of calm, holding onto it tightly and said, "We should check in the village. See if anyone saw anything. We can go. Tomorrow."

She nodded. "Yes. And Baba might be able to–"

"Scarlett!" he shouted at her. "Stop! Listen to yourself! Was dosing your family with a sleeping potion not enough?"

"But if she can help–"

"Do you know who you sound like?" When she didn't ask for more, he told her anyway. "Your father."

Her mouth opened with shock.

"So one-track minded you can't see beyond the tip of your fucking nose."

"That's not–"

"It isn't? Maybe you haven't imprisoned anyone, but you're addicted to the magic and need it to keep control of everything around you, even to the detriment of those you love."

"That's not–"

He grasped the back of his neck and turned his back to her, reason and calm fleeing. "You've never listened to me," he said, more a lamentation than accusation.

"Tomas, that's not–"

He spun back to her. "Was it pity? Is that why you've stayed with me? Because you felt sorry for me?"

"No. No!" She shook her head. "I love you."

He shook his head and waved a hand. "I'm not sure this is love, Scar." He huffed, the anger a beast writhing and alive inside him, then waved a hand. "Do what you're going to do. I just..." He stopped and shook his head again. "It's your life."

"No. It's ours," she replied, reaching for him.

He stepped away from her touch. "Is it? Has it ever been?"

He waited for her to respond, but when she didn't—her face slack with surprise—he walked past her, through the house to the back room where he usually took his bath. Rather than bathe, however, he stood there breathing like he'd raced home through the woods, his eyes burning with the horrible awareness that his life had always been hers, and now he didn't know who he truly was either way.

Scarlett stomped out into the blue twilight as night fell, anger and hurt fueling her steps. Incredulity and justification inspired her forward. How could Tomas accuse her of being like her father? The king had trapped her in a tower, and in his madness, planned on making her his wife.

You trapped your family in a spell.

She stumbled, catching herself against the barn wall, her breath suddenly coming in gasps. No. No. It wasn't the same. She was trying to protect them.

You trapped your family in a spell.

Tomas's words lurched through her: *Just like your*

father. Was it pity? The reason you stayed with me?

A sob bubbled up from the depth of her soul as she sank down to her knees on to the cold ground. Leaning against the barn wall, forehead pressed against the wood-plank siding, she cried. She loved Tomas, absolutely loved him. She tugged at her coat in her grief, the breeze in the trees—a hollow whirl rustling the boughs of evergreens—the hum of the River Grimz in the distance, and the crickets somewhere chirping in the night mingling with her thoughts and tears.

"You were right," she sobbed out loud to the old witch, even though she was just outside the cottage and knew the old woman wouldn't hear her.

Baba had told her she would lose everything, and that was exactly what was coming to fruition. Scarlett had been so focused on her need to keep them safe, she'd ignored the warning.

Tomas had told her to tell their children. She hadn't listened.

Obsessed, just like her father.

She nearly gagged at the realization, wanting to deny it but couldn't. She had imprisoned her family in a spell, and though her intentions had been to keep them safe, it wasn't a far cry different from what her own father had done to *keep her safe.*

When the weeping subsided, the power of that pain waning, she sniffed and sat back onto her heels, still kneeling in the ground outside the barn.

Her first impulse was to get to her feet and stomp into the woods to demand answers from Baba, but then she turned to look at the cottage, the windows dark but for the single window upstairs where she knew Tomas was.

Has it ever been our life? he'd asked.

The thought grabbed hold of the air in her lungs, and she gasped, trying to draw a breath, looking back at the barn wall. Had it? Every choice, every decision she'd made since running from her father, from Crue, had been to hide them, keep them safe. She had relied on the witch and the magic to do it. They were living in the cottage amid the Whitling Woods for that very reason.

Tomas was right.

She glanced at the glowing window like a beacon in the darkness once more.

Tomas.

When she walked into the main room of the cottage, depleted of indignation and the lies she'd been telling herself, it was dark and cold. The fire had gone out. She removed her cloak and hung it on the hook Tomas had installed for her, then shuffled through the front room to the back, noticing each and every spot had been touched by Tomas in some way. The table he'd built. The kitchen he'd changed. The stove he repaired. Every bit of this cottage was a home he'd built for her. For them.

She was struck with an understanding so deep it barely rose to the consciousness of her mind, only in fragments coalescing rather than the whole picture that might overwhelm her though the essence of the truth was there. While she'd been living to protect them from Crue, Tomas had been living for her, for their family.

This isn't love.

Her knees nearly buckled, and she grabbed the wall at the bottom of the stairs to keep her upright as tears burned through her body once more. These weren't heavy sobs, but quiet tears laced with regret and shame.

She did love Tomas. She needed him to know that.

When the wave of tears passed, she wiped her face and looked up the dark stairwell to a faint glow seeping under the door at the top. Speaking to Tomas was paramount, so she climbed the stairs, the wood creaking with her steps, hoping that it wasn't too late to find a different path forward, to tell him she wanted to be different.

But when she was a few steps from the top, the light went out, casting everything in darkness and shadow.

Her throat tightened at the thought that perhaps she'd crossed the point of no return with him.

So she retreated.

When she reached the room she'd shared with him for the last twenty-eight years, her heart dipped into her belly and burned with anguish. Though they were in the same house, she felt alone. She wanted to stomp back up the stairs and rage at him, tell him where he belonged, but the indignation died in the truth of what she'd done fueling her guilt. He'd said he doubted that she loved him. That was her fault.

She stripped off her dress and garments and slipped into the bed to spend another night alone.

Then another.

Followed by another.

Tomas never returned to their bed at night and spent the days avoiding her. He was gone before her, and silent and sullen, retreating out into the barn or up into the attic room.

But he'd asked for time, so she gave it. For the next two weeks, she lay in their bed missing him. Missing his large body curled around hers, the safety of being in his arms. Missing the feel of his calloused hands on her body. Missing his kiss. Missing the way it felt when his body invaded hers, filling her. Besides the birth of the children, they'd never gone this long without one another before. And while sleeping without him was horrible, the longer the time stretched, the more restless her sleep turned, her dreams brimming with dark imagery.

And worse yet, in that time there was no word from Crue or Lachlan's man about Jessamine.

One morning, Scarlett woke up with a start just before

the sun rose and lay there trying to catch her breath as the dream overran her thoughts. Dark flowers were blooming and taking over everything in her garden. It didn't matter how much she yanked and pulled, they squeezed out all that was good. When she looked closer, the healthy plants had the faces of her family. By the time it drifted away, she got up and slid into a chemise, then shuffled through the door into the kitchen to start the fire and put on the water for coffee.

To her surprise, Tomas was in the kitchen, pumping out water from the sink, his pants hanging at his waist, suspenders draped over his hips and his mouthwatering torso bare.

"Oh," she said, pulling up short at the sight of him.

He turned and looked at her, his eyes skimming over her nightshirt, his gaze heating before he looked back to his task.

Scarlett glanced at the potbelly stove and noticed the crackle of a fire alive with heat and fuel. "You lit the fire."

He grunted and turned, holding a full kettle.

"Thank you," she said, recognizing he had always lit the fire, in more ways than one.

His eyes jumped to hers as he crossed the space to set the water on the stove, but he didn't say anything, just offered her a nod.

"About the other night," she said, taking a step toward him.

"Scarlett." He held up his hands and took a step away. "I can't."

"Can't what?" she asked, afraid to know what that meant.

"I can't do this right now," he said and started across the room.

"But we need to–" Scarlett started, only to be interrupted by a knock at the door. Her gaze bounced from the door back to Tomas, who'd stopped.

Her heart skipped, tripped, then raced.

"Are you expecting someone?" he asked.

She shook her head. They both knew Jessamine wouldn't knock. "Maybe it's news?" She walked over to the couch, pulling a blanket draped over the back, and throwing it around her shoulders like a shawl.

Tomas shrugged into the shirt he'd dropped on the table, then stopped at the threshold of the closed door. "Who is it?" he asked.

"Trevis, sir. Come to fetch Miss Scarlett for Mimi."

A deflated sigh filled with possibility left her, and tears cut the back of her eyes.

Tomas glanced over his shoulder at her, then opened the door to the boy who worked at the stables of the Copper Pot Inn. He swung his overgrown blond hair from his eyes and flashed a brilliant smile unaware that anything was amiss.

"Mimi is in labor?" Scarlett asked him.

He nodded. "Credence sent me."

"Let me get my things," she said and started back to the room to dress.

"What happened to the hedge?" she heard the boy ask as she shut the door. Tomas's deep voice rumbled as he answered.

With a sigh, she pushed away from the door disappointed that she couldn't have this conversation with Tomas now, but perhaps some more time was best for him. Here the universe was offering it.

When she came back out into the main room of the cottage, Tomas was still there waiting with Trevis, surprising her. Both of their faces turned when she opened the door.

"Ready then," she said and though she said it to Trevis, her eyes sought Tomas.

Her husband scratched at his brown beard he always kept neat but looked like it needed a trim. He glanced at her for a moment and ran a hand through his brown hair. Like his beard, it was a touch too long, curling around his face. She was the one who usually trimmed it, but he hadn't asked. "Well then," he said.

She wanted to scream but just ground her teeth together and met them both at the doorway. Living like this was going to tear her apart, she decided. Living their lives together but separated wasn't going to work. Though she was trying to be patient and give him the time he needed, neither of them deserved to live in this purgatory.

Without looking at him, she said, "It could be a couple of days. Mimi's first baby."

"Alright," he said quietly and nodded, his eyes on the floor between her feet.

She wanted more, but he wasn't going to provide it. So she started through the door, but Tomas stopped her, a strong hand wrapped around her arm. She looked up at him.

"Is it safe?" he asked quietly, his eyes bouncing to Trevis, who had wandered out into the yard, then back to her.

Scarlett wanted to imbue those words with hope, but it struggled to stay afloat. "Does it matter?" she asked but didn't wait for Tomas to reply, leaving the cottage behind but taking her heartbreak with her.

Tomas

'Does it matter?'

Scarlett's question plagued him the whole of the day after she left for Sevens. He knew where she was: the skinhouse. Mimi was a worker that Scarlett had been monitoring since the young woman had learned she was pregnant.

Even knowing where Scarlett was, watching her walk away ate at him.

Everything ate at him.

He'd left for the forest to collect wood to repair the lean-to and firewood for a few of the merchants in Sevens. The giant trees rose up around him, and he felt judged. Since his fight with Scarlett about the witch, he'd taken the distance he'd asked for. While he'd hoped it would offer him clarity, maybe even provide him direction, it only served to make him long for his wife. That was confusing, considering all she'd done.

And yet, he understood it.

She'd been abused, lied to, threatened, tricked, chased. She'd always needed to control the outcome of things, hadn't ever lied to him about wanting to be a better parent than her own—to protect her children. While he knew his understanding didn't excuse her choice, it helped his hurt and anger fade some.

The truth was that Scarlett had fallen in love with him before he had been a full-sized man. She'd extended grace to choose him regardless of his size. It had been the witch who'd given him that gift. If anyone understood the lure, the call, and the danger of magic, it was him. Considering all the ways Scarlett had been hurt and how magic had been the only means to protect herself, perhaps it hadn't been fair of him to be surprised that's where she defaulted to find Jessamine.

Did it matter?

When she didn't return that night, Tomas sat in the cottage watching the fire and wondering what to do. His heart and mind were wild with worry, but he resisted the urge to saddle Ferdie and visit the skinhouse to make sure

Scarlett was safe. While he didn't chase the impulse, it offered him some truths. First, that he cared about Scarlett and her safety and second—that wildness inside him was more than just concern.

He pictured her walking into the kitchen that morning in her nightshirt, her hair mussed with sleep, knowing she'd been bare underneath. It was how she always slept. His innards had tilted, his equilibrium unbalanced at the way he missed her. Sleeping apart had become a burden, and though he thought it was what was best to get a clear sense of the path forward, each night away from her had become harder and harder to bear. The time was ripping the hole in his chest bigger and wider. Being stuck in the uncertainty of in between was no way to live.

He wanted his wife as much now as he had twenty-eight years ago.

He cared for Scarlett's well-being.

The truth was, he loved her. He'd never stopped.

So yes, it fucking mattered.

She'd tried to talk to him, and he'd been the ass to rebuff her attempt.

As soon as she returned, he decided. They would talk.

The following day, he stayed close to home, hopeful for her return. But as he chopped wood and stacked it in the cart, she didn't appear in the lane.

She still didn't return after he'd finished lunch. His

anxiety spiked at thoughts that she was in danger, that Crue had found her and stolen her away.

By the time Tomas finished with firewood orders, he couldn't contain himself—he saddled Ferdie and raced into Sevens, his mind racing as the gelding galloped toward town.

He hitched Ferdie to the post outside the skinhouse. He wasn't completely comfortable going in, never having visited before, but his need to know Scarlett was safe overrode any discomfort. He turned the doorknob and entered.

It was nice. A comfortable entry, tastefully decorated, though he wasn't sure what he would have expected, not having any experience about it either way. In his first twenty-two years, he'd met one woman who'd sold her body—Glinda had been her name. Tomas had hitched a ride on her shoulder, and while Glinda had hinted at the struggle to survive which necessitated her profession, she'd been a kind, funny, and accommodating companion.

"Mr. Fareview!" The proprietress of the establishment smiled when she looked up from the settee in the entry. "I didn't think I would ever see you here." Stella laughed as if she'd made a good joke. "I assume you're here for Scarlett."

He didn't answer, just nodded tightly at her, his eyes skimming the long hallway, the stairwell, the bar area. "She's okay?"

Stella's smile widened. "I'd expect she's exhausted. Baby is taking its time, and poor Mimi is having a rough go of it being her first babe and all. Would you like me to get her?"

Tomas shook his head and backed away. "No. Don't want to interrupt. Just checking on her."

Stella's brown eyes twinkled.

He nodded his head though nothing had been said and withdrew from the building, looking up at it once he was outside, his heart racing with... trepidation? Fear? He wasn't sure. He knew where Scarlett was, so why did he feel so unsettled?

Instead of returning to the cottage, he retreated to the Copper Pot and bellied up to the bar, where Horance poured him an ale.

"Everything alright, Tomas?" Horance asked, wiping his hands on a cloth. Horance's bulk blocked much of the view of the tapped kegs were lined up along the wall. Tomas hadn't met many men as big as he was, but Horance was close.

Tomas nodded. "Fine."

Since Horance wasn't a man of many words and neither was Tomas, they existed in companionable silence as he finished his ale. He still didn't return to the cottage, staying to have another ale, and then another. As he drank, he meandered his memories and realized he'd spent most of his first twenty-two years alone. Sure, he'd grown up with his parents, who he'd left when he'd turned fourteen. Then he'd done what he could to get by, relying on cleverness and charm to make his way in a giant world.

But those interactions had always been transactional. He'd never had anyone to call home. Until Scarlett. So going back to an empty cottage wasn't what he wanted, and he was beginning to suspect it wasn't what he needed either.

Scarlett

The baby howled his first cry shortly before dawn on the third day. Though Scarlett had known Mimi's birth would take some time, she didn't understand why she was feeling the way she was about it. But as she reflected further, she realized it was because things were so uncertain with Tomas. It made her nostalgic for when everything seemed so clear when their children were young. She'd left things with Tomas unresolved, and it didn't feel right.

After making sure Mimi and the baby were tucked up and surrounded by people who loved them, she descended to the lobby, ready to go home.

Stella stood, wrapped in a robe, waiting, and handed

Scarlett the promised luri. "Thank you, Scarlett. I don't know what we'd do without you."

"Find a way," Scarlett said, wondering what she would do if Tomas decided that he no longer wanted to remain partners. Though she had a trade to support her, life without him felt bleak. She would find a way too, she supposed.

"By the way," Stella said, "that husband of yours is a treasure."

The mention of Tomas stopped her. "Excuse me?" Scarlett knew that to be true but tilted her head at Stella, who read the question in Scarlett's gaze.

"He was here last night."

"He was?" Her heart bounced inside her chest. "Did he say why?"

"Just came to check on you." Stella tightened her robe. "Didn't say much but wanted to make sure you were safe, I'd guess." Stella smiled. "Keep that one close. Not very often a good one comes along."

Scarlett nodded. "Oh. Yes. A good one," she mumbled, dumbfounded, and backed out beyond the front door, her mind tripping over why Tomas might've come. He'd known where she was, what she was doing. Maybe there was news.

She whirled around, to find Tomas standing in the middle of the road, leaning against Ferdie. Her heart stopped. Then it raced. He looked as he usually did. His dark boots crossed at the ankle, muscular legs filling dark trousers held up by suspenders, though she knew he didn't truly need them. His broad chest and shoulders were covered with an ivory tunic she'd made him, and though there was chill in the air, he hadn't worn a jacket, his sleeves rolled to his elbows, his strong arms on display. His head was tipped down, his chin to his chest as if he were asleep, leaning up against Ferdie.

Tentative hope and light burst inside her chest as she took a step toward him.

Then he looked up, and when he saw her, he straightened. Ferdie side-stepped at the loss of Tomas's weight, the animal obviously leaning into him as well.

"You're here," she said.

He grunted, stepped forward, and took the bag from her hand. "Yeah," was his reply.

She was bursting with the need to ask him all the questions on her mind but was afraid to break the spell that wove its way between them—its own kind of magic. So she didn't say anything, just waited, giving Tomas the lead.

"Thought you might be tired." He set down her satchel at Ferdie's feet, then turned and held out his hand.

Scarlett took it and stepped toward him. "Yes. Thank you. Have you been waiting long?"

Tomas captured her waist in his hands and lifted her

onto the gelding's back, his hands lingering a moment before he bent to retrieve her bag and handed it off.

"Spent the night at the inn." He climbed up onto the horse behind her, then adjusted to accommodate the both of them, settling her a touch closer between his spread thighs, her legs draped over one of his. Nestling her body safely between his arms, he clicked his tongue, flicked the reins, and turned Ferdie around.

"The inn?" Scarlett asked as the Ferdie clomped through Sevens.

"Drank a little too much with Horance."

"Horance drank?"

"No. He just served me and laughed at me when I could barely stand."

"You drank?"

He hummed an affirmation. "Let me sleep it off there."

The sun was just hinting at the horizon, the sky above the sharp treetops a thin blue touched with streaks of pink, orange, and yellow. There wasn't a cloud in the sky—strange for Sevens—but it was going to be a beautiful fall day. It was so early, the thoroughfare was empty but for the sound of Ferdie's hooves hitting the packed earth.

Scarlett rifled through her bag for an herbal candy she'd made for the effects of a hangover. "This might help," she said and held up the sweet drop in her hand.

Tomas's eye dipped to her open hand, but instead of

grabbing it, his eyes jumped up to hers, and he opened his mouth, his command clear.

Scarlett swallowed but lifted the drop to his lips, her gaze trailing the movement of her hand to his mouth. His lips closed around her fingers, his tongue caressing her skin as it curled around the sweet drop. Her heart quickened in her chest, a shimmer of a dance filled with buoyancy, and she looked up at Tomas whose gaze was filled with heat.

Scarlett didn't speak, afraid to, but looked to the lane ahead of them as she relaxed against Tomas's chest.

He didn't speak either until they'd turned onto the lane toward the cottage. "How did she do?"

"Mimi?" When he grunted, she answered, "A rough go. Got a little worried, but she made it through."

"She had you," he said.

She turned her head to look at him, moved by the pride she heard in his voice. "Stella said you came."

He grunted again in acknowledgement, his cheeks tinted with a blush.

Scarlett looked back at the road ahead and pondered this information. Tomas had come to the skinhouse to check on her, he'd ended up at the pub and drank so much he couldn't get home—uncharacteristic of her husband—then he'd waited for her, and now he blushed that she knew. She nestled closer into him, going so far as to lean her head against his chest—partially to test if he'd allow it, partially because she was so tired, and mostly because she needed him.

He did allow it, one of his arms wrapping around her, to hold her steady. "Rest," he said.

She needed to, but her mind was buzzing with all the things they needed to talk about. There so much she wanted to say.

But she realized Tomas wasn't a man of words. He was a man of action.

Her words died before they were said as she realized she needed to show him, prove she wanted a way forward between them. So she just rested her head against him, listening to his steady heartbeat.

A little while later, Tomas hummed a happy noise that reverberated through his chest and into Scarlett, and Ferdie nickered, huffing excitedly. "Scar?" he said quietly.

She sat up and looked at him before turning to see what he was smiling at. Standing at the door of the cottage were Brinna and Auri, Lucian with them.

"Hello!" Tomas called as he brought Ferdie to a stop and dismounted, helping Scarlett down from the horse to the ground. His face was beaming with delight, but anxiety gripped Scarlett.

She bit her tongue from asking if there was news, and shut her eyes, resetting. Choosing forward met being more patient, she decided. When she opened her eyes, Tomas was watching her.

"Morning, Father." Brinna curled up into her father's embrace, then made way for Auri, who did the same. "Mother," she said.

Scarlett looked at Lucian, still by the steps to the doorway. He looked hesitant to leave. "Afraid I've got another spell up my sleeve?" she asked.

His eyes narrowed. "Truthfully, Scarlett. Yes."

"Fair enough," she answered.

Neither of her daughters embraced her.

"I'll help you with Ferdie," Auri told Tomas, never meeting Scarlett's gaze. "I'd like to see Wilhemina too."

Scarlett watched Auri and Tomas walk toward the barn, then turned to Brinna and Lucian. "You're here early." She led them into the cottage.

"You were on a call?" Brinna asked, her eyes dropping to Scarlett's satchel.

"Mimi Wills had her baby."

Brinna smiled and glanced at Lucian, then blushed. "We just came to check on you. See if perhaps Lachlan's guard had returned."

The hope that had started with the sunrise remained as Scarlett set the satchel on the table then moved to get a fire going in the hearth. "We haven't. I'd hoped perhaps you had news." She stuffed the tinder in the kindling.

"No. But Lucian's sister—Lexa—thinks she knows

someone to help us learn how to use the magic," Brinna said.

"Tarley and Mattias, too?" Scarlett lit the tinder and leaned forward, blowing on it before looking at Brinna when it caught.

Brinna nodded. "Yes."

"They're... alright? You're all alright?" She swiped at her dress swallowed the guilt and rose up inside her.

Brinna frowned and glanced at Lucian, who was also frowning. "No, Mother. We're not. Auri and Nix most of all."

She nodded, knowing now that she'd planted a terrible harvest, and this was what it was reaping. "I didn't know."

No one said anything. What was there to say to that, really?

Scarlett moved back to the table, trying to do something with her nerves, spending the energy on something rather than standing idly waiting for the next words that Brinna might say that would deflate her hope further. Grabbing her satchel, she began organizing its innards, pulling emptied containers to discern what she needed to refill and make more of.

"Mother?"

She stopped and looked at Brinna, waiting, unwilling to offer up any more words that might increase the distance between her and her daughter.

"How are you?"

That hadn't been what she expected. Tears filled her eyes until Brinna blurred before her. Before Scarlett could catch them, several slipped down her cheeks. "What?" was all she could push past her thick throat. Then she whirled back to the fire and added several chunks of wood.

Suddenly Brinna, her sweet, sweet Brinna, grabbed hold of Scarlett and helped her into a chair at the table. "Sit." Brinna pulled a chair so she was facing Scarlett, so close their knees were nearly touching. Then she gathered Scarlett's hands between her palms.

"I saw your dreams," Brinna said. "During the spell. And Lucian" –she glanced over her shoulder to look at the golden god, watching the exchange from several feet away before looking back at Scarlett– "saw..."

Brinna stopped and swallowed, looking down at her lap and shaking her head as if to dispel whatever she saw in her mind's eye.

"I uncovered your story," Lucian said simply.

Brinna lifted her eyes filled to the brim with emotion and nodded. Tears slipped down her cheeks.

Suddenly, their reaction after the spell had been broken made sense. Their understanding.

Scarlett wasn't sure how she felt about that, having wanted to protect her children from that awful truth. She would have taken it to her grave if it had been possible to save them from the horrible awareness. But now the truth was theirs too.

There were parts she was ashamed of—like falling prey to Crue—but now, nearly twenty-eight years later, she recognized she'd always been the victim and shouldn't carry the blame, even if knowing it didn't always reconcile with living it.

More tears slipped from her eyes. "I just wanted to protect you from it. From him."

Brinna squeezed her hands. "Only now, you don't need to anymore. Now we just need to focus on getting Jessamine back."

Scarlett's eyes flashed to Lucian, then back to Brinna. "I've ruined everything," she whispered.

Brinna glanced over her shoulder and offered the god a teary smile. "I think Lucian has some wisdom he could share about that."

The golden god smiled at Brinna, a brilliant look filled with love and adoration. He closed the space until he was sitting at the table next to Brinna, wrapping a hand around the back of her neck. "The story starts with a young god named Nixus and his villainous older twin brother, Lucian." His gaze jumped to Scarlett. "Thinking I was doing the right thing at the time, I cast a spell that trapped him for over ten years. He almost didn't make it out but for a plucky key keykeeper named–" He stopped and looked at Brinna expectantly.

Brinna smiled, bumping against him with her back. "Aurielle Fareview."

Chills raced across Scarlett's skin. "Auri?"

"The Great Nap Escapade," Brinna clarified.

Scarlett's eyes jumped between Brinna and Lucian. "The key she wears?"

Lucian nodded. "That is where she and Nixus met, where they were god-yoked. The spell was my fault, you see."

Scarlett disconnected from Brinna's hold and covered her mouth with a hand.

"I understand regretting a choice," Lucian said, "but someone taught me that you can't get stuck there." He cleared his throat and glanced at Brinna, who nodded. "I saw your father," he added.

Scarlett jumped up, her chair hitting the floor with a loud bang. "How?"

Lucian held out his hands. "Clarification. He's in the Netherrealm, long dead from the world. He can't hurt you."

She nodded even though her heart raced, and she shook with the need to flee.

"He was stuck even in the afterlife, a husk, I'm sure, of the good man he'd once been, but fighting with all the versions of the man he'd become. Stuck in his mind and his obsession with your mother."

Scarlett nodded, her stomach swirling with nausea, her

hand still pressed against her mouth.

"And I tell you this to say that the choice you made, the choice I made—albeit terrible ones—don't have to keep us stuck. We can make other choices, better ones. Ones that heal and grow."

The dark flowers in Scarlett's dream surfaced in her mind.

"I forgive you, Mother," Brinna said, "and I understand why, even if I don't agree."

A sob rasped and caught in Scarlett's throat. She covered her face with her hands, unable to hold back. When Brinna's arms wrapped around her, Scarlett leaned into her child, finally understanding what Tomas had been telling her all along.

Tomas

"Are you alright?" Tomas asked Auri as they walked into the barn, leading Ferdie behind them. "Is it nice where you are? Safe?"

Auri glanced at him. "I should be asking you that."

"Why?"

"Because you're stuck here with her."

"Auri–"

She huffed a breath. "I'm sorry. I am. I'm just so angry."

"Go get me the brush," he said and watched Auri walk across the barn. She stopped to give Wilhemina some affection, and he led Ferdie into the paddock.

"Good boy," he hummed and patted the gelding, unbuckling the saddle and pulling it from the horse's body along with the blanket to drape them over the railing.

"Your anger is justified," he said. "For both of us."

Auri appeared in the doorway, then shut the gate behind her. "You?"

"I kept her secrets, Auri. From you. From you all."

"Why doesn't that feel as bad?"

He shrugged.

Aurielle sighed. "I knew something was up, right away. Nixus–" Her voice caught, and she swallowed which made Tomas unsure and unsteady for her.

Using the brush on Ferdie's fur, Auri appeared to reset, her features softening. "Anyway, Nix told me there was more to the story, and he was right. And I just knew, every time Mother would say something, that it wasn't the whole of it. It's that power, this knowing, like she said." Auri held her hands out in front of her, and though they were empty, it was like she could see what lay in her palms, the brush included. "I can see all these puzzle pieces in my head and when one is missing or one is more important, it stands out."

Tomas took the brush from Auri and smoothed Ferdie's other side with the thick bristles.

"Yes. We're safe," she said, finally answering his initial question. "Lucian's home is beautiful. And Lexa, that's Nix and Lucian's sister, knows someone to help us with the magic."

Tomas frowned, handing the brush back to Auri, hating the magic for no other reason than what it had wrought on his family.

"I remember Lexa," he said, recalling her from the meadow where she'd descended as a dragon. He removed the bridle, unbuckling the harness from the horse's head and drawing the bit from Ferdie's mouth. "A good thing?" He rubbed the gelding's velvet nose.

"If it can help us get Jessamine back, I think so."

He nodded, and they finished up with Ferdie. Auri gave him grain and feed while Tomas put the tack away. When he re-emerged from the tack room, Auri was standing at Wilhemina's paddock, speaking softly to the mare.

"Your mother," he said, surprised he'd started that way, but the conviction to still support Scarlett was heavy on his heart.

Auri looked up. "I know the story."

"Knowing the story and understanding the story are two different things. Like your power. You might have it, know it's there, but being able to use it requires a deeper understanding."

She swallowed, nodded, and pressed her forehead to Wilhemina, a position he found himself in a lot.

"I met her just after she escaped the tower." He paused, leaning against the wall across from his daughter. Looking at the floor, he tracked the grain of the wood near her feet, trying to find the reason he was speaking about this at all, unsure where his memories were taking them. They felt important somehow, whether it was for Auri or him, he didn't know.

"She was so afraid," he continued. "I'll never forget that." He frowned remembering that visceral fear on her face. "I'd been a selfish prick up to that point in my life. Really only cognizant of myself and my own needs, and this beautiful woman dropped into my world—literally—and needed me. I felt seven feet tall."

"You are nearly seven feet tall," Auri quipped.

Tomas offered her a short smile. "That's the thing about your mother. She never made me feel small, even when I could fit in the palm of her hand. She never looked at me like I was less than."

Even if her actions had of late —but he could see it had been an act born of her desperation, and Scarlett backed into a corner was a feral creature. He'd been the one to see himself as small. That wasn't her fault.

"Why are you telling me this, Father?"

Tomas sighed. "Things change," he said quietly, more to himself than to her.

She looked a bit taken aback by the statement. "What does that mean?"

He looked up at his daughter. "Things can't remain unchanged. I changed when I met your mother. I wanted to be better for her. Now she's changing. Our whole family is changing. It's the law of living, I suppose."

Auri was quiet.

The horses snuffed and nickered, wanting attention.

"Do you still love her?" Auri asked.

"Yes," he said without hesitation. "That is one thing that remains unchanged, but love evolves, I think, as we do."

"Right," Auri said, pressing a hand to her heart. "I'll have to try."

Tomas didn't understand what she meant by her words—not completely—but it connected to his heart somehow, the final missing piece of a puzzle dropping into place.

After Auri, Brinna and Lucian left, Tomas's eyes found hers.

"I'll be heading into the village tomorrow," he said. "Ask around about Jessamine. I'm tired of waiting."

She nodded. "Okay. I'll be ready."

He nodded, then walked away.

"Tomas?" she called.

He stopped and turned back toward her.

"Should we talk? About us?"

"Yes," he said, backing away. "I just need to get my thoughts in order." He disappeared once more up the stairs.

Scarlett watched him go, wanting to push him into

doing it now. But it was his turn to lead them, so she didn't and spent another restless night without him.

The lack of hedge was still strange as they set off the next morning. The safety of it had been part of their existence as long as they'd lived in Sevens. That protective fence had offered her security, and now that it was stripped away, she was exposed.

"Do you think Crue will look for us?" Tomas asked as they started down the road toward side by side.

Scarlett hummed a response, more to give herself time than as an actual answer. She didn't want to talk to Tomas about Crue, but finding Crue was how they would find Jessamine. "No. He has what he wants."

"Not everything," he said, glancing at her.

"He has Jessamine."

"Do you think he'll..."

"Consume her?" Her voice shook as she said it, unsure how to answer and unable to offer any more solace than she could provide herself. "I don't know what he'll do."

They walked in silence for longer than was comfortable.

"Tomas–"

"We need to–" he started at the same time. "Sorry," he said. "You first."

"I do love you," she said, unwilling to allow him any more time to think that wasn't so.

"Why did you lie to me?"

"I didn't tell you about the potion because I knew you would disagree and you'd fight me on it."

"So you just don't trust me?"

"I do."

"Just not enough to also have our children's best interest at heart? Or yours? Ours?"

Her eyes burned with tears hearing his words. She could see his point, and while it was fair, she wasn't sure how to reconcile her choice with his needs. It was a fair question. "I do trust you, I didn't want to take the risk–"

"–which still led to Jessamine being taken by Crue."

"Yes," she bit out. "Had I considered that…"

"If you'd asked me, you might have."

The bitterness was evident in his voice, and it made Scarlett feel defensive. "I just did what I thought was right."

"But that's always the case, isn't it, Scarlett. It's always what you think is right. Your decision, your plans, your way or no way."

She bristled against his observation, wanting to deny it, but she'd damned herself. She had nothing to hold her up. "I was just trying to protect them." And failed.

They walked in silence, Scarlett pondering what he'd said and hating how it convicted her, hating that she knew he was right. She'd made it easier for Crue to get his hands on Jessamine. Her fault. And the sensation of having alienated Tomas was a rendering of what made her whole.

"Why do you think he only took Jessamine?" she asked.

"As opposed to both of you?"

"Why leave at all?" she asked. "He made it through the hedge. Got to us."

They walked in silence, her mind working it over. What she knew of Crue was that he wanted the powers she'd taken, he wanted the godlight. Jessamine held the godlight, but not the powers.

"Timing and ability, I'd guess," Tomas said. "If Lachlan, Nix, and the other one came through the hedge around the same time. Maybe he didn't have time."

"But he could have incapacitated them. Locked the cottage."

"Even the gods?"

Scarlett nodded. That was true. Perhaps not, but that didn't make sense to her.

Then it hit her. She stopped short. "He doesn't know."

"Know what?" Tomas stopped a few feet away, turning when he noticed she wasn't next to him.

"That I don't have the powers. He wants them back. Not just the godlight."

"He thinks you have them."

"And maybe Jessamine is his leverage."

"Which means we will hear from him."

She nodded and started toward him. "And she will be safe, at least as long as he thinks he can control me."

Tomas

"What did you want to tell me?" Scarlett asked as they continued down the lane toward the village.

Tomas glanced at his wife ready to change the strife between them, tired of the distance.

"Tomas?" she asked, drawing him back to the lane.

"I'm sorry for hurting you," he said simply.

"Hurting me?" She sounded confused. "About my father?"

"On the table." Her breath hitched, and he glanced at her. "I didn't mean to be... rough." Only it felt like a lie. He had wanted to be rough. He wanted to be rough now.

"I wasn't hurt," she said quietly, her cheeks colored with

a sweet blush. "You didn't hurt me." Who knew his wife would blush after being together for twenty-eight years?

"But you were crying."

"I told you it wasn't that." She glanced at him and offered a wan smile. "I was just overwhelmed."

"Because of Jessamine?"

"Yes. But being with you felt like such a relief. It felt so… good, I didn't feel like I deserved it."

He hummed a sound as they walked into Sevens, pondering what she'd said. *She'd liked it.* She thought she didn't deserve to be with him. It upended what he'd always thought about how he should be with his wife, intimately. He glanced at her with curiosity but held his tongue and considered that perhaps that filtered into other areas of his life. His deference to her control had often ruled his choices, and when she'd pushed against his pushback, he'd often given way.

By the time they reached the mercantile, Tomas was even more unsettled by this realization. They checked in with Mr. Koffi, who hadn't seen Jessamine.

"Is she alright?" Mr. Koffi asked.

Scarlett exchanged a look with Tomas but then bit her lip, uncharacteristically withdrawing from the conversation. Seeing her unsure felt strange, but Tomas took charge. "No. We think she might be in danger."

Mr. Koffi's eyes grew. "What can I do?"

"Keep your ears and eyes open," Tomas said. "Anything different or strange comes through, anything said that just doesn't sit right, would you let us know?"

"Absolutely," Koffi said. "There's been so many strangers through here lately with the Queen's visit and the wedding–"

Tomas nodded.

"But yes, of course, you'll have my eyes and ears."

When they walked out into the dull gray of the afternoon, snowflakes were beginning to fall intermittently. "Should we split up?" Tomas asked.

Scarlett took his hand in hers and shook her head.

With his wife's hand in his, they stopped at the blacksmith and metalworks, the baker, and every other shop and home along the way. Tomas wasn't surprised that there hadn't been any sighting, but it felt good to know that their village community was willing to help. They finished at the Copper Pot Inn, speaking with Credence and her brother Horance.

"Have you checked in with some of the homes on the outskirts of Sevens?" Horance asked.

"Not yet," Tomas said.

"Send those soldiers Ollie... I mean, Prince Lachlan left," Credence suggested. "We'll keep our eyes and ears open here."

"Let me grab Trevis," Horance said, setting down his

drying towel on the bar. "He mentioned something about new tenants." The barkeep set down a tankard of ale for Tomas and started around the bar. "Might be a few of those along the way with all the new people up this way. And if Jessamine was taken, someone might have seen something."

"That's a good idea," Scarlett said, her eyes jumping to Tomas's as he took a sip of the ale.

A few minutes later, Trevis walked in on the heels of Horance, dusting snow from his hair. "I think it's the first true snow of the year."

"Afternoon, Trevis," Tomas said and smiled at the boy, a few years younger than Mattias.

"Sir. Horance said you're searching for Jessamine?"

"Aye," he replied. "Think she might be in some trouble. Horance here said you mentioned there are new tenants we might check with?"

"A couple. People talk about working for a few. There's Midlord Applegate over in the old Clawsen Chalet. And there's a Highlord Ramslow in the Pickering Manor. That's two I know of—the closest."

Scarlett turned to Credence. "Would you pass that message onto the two Jast soldiers?"

"I'd be happy to. Send them out as soon as it's possible to travel. How bad is that snow?" Credence asked Trevis.

"Just starting to come down."

"We should probably start home," Tomas said and

finished the ale.

"Can I give you a ride?" Trevis asked.

"No. No. We should beat it," Tomas said.

But halfway home, the light snowfall just shy of a blizzard, and they'd only worn their fall outer garments.

"Faster, Scarlett," Tomas ordered.

"My toes are frozen," she said. "We should have known better. How many years have we lived in Sevens?"

Tomas grunted. "We're almost there," he said, hopeful that was true. While he knew the road between Sevens and their cottage as well as the back of his hand, the road looked different in the snowfall. And now, without the hedge, they needed to get there before the dark set in. There weren't any lights on in the window—which he should have considered without anyone else at home.

"Maybe you should run ahead," she said. "Light the fire and the lanterns."

"I'm not leaving you," he growled. "Just move faster."

When the cottage finally came into view, the wind had picked up, and seeing the dark outline of the cottage amidst the snow felt like a miracle. Tomas grabbed hold of Scarlet, tugging her into his arms, and shuffled through the deepening snow to get her inside.

It was freezing, and both of them were wet.

"Strip," he told her. "I'll get the fire started."

By the time the fire was growing in the fireplace, Tomas

stood. "Scar?" He spun, and she stood a few feet away, dressed only in her chemise. The ivory fabric hung off her shoulder, and she shivered, her arms wrapped around her.

He held out a hand. "Come."

She took his hand and let him lead her to stand in front of the fireplace. He rubbed her arms with his hands.

Through chattering teeth, she said, "You need to get your wet clothes off."

He nodded.

She helped him remove his coat, dropping it on the floor.

"I'm sorry for not taking Trevis up on the offer of a ride," he said.

"It's okay."

He shook his head. "I know better, about snow in these woods."

She shrugged and pushed on his suspenders. "We both do. And this is a bit early."

He drew his arms through the loops and let them drape over his hips, then pulled his tunic from his trousers as she unfastened the buttons at his neck. She helped him pull it over his head.

"Your boots," she said.

He sat on the couch.

She knelt to help him.

"I can do this," he said, though his eyes greedily took in

Scarlett on her knees before him. He swallowed.

"I want to help," she said, pulling at one boot. "Let me take care of you."

He started to say he could do it but stopped.

"You have always taken care of me," she continued, removing his second boot, and setting it next to its match. She slid her hands from his ankle up his shin. "Your pants are soaked."

His heart raced at her touch, needing it more than he wanted to admit, but leaned back, his hands fisted on either side of his hips.

Still on her knees, she leaned forward and unfastened his pants with a soft touch, tugging them down. Tomas lifted his hips to help her, watching as she removed not only his outer garments but his under as well.

She folded and set the clothes in a neat pile near his boots, then studied him before walking closer on her knees so he had to spread his legs wider to accommodate her.

The light of the fire offered him the shadow of her body under her chemise, the neckline hanging to afford him the view of her bound breasts. He thought about reaching for her but didn't, his heart a cacophonous beat in his ears and vibration in his chest.

Her hands glided across the skin of his thighs.

"Scar?" he asked.

She cupped his sack in her palm and looked up at him

through her lashes. "Is this alright?"

He hesitated—not because he didn't want it but because he wanted it too much. Despite his fear that giving into what he wanted to feel with her might cloud his judgment, he nodded.

She kneaded him with her hand and leaned forward, sliding her tongue along the underside of his cock from root to tip. Having missed this intimacy with her, Tomas sucked in a harsh breath and moaned, drawing his wife's gaze before she took him into her mouth.

Scarlett

With a fervor to please him, Scarlett wrapped her mouth around Tomas's cock, and it swelled inside her mouth, stretching her as she slid down his shaft toward the base. She moaned with desire, her own wetness pooling between her legs, as she shifted her tongue to accommodate his girth, dragging it over his velvet skin, wanting this, wanting to worship him with this offering. She drew back up to his tip and released him, sliding her thumb over his head, slicking her finger with his wetness.

"You're beautiful," she murmured and licked his head.

"Scar," he groaned. "Fuck. Look at me."

She did while she took him as deep as she could into her

mouth.

His eyes were hooded, dark with desire as he watched her.

She'd been seventeen and pregnant when they'd met and just shy of her eighteenth birthday when they'd found Baba, who'd reversed the wish Tomas's parents had made. He'd been small his whole life, all twenty-two years of it by then, and had never been with a woman. Her own sexual experience had been limited. She and Tomas had learned together. They'd grown up together.

Earlier, as she'd stood in the living room of the cottage watching Tomas make her a fire, she'd realized they were alone for the first time since Jessamine had been born. Scarlett had watched him move, recalling the strength he'd shown all day as he'd talked to villagers in Sevens, thinking about him standing at the sink bare chested, considering all the ways in their lifetime together that he'd been her foundation. Remembered the dominant way he'd been with her that day and knew she needed him, wanted to serve him.

Now, she lowered her head down his shaft, taking as much of him as she could into her throat, and with her hand wrapped around his base, she used both her mouth and her hand as she drew back up to his tip. She repeated the action, deliberately slow and with pressure until he groaned with pleasure. It struck her how infrequent she'd offered her adoration to him this way—even if she felt that adoration keenly.

Tomas hissed. "Fuck." His head fell back onto the couch.

"Touch me, please," she said before driving back down his shaft.

One of his hands dove into her hair, his fingers curling and tugging at the strands. The pressure of it excited her, and she moaned and swirled her tongue on the underside of his cock, driving down on him again as her core throbbed with heat.

Tomas growled and shifted, his hips lifting from the couch, sucking in a breath as she drove down onto him again, adjusting her speed.

She wanted more. She wanted all of him.

"Fuck my mouth, Tomas," she said. "Use me." Her heart snapped hard against her chest with longing.

"Scar?"

She slid down his shaft again, looking up at him, then scraped his skin slightly with her teeth on her way up.

He hissed.

Then she stopped, her lips resting on the tip of his cock as she waited for him to take control. "Tell me what you want."

Tomas hesitated, then understanding unfurled on his features. He swore, picked her up, and flipped their positions so she was on the couch, and he stood over her.

"Open your mouth," he snapped. "Wider."

She did, one hand reaching up to grip his cock, the other grabbed one cheek of his taut ass.

"Touch yourself, Scar. Not me," he said, and with his hands holding her head, he pushed his cock into her waiting mouth, groaning as he did. "Fuck, you feel good."

She gagged at first, but breathed through it, relaxing to take all of him down her throat. He waited as she adjusted, then tested her with a gentle pulse of his hips. When she used her tongue against his skin, he pulled back, then sank into her throat, groaning as he did.

She moaned around him as he did as she asked, fucking her mouth as her eyes watered and saliva pooled. Then she reached between her legs, pressing and caressing her aching clit with her fingers like he'd told her, reaching between his legs and caressing his sacks, the skin between his sacks and his ass.

"Fuck," he shouted. "Fuck. Fuck, Scar. So good–"

His cock hardened further inside her mouth.

Her fingers slid through her slickness, bringing her close to the brink, when Tomas threw his head back with a loud groan, and fell forward, his hands gripping the back of the couch on either side of her head. "I'm coming," he grunted, and his shaft pulsed as it released his cum into her mouth.

Scarlett swallowed it, every drop, then grabbed his hip

as she released him from her mouth, licking anything left, cleaning him with her tongue. When she was done, she looked up at him.

Tomas's eyes—so dark she couldn't discern the color—watched her.

He went onto his knees before her, grabbed her hips, and yanked her to the edge of the couch. "Spread your legs, wider," he ordered.

"Tomas. I don't–"

"Hush," he commanded. "I'm doing what I want. You're doing what I want." He looked at her, waiting for her capitulation, and she gave it, needing it, spreading her legs to allow him entry.

He shoved her chemise up to her waist and tugged her undergarment down until she was bare for him. "Take it off," he said, pushing the chemise over her breasts.

She did, pulling it over her head, then removed her wrap and shivered with adrenalin, hot all over.

He grabbed a breast with one hand, while the other pushed against one of her knees, spreading her wider. The firelight illuminated the room with soft, warm light, undulating against Tomas's skin as he studied her sex.

She shivered.

"You're glistening. So fucking wet." He looked up at her face. "Did that turn you on?"

She nodded and breathed, "Yes."

Tomas swallowed, then growled as he leaned forward and closed his mouth around her clit.

She gasped. "Oh. Yes," she moaned, grabbing the back of his head, her hand sliding through his hair.

"Fuck, Scar." He let go of her breast and used his hand to press against her belly, stretching her sex. The sensation made her even more sensitive. With his other hand, he spread her wider, then, leaned forward and licked her clit, flattening his tongue, putting more pressure on that bundle that brought such pleasure.

"Oh," Scarlet cried out, rocking against his mouth.

Tomas inserted a finger inside her, then another as his tongue worked magic, growling and groaning as he did, as if she were a feast and he was a starved man. "You. Taste. Like. Heaven," he said between licks.

Already sensitive, Scarlett felt her own climax too soon. "I'm close," she gasped. "So close. Tomas. Yes." She frantically rolled her hips against his face as he fucked her with his tongue and his hands. Suddenly she was there, all the sensations gathering up into a tight knot inside her. "Please. Please," she chanted, then screamed, "I'm coming," her body exploding as everything tensed.

Tomas continued to work her through it, and though he gentled, he didn't stop.

She continued writhing and grinding against him, moaning and gasping as the orgasm lingered, unwilling to let go.

Tomas slid up from between her legs, wiping her pleasure from his face on the skin of her belly, her tits, until he leaned over and kissed her. The taste of her own pleasure grabbed hold of her insides, yanked her into the moment with him as he grabbed her legs, spreading them wider before he speared his cock into her body, driving home with one thrust.

She gasped and moaned, grabbing hold of him.

"You take it like a good girl, Scar," he said through his clenched teeth, his lips against her neck. Then he bit down, testing their connection.

Scarlett whimpered, loving every sensation rioting inside of her. From his teeth on her neck, to his skin slipping against hers, to his hips grinding against her inner thighs, to his cock spreading her wide, she was an exposed nerve, crying out with each movement. She lifted her legs, widening them even further, and pressed her heels into the back of Tomas's back. "Fuck me, Tomas," she groaned. "Harder."

He sat up and grabbed her hips, his fingertips biting into her skin, squeezing her as he fucked her.

Abruptly, he withdrew.

"No," she gasped.

But with fervor she couldn't remember from Tomas, he pulled her from the couch and flipped her onto her belly, pulled her hips up, and drove into her cunt from behind.

She cried out. "Yes. Yes."

His movement was frantic, needy, the rhythm lost as he fucked her. "Play with your clit. I want to feel you milk my cock," he growled.

Scarlett reached between her legs and touched herself, sliding through the slick around her core, feeling Tomas's cock as he drove into her again and again. As she climbed toward another orgasm, she relished every sensation, grateful for it, grateful for Tomas, needing this release to reclaim something that felt lost. She cried out. "I'm coming. I'm coming."

"I'm here," he grunted, as if he'd read her mind. But then he groaned as he tensed. "I'm here. Fucking milk me, Scar." Then he gasped, pushing into once more and stilling as his cock pulsed with his orgasm inside her.

Tomas

"Fuck," Tomas breathed, his body depleted as he held Scarlett's hips, her backside pressed tight against his pelvis, his mind whirling in the post-coital haze. He couldn't remember the last time it had been this way: frantic, needy, and so godsdamned good.

When Scarlett shuddered, then gasped, Tomas came back to himself, looked down at his wife, and noticed her shoulders shaking.

"Scar?" He pulled his softening body from her, and lifted her, turning her toward him, both of them on their knees facing one another. Concern slammed into his chest at the tracks of tears on her cheeks. He grasped her face between his hands. "What is it? Did I hurt you?"

She shook her head.

He smoothed her hair back away from her face. "What is it?"

Her watery eyes lifted to his, their gray depths an ocean of unshed tears. "I just love you so much," she whispered. "I hurt you."

His heart slammed up against the inside of his chest with cataclysmic force, and he gathered her against him. "I love you too."

"I'm so sorry for what I did."

Tomas leaned back and pressed a kiss against her cheek. When she looked down, he gently tilted her face so he could meet her gaze. "I forgive you, Scar. I will always forgive you. You are mine. I am yours. Forever."

Tears slipped from her eyes, and she offered a faint smile.

Taking the blanket draped over the couch, Tomas wrapped them together and they sat side by side, backs against the couch.

"Tell me what happened," he said.

"With?"

"Baba."

"I didn't go."

He turned his head to look at her, surprised. "You didn't?"

She shook her head and looked down at her hands.

With his fingers under her chin, he raised her eyes to his. "Tell me about the potion."

She hesitated a moment, her eyes lingering on the flames in the hearth. "I told her what I wanted to do, and she advised me against it."

"She did?" This surprised him, though his experience with Baba was limited to the one and only time he'd ever met her—the day she'd reversed his parents' wish.

Scarlett nodded. "She said I'd created a house of cards. That I should face Crue."

"Why did you discount her advice?"

She shrugged, then shook her head as if having her own internal argument.

Eventually, she turned and looked at him. "I was afraid. Afraid that he could take everything from me. You. The kids." She looked back at the fire. "The ridiculous thing is he did it without having to do anything. I did it for him." A sob caught in her throat. "Just like my father."

Tomas tightened his arms around her. "You aren't your father, Scarlett. I'm sorry I said it."

She shook her head. "No. You were right. It was awful to hear, and I might not be him, but I was acting obsessed like he was... before–" She sniffed and swiped at fresh tears, then leaned her head against his shoulder. "I'm sorry."

He squeezed her tighter against him, feeling clearer and

more cognizant of his place in the order of things for the first time in years. Everything was out in the open, the magic that had dominated their whole life together was gone, and all that remained was them and this new normal.

"We'll find her," he said, absolutely convinced that this was the truth. As much as he needed it to be true, he felt it. "We'll find him and end this."

Scarlett turned her face and looked at him, her gaze finding his.

Tomas leaned into her and pressed his lips to hers, before saying, "Together."

She turned in his arms, facing him, her eyes searching his face. Then she nodded. "You and me. Always." Then she kissed him as the first winter storm raged outside.

Tomas hadn't known he could find that inner fire again, but his body responded to his wife once more.

And for the first time since the wish had reversed, he felt at home in his body, big enough to match the size of his heart.

173

In the Shadow of a Kiss

Brinna & Lucian

By Maci Aurora

176

Brinna's eyes burned with unshed tears as Scarlett finally told them the truth. The visible toll it took on her mother only added to Brinna's emotions. What Lucian had discovered as they'd dreamed was real: the mad king, her mother trapped in a tower destined to be a demented version of a daughter-bride, a sorcerer who'd tricked Scarlett.

Brinna's breath hitched audibly as her tears spilled, and Lucian's warm hand curled around hers, pulling her a touch closer against his side to remind her he was there.

Bright warmth sizzled up her arm at his touch—a real

touch not lost in a dream—that burned right to her heart, filling it with heat. There weren't many instances in her life when she could remember someone offering her comfort rather than the other way around. This awareness—along with the heat—stitched up the eviscerated bits of her heart, piecing the fragments back together despite the pain caused by Scarlett's duplicity and the truth that had just upended everything.

Her siblings were angry, but all Brinna could think about was the dream.

About already being aware of her mother's painful past.

About Lucian reviving her. "Mi Alora, *I love you,*" he'd said. *"Come be in the true world with me."*

Brinna squeezed Lucian's hand a touch tighter, afraid, suddenly, that he might be torn away from her. That she might still be sleeping. Discerning what was real was suddenly difficult.

But a few breaths later, they still stood in the cabin amidst the tears.

Their father stood, admitting he'd known. And after an apology, he disappeared out the door of the cottage into the woods.

"Don't blame him," Scarlett said.

And the world continued to collapse around Brinna. All but Lucian, who stood at her side still holding her hand—solid and stable.

In the aftermath of the truth, somehow Brinna listened as a plan was put together. Only it meant—for the first time—they were all leaving the woods, the cottage, their parents. She and Auri would go to Sol with Lucian. Tarley and Mattias were going to New Taras with Lachlan, though Nixus would ferry them to Sol later. And Jessamine…

A sob caught in Brinna's throat.

Their mother and father would stay at the cottage in case there was news—await the return of Lachlan's man. Or hopefully Jessamine.

The tears came too easily, Brinna realized, and she swiped at her cheeks yet again as Lucian whisked them away on a whisper, his power carrying them from the Whitling Woods to Sol as if it were as easy as taking a breath. She couldn't seem to stop the tears.

Sol's atrium materialized around their party as they stood at the entry of one of the skybridges. The space was just as she remembered. The massive room stretched around them, outlined with the twelve Elsewhere Doors at even intervals, the four skybridges that led to the various wings, and at the heart—where they stood—the wilderness of the atrium underneath the glass dome arched high above them.

Auri turned in a circle taking it in, her mouth open. Her sister looked awful. Her dress—not dirty, per se—was covered with a sheen of something otherworldly. It was as if the spell had frozen them in time somehow, and the shattered magic coated her skin with cobwebs. Her sister's nest of dark hair had Brinna reaching up to touch her own. She would be lucky to get the knots out. Even Lucian and Nixus were a mess, their skin nicked with scratches and cuts, clothing torn, the exertion of having navigated the magical hedge apparent.

Still, no one moved.

A fear of separation stole through her. She shuddered at the fear of isolation the dream had created, at the memory of reliving each of her family's nightmares. She was certain Auri was remembering too, that and in pain at the loss of Nixus, who couldn't remember her. What loss she must be feeling! But Nixus was also quiet. Perhaps for a different reason, considering the confusion written on his face every time he snuck a glance at Auri.

Lucian squeezed her hand again as if to say, *I'm still here.*

"I need a bath," Auri mumbled and shook out her green skirt, as if it would help, then wrapped her arms around her middle.

"Do you think Jessamine–" Brinna started, her mind turning back again to their oldest sister. She dried her wet cheeks on the back of her hand, pretty sure she'd left streaks. "I keep thinking about what the wizard–" But she stopped.

"She's okay," Auri said with force and a determined nod, as if willing it to be so. "She's strong."

"Crue wants the other powers, and he thinks your mother has them. Jessamine is his bargaining piece. He needs her," Lucian offered.

Brinna moved into the skybridge, no longer afraid of the way she felt suspended in the sky when she stood and looked through the glass. *Where are you, Jess?* she wondered. It was night in Elcadia, the stars blinking in the dark sky like golden heartbeats. She glanced over her shoulder at Nixus, who was studying Auri without her being aware, his brow contorted.

Then, as if he felt Brinna's look, his gaze flicked to hers. He pasted on a smile, a blush warming his golden-brown cheeks, pretending that everything was normal.

"The night is beautiful at Sol," she told him.

"You should see it at Ombra." He puffed up.

"What is that?" she asked.

"His godseat," Auri answered without looking at Nixus.

"How–" Nixus stopped, his brow furrowed, and frustration lined his mouth.

"You told me," Auri replied, glancing at him.

He looked discomfited, his usually flippant and arrogant air giving way to a fleeting moment of insecurity. Then he shuddered, cleared his throat, and ignored what Auri had said. "Ombra is perfection."

"Sol is perfect," Lucian said, the frown deepening on his face.

Brinna looked at Lucian. "It's my favorite." Warmth flushed her like a flood recalling they'd come here in their dreams. What they had experienced together in their shared dreaming.

"You haven't seen Ombra," Nixus replied.

Lucian made a grumpy noise, but his eyes never left Brinna as if he were thinking of the same thing she was. Her thoughts relived peeling away his clothing. Of kissing him. Of using her body to speak reality because everything else had been a dream.

But guilt stopped her.

Turning back to the window, she could see her reflection and those made by the people behind her. She sighed, unsure what to say. Her heart was so heavy, her chest was caving in. Yet here she was at Sol with Lucian, the literal man of her dreams who'd confessed his love. A truth. She was standing once more in the real world because he loved her. And she loved him back. They were god-yoked. Except, how could she accept such joy considering such sorrow?

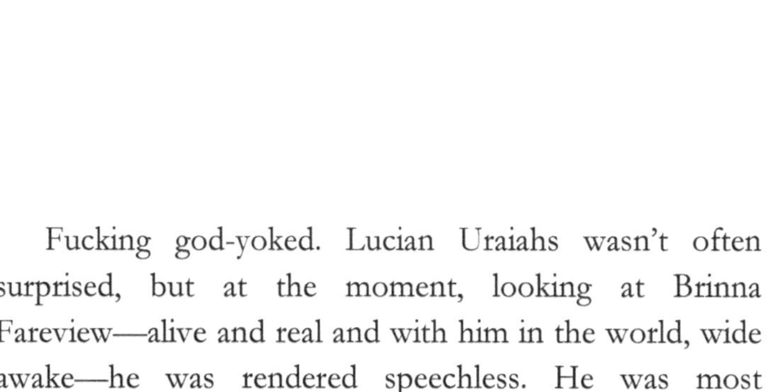

Fucking god-yoked. Lucian Uraiahs wasn't often surprised, but at the moment, looking at Brinna Fareview—alive and real and with him in the world, wide awake—he was rendered speechless. He was most assuredly dreaming, except here she was, standing an arm's length from him staring out a skybridge of Sol. She was really there. With him.

How had he gotten so lucky? They'd dreamed together, solved the riddle of the spell, broke it, and now they were standing together in true flesh and blood at the heart of Sol. God-yoked. He could reach out and touch her if he wanted. Kiss her. He pressed his fingertips to his chest, a warmth encasing the whole of his heart.

The shock of the truth of it startled him.

He was god-yoked. Him! The god who'd spent his entirety Roaming to escape reality and responsibility. Add to it the fact that it was Brinna. The realizations offered him the strange sensation that he was both floating and falling simultaneously. He loved her—obviously. She was standing with him, tangible and substantive because that was the truth. Except in real life, they'd never been very good together. Aside from one night in bed together talking, he'd mostly teased, cajoled, insulted, and angered her.

Then he'd always run.

Luc tensed. He might love Brinna, but he knew without a doubt, he didn't deserve her, which terrified him.

The atrium glowed with soft light from the sconces and fluttering torches, and she looked more beautiful now than even in his dreams. An ethereal quality drifted around her gentle features and highlighted not only her beauty but her goodness. Even if she was as in need of a shower as he was. Her burnished copper hair was a mess. Her large, gray-blue eyes were sallow and sunken. Her usually lush lips were turned down with her heartache. These things didn't make her less beautiful in his eyes, but more so. She was strong, kind, and compassionate. She loved her family fiercely. They had been through the Netherrealm—though Lexa would argue the comparison—and returned. Alive. He wanted to gather her in his arms, hold her, and ease her hurt.

Her world was shattered. Her mother had tricked her family into taking a sleeping potion, willing to let them waste away in their nightmares. Her sister was missing. And even still, Brinna's first impulse upon learning Scarlett's secret was true was to cry for her mother. Not only because Brinna was heartsore for herself, but because she empathized with the pain her mother's secret carried.

"Would that be alright? Lucian?"

Brinna's hand on his arm dragged him back to the atrium, away from his thoughts.

He glanced at her slender hand resting on him, her touch creating an earthquake inside his chest, and he gave her the pulse of an awkward smile. "Sorry. What were you asking?"

Stars, she was beautiful. It made it difficult to think straight.

She tilted her head; her gray eyes held a question. "Would it be alright if we went to our rooms? To clean up?" she asked, and her cheeks brightened with a blush. "Before we convene for the family meeting?"

He glanced at Aurielle then at Nixus, who stood apart from them, leaning against the entrance to a sky walkway. He looked bored, but Luc knew his twin better than that. He hadn't been able to take his eyes off Aurielle since the spell had ended even if he couldn't remember her. "Yes. Of course."

"I'm not staying," Nix announced, shoving off from his excellent lean. "I'll shuttle the others here, but then I'll go home. To Ombra. I don't need a room."

Luc, facing Aurielle, saw her flinch. Her back was to

Nix, so he wouldn't have noticed, but guilt cut acutely into Luc's bones. He'd done that to them and had to find a way to undo his brother's locked memories. He wondered if an *oblitorium* could be reversed, making a note to check.

"You sure? I have plenty of rooms."

The problem was the god-yoke that Nix didn't remember required he and Aurielle remain near one another. The spell had nearly killed them, so Luc wasn't sure what kind of distance they could endure with the weakened tether.

"I miss Ombra." Nix's eyes flashed to Aurielle, then he frowned even as his shadows flickered like dark hands toward her as if they understood the truth. "You can just summon me."

"Right." Luc nodded, knowing it was best not to back his brother into a corner. He shoved his hands into his trouser pockets. "Summoning takes time, though."

"So?"

"Considering the circumstances—what we need to do now with shuttling Brinna and Aurielle's siblings to and from Sol—I think we'll need you. A lot. Might be easier to stay."

Aurielle's gray gaze heavy with turmoil leapt from the floor up to Luc. Gratitude softened her features—and that felt like a first. She had every reason to hate him more than anyone. He'd trapped Nix in the spell, but he'd also lured Aurielle into the trap as the key keeper. That was the reason she and his brother were god-yoked, which Luc had been told neither of them would change, but it had indeed caused them both suffering. Including this latest development: locking away Nix's memories of her.

Luc looked from Aurielle to Nix, whose own dark gaze jumped to Aurielle, then away. His brother might not remember her, but he was clearly attracted to her as his reaching shadows suggested.

Nix shrugged. "Fine."

Luc clapped his hands together in a weird way and hated that he'd done it. "Excellent." He swiped his palms over his torn, dirty shirt as if to get rid of the awkward tension. "Nix, you can stay in your usual room." He pointed toward the skybridge to the east wing of the villa.

His brother huffed an acknowledgement.

"And Aurielle," he paused, pretending to think. "I think in a room by the pool."

"The West Wing?" Nix scoffed, incredulous. "It's too hot in that wing in the afternoon light."

Luc gave his brother a confused look even though Nix was walking right into his intentional trap. "You have a better idea?"

A line appeared between Nix's eyes as if his outburst had confounded him. His gaze drifted again to Aurielle with that same perplexed look, then away, shoving his hands in his pockets with a shrug. "Whatever."

"You might be right," Luc said, feigning thoughtfulness. He had a strong suspicion that the more time Nix spent in the company of the love of his life, it would help him remember. The trick was making it Nix's idea. "I think the wing you're in, Nix, is probably the most comfortable at this time in the rotation. Would you show Aurielle the room across from yours? I'll escort Brinna to the north wing."

Aurielle glanced over her shoulder at Nix, then back at Luc. "Or Brinna can show me–"

"No!" Luc yelled at the same time Brinna did. They glanced at one another, and Luc's neck got hot.

"I don't know where it is," Brinna said, her cheeks ripening with bright color.

Aurielle glanced between them and nodded, her frown deepening.

Nix straightened, removing his hands from his pockets. He held out his arm. "Shall we?"

Aurielle looked at his offered arm but didn't take it.

Nix appeared confused by her response. "What is it?"

"Just show me the way, please," she snapped, flinging her hands in a motion to get him going.

As Luc watched his brother lead Aurielle back through the atrium, his anxiety resurfaced.

"It isn't your fault," Brinna said, her shoulder bumping against his arm, offering the converse of what he thought.

He turned his head to look at her, falling into her stormy-sea eyes. "It is. Actually. Let's not absolve me of my sins just yet," he said with a frown and watched the retreating form of his brother as he disappeared across the skybridge. "But I'll concede your point"–he offered her his arm– "that it had to be done to keep them both alive."

She slid her arm through his. "And we'll do what we can to help them."

"We?" He squeezed her hand around his arm against his side, wondering if he'd ever trust the sound of that.

They started through the atrium's garden. The path

meandered through the greenery lit by glowing lamps, offering light under the canopy surrounding them. The small brook flowed through the parkland, and they crossed an arched bridge over the water.

"Of course," she said. "Hasn't it been a *we* this whole time?" She smiled but didn't look at him.

"Yes. It has." They had dreamed together. They had put the pieces of the puzzle together so that he could break the spell.

When they reached the central point of the atrium's garden, Brinna stopped, her hold pulling him to stop as well. It was darker there, the hood of the trees blocking much of the light above so that the lamps offered diffused light by which to see.

"We dreamed of this place."

"We did."

"We kissed here," she added, and her eyes jumped to his, her cheeks pink with her blush.

"We did." Luc's body felt hot and needy, and he took a step closer.

Brinna blinked and took a step back. Away.

His heart tightened in his chest. Luc didn't like that at all, but he decided he needed to consider her place. Before they'd dreamed, he'd mostly been an ass. He'd spent so much time goading her, running from her, was it a surprise she might be hesitant? Adding all that she was going through at the moment, why would he think she might be amenable to his affections, even if they *had* shared them in the dream?

"What is it?" he asked.

"I don't know how to feel," she said and swallowed.

Confused by her words, and suddenly hot with frustration and worry, he took a step toward her. "What are you saying?"

"I feel… guilty for feeling happy."

His ire cooled, and he reached out and took her hand to lead her to her room. Though he wanted her in his, he didn't want to presume. "Because of Jessamine?"

"And my mother. My father. My siblings. All of it." She walked silently next to him as they crossed the skybridge. "How can I feel such joy amidst such sorrow? And what, then, does that mean about me?"

Luc stopped outside her door and turned to face her. He cupped her face between his hands, tilting her head so he could gaze into her eyes. "It is possible to feel it all, Brinna. I can both love my brother and be frustrated by him. I can both find joy to have you here with me and feel sadness for the circumstances. I know that I can both love you and feel afraid that perhaps you might not love me back. Just as existing in our dreams together was also simultaneously reality. It's a fallacy to think life must exist in eithers and ors."

Brinna gripped his wrists, rose onto her toes, and pressed her lips to his.

Had Brinna imagined that one day she would be standing in a floating estate in the sky kissing the god of day and light after he'd said he loved her, she'd have laughed. Her imagination had always tended to run away with her, but this was beyond her wildest imaginings. Except Lucian's extraordinary kiss slipped between her doubt and reinforced the tether that existed between them. They were god-yoked! She hadn't known she was godblood—confirmed by her mother—but now it all made sense.

"Get out of your head, Brinna," Lucian ordered, then pulled her bottom lip gently with his teeth. "Be here," he said, letting her go and speaking against her mouth, his supple lips reminding her of what was real and right in front of her. "With me."

Though she'd started this kiss, Lucian took control of it, his mouth, his tongue, his teeth reinforcing who she belonged to. Her dreams of him, of this, had been marvelous, but this—the reality of kissing him—was infinite like the cosmos, something bigger than she could even understand.

His mouth was somehow both dominant and submissive. When his tongue demanded entrance, she acquiesced, happily, adding to the sensations curling through her, which filled her with heat, bright and addicting. Unable to contain the spreading forest fire inside her, she moaned, then whimpered, grasping onto Lucian's tattered shirt to keep herself standing.

He growled and maneuvered her until her back was pressed against the door behind her, his hips pinning hers as his mouth strayed to her neck and his hands roamed, discovering her peaks and valleys.

"Lucian," she moaned, tilting her head to give him more access. "I love you, too," she said. "So much."

Lucian dragged his mouth from her skin and pressed his forehead to hers. "Say it again."

"I love you." And she kissed him so he would feel that love.

With her hands, she held his face until she needed to be closer, then wrapped them around his shoulders, pressing her breasts against his unforgiving chest. "Lucian," she murmured into his mouth.

His hands slipped down to her hips and squeezed. "I'm

here," he answered.

When she drew back, still holding onto Lucian like he might slip away, she whispered, "This feels like a dream. I'm afraid to trust it. With everything else, I'm struggling to understand my feelings. But not about this, Lucian."

Lucian drew her into his arms and held her against him, his strength enveloping her. He didn't reply, his silence communicating so much more than just understanding.

They stood that way in the hallway of Sol, just holding onto one another.

Eventually, Lucian broke the silence. "You can trust that I love you," he said quietly, his lips against her temple and his hands skimming her ribs, her hips, her back, offering the comfort of his touch. "That though we discovered it within a dream, it makes it no less real in my heart."

Her throat closed around her feelings, locking them up because she understood his words so keenly. She did love him. It was why she was standing there in his arms even now. Why Auri was with them at Sol. Why Tarley was with Lachlan. Why Mattias, her father, her mother were all awake. Tears pierced her eyes.

"I don't know how to move forward," she gasped against his chest, holding onto him as if letting him go might mean she'd float away.

"Then we'll find a way to do it together," he said, pressing a kiss to her hair, then sliding a hand over the strands. "But maybe we should get cleaned up first?"

She felt him smile and nodded but hesitated, suddenly afraid to be without him. A remnant of the dream, she supposed. "Would you come with me?"

Lucian leaned back, his gaze molten. "Bathe together?" He offered a predatory grin.

"Luc!"

They both turned as Nixus stalked across the skybridge toward them, his features as dark as the shadows swirling around him.

Lucian growled and looked at Brinna, then sighed. "Save that thought. Meet me in the kitchen?" He squeezed her hip one more time before stepping back to face Nixus.

"I need to talk to you," Nix demanded.

Lucian looked at Brinna.

"The kitchen," she repeated, then watched Lucian move through the door across the hallway, Nixus just behind him.

Brinna was left with the whirlwind of thoughts and feelings raging through her like a hurricane. There was so much to wrap her mind around, she didn't even know where to begin. But a bath—that could help her start, she supposed. It wasn't sleeping, just bathing.

She stripped out of her clothes as warm water filled the tub, steam making the air in the room pleasant. Once she was submerged in the warmth, she worked the sheen of the spell from her body and her hair. It was sticky like tree sap, lingering not only on her skin but inside her as well. With a shudder, the memories of being trapped flitted through her mind: her inability to change their circumstances, her family trapped inside their nightmares, and her inside their dreams with them, the powerlessness.

Only there'd been Lucian.

She slid deeper into the water and leaned her head back against the lip of the tub. The warm water slipped around her, bubbles skimming the surface, and she thought of him there with her. Wished it were so, but she didn't close her eyes to imagine him, afraid of finding herself trapped in sleep once again. With her eyes open, she thought of his kiss, his hands as she touched herself. She thought about Lucian's mouth, the sensations igniting a fire inside her, only now, it wasn't a fire but an empty reminder he was missing.

With a sigh, she sat up, the water sloshing around her, and wrapped her arms around her knees.

She considered her feelings for Lucian, the joy he inspired in her, then the sorrow of what was happening to her family.

It's a fallacy to think life must exist in eithers and ors, he'd said.

He was right, she knew. Just as dreaming had proved she could exist in a dream that was real, it was possible to experience both joy and sorrow. She just wasn't sure how to navigate the duality.

Then we'll find a way to do it together, Lucian had said.

With a deep, cleansing sigh, Brinna washed away the remnants of the spell and her doubt. She was ready to find her Lucian in the real world. It was time to talk.

"You did something to me."

Luc glanced at Nix over his shoulder as he unbuttoned his ruined shirt. "I told you I did."

Nix narrowed his gaze.

"You should go bathe," Luc told him, eyeing Nix's tattered shirt and pants. His brother's hair was an unruly mess on his head, though that wasn't abnormal.

Luc shrugged out of the shirt, dropping it on the floor to dispose of later, and started on his pants, wishing he was climbing into the bath with Brinna instead. He imagined her naked body—a body he'd only experienced in a dream—slick with water, then took a deep breath to keep his semi hard-on from getting any harder.

"I know you did," Nix snapped. "I just don't believe you."

"Then why are you here?"

"Because you definitely did something. I feel strange."

"Alright. Tell me," Luc said and left Nix behind in the bedroom as he went into the bathroom, where he started the shower and climbed underneath the spray. It felt so good, washing away the dirt from their trip through the hedge.

"Why would I tell you? You're so good at using things against me. I don't fucking forget things."

Luc glanced at Nix, who was leaning against the doorframe as if holding it up with his shoulder. "I promise you, Nix, I haven't done anything you wouldn't have done for me."

His brother growled, stalking into the room, and slumped against the counter. "I don't know how I'm here."

"Here? As in Sol? You just came with us from Sevens."

Nix shook his head, looking down at his hands, his shadows uncharacteristically subdued, hidden. "How I'm not in the spell," he said and looked up, catching Luc's gaze through the glass. "Don't say it."

"What? That you've forgotten?" Guilt slammed into Luc so that he had to look away.

With his head in the water's spray, Luc wished he could alleviate the heavy regret that held him under and made him feel like he was drowning. He *had* locked away Nix's memories. It had seemed a kindness as opposed to severing them completely, but maybe the oracle had been right. Perhaps the lingering essence of the locked memories was battling against Nix's awareness and the ramification would be dangerous.

"I don't forget," Nix snapped. "It's not like forgetting. It's like I remember being in the spell's labyrinth. I remember drinking myself silly. Next thing I know, I'm waking up in Father's office like I've been brought back from drowning, and I don't know how that happened."

"I told you," Luc said, shutting off the shower. He grabbed a towel and dried the water from his skin and hair. "I locked the memories up. It was either that or let you die. Let Aurielle die."

"Right. The god-yoke." Nix said it like it was a joke.

Luc sighed, wrapping the towel around his waist. "Look. I get why you're hesitant to trust what I'm telling you—"

"Hesitant?" Nix shouted; his shadows burst from him like a dark, angry cloud. "You trapped me in that spell. You and Poe tricked me, and I'm just supposed to believe what you're telling me now? I'm just supposed to forgive and forget what you did?"

Luc's breath caught. Nix *had* forgiven him already, but that memory was locked away.

I forgive you. I forgave you long ago. Stop punishing yourself.

This Nix didn't remember those words he'd given to Luc before sliding toward death. They'd been in the meadow of the Whitling Woods awaiting the witch who'd helped Scarlett, and Nix had said, "If it hadn't happened, I never would have found Auri." Then his brother had smiled, warming Luc to the bone. But this Nix was the Nix still trapped in the spell, the one who hadn't met Aurielle.

The one who hadn't yet been changed by love—her love. This Nix was a god ruled by vengeance.

"What do you want to do? Kill me?"

"Yes. Actually. I kind of do." Nix stood, his shadows writhing around him like a dark aura.

Months ago, Luc would have let Nix kill him. In fact, he'd been ready to place himself on the altar of sacrifice for what he'd inadvertently done to his brother. But everything was different now. He was different. And now there was Brinna. If he died, Brinna died.

"But for some reason I'm not in the spell anymore," Nix added.

Luc pressed his teeth together, wanting to goad his brother about why he wasn't but sensed it wouldn't help matters, that his usual impulsivity wasn't going to serve him or the situation. Besides, he was going to be taking on his father's mantle, and he vowed to be a better god. Brinna deserved that. Everyone did. And that meant so did Nix.

"I want to fix it," Luc said, instead. "I did this to you. Let me fix it."

Nix glowered, which he was very good at, especially this version of Nix. Then he grunted and disappeared through the doorway, his shadows trailing behind him. It wasn't until the bedroom door slammed that Luc took a deep breath and swiped a hand over his face.

Yes. He was going to have to fix this somehow. The bigger and more plaguing concern was how.

After dressing in clothing stashed in the closet, Brinna retraced her steps from her room, across the atrium to the kitchen where she found Lucian. He'd also bathed, his blond hair wet and dark, curling around his face.

Nixus was nowhere in sight.

Lucian smiled at her when she walked into the room, a brilliant smile that warmed her insides and offered her ease. She might not know how to make sense of anything in her life just then, but she could make sense of that beautiful smile that made her feel wonderful.

He walked to her, grabbed her by the waist, and pulled her against him so he could press his lips to her neck. Then he leaned back and studied her, twirled her around by a hand, and hummed a note of appreciation. "You look beautiful."

His words, his grin, his appreciation sent that heat already warming her into every nook and cranny of her body. "You're a sweet talker, Lucian Uraiahs."

He grinned, his dimple showing, and he pulled her into the kitchen. "I'm cooking. If you don't want to help me, that's alright. I just want you with me."

"I'll help," she clarified.

His smile widened. "Our first time." He sounded delighted, and his eyes sparkled as he leaned to kiss her cheek. "Would you chop these?" He pointed at a bulb of garlic.

But she was thinking of other first times to come. Of their kiss. Of what she wanted, the pulse between her thighs an incessant reminder. Though they'd been together in the dream, it was as if they were starting over with an entire lifetime of history between them.

She cleared her throat. "What are we making?"

"I figure something comforting is in order. Soup. Besides, the piskies made some bread, and we wouldn't want it to go to waste." He glanced over his shoulder.

She followed his gaze to two beautiful golden loaves on a cooling rack. "What's a piskie?"

"Creatures whose sole purpose is to keep the world clean and taken care of, but"–he moved to the cutting board where he'd been working– "they work in secret."

"So you don't know they are here?"

"Exactly. I just know because I find the evidence of

their work." He grinned and plopped meat onto the board.

"And what do piskies get in return?" Brinna asked.

"Whatever they want, I suppose," Lucian said. "Food. Trinkets. A place to live." He shrugged, then used the spoon in his hand to point at a bulb of garlic. "Would you crush me a few cloves of that, *mi alora?*"

Brinna stalled at the term. He'd used it in their shared dream. He'd even used it once when they'd danced together, long before they'd ever shared a dream. She reached for a knife and the garlic he'd set out. "What does that mean?" she asked.

"What?"

"*Mi alora?*"

He didn't answer her immediately, as if he were holding onto it for the time being, perhaps nervous himself, but she couldn't be certain. She had never read him very well.

Then he seemed to decide because he turned his head toward her. "It means *my heart.*"

Her own heart jumped then raced, her skin heating pleasurably at the thought. Her hands were slightly unsteady as she pressed the flat part of her knife against the garlic clove to break it open.

"Is that... alright?" he asked.

She nodded, unable to suppress her grin as she chopped the crushed garlic. "It's... beautiful."

Lucian smiled too, leaning toward her and pressing a kiss to her neck once more, as if he'd found a favorite spot. "Done?" His husky tone dove straight into her belly.

She met his gaze. "With the garlic." She pointed at the pile of them with her knife. There was a variation of roots and bulbs of beautiful colors. "The rest of the vegetables?"

He nodded, his gaze reading her features before taking the garlic and adding it to the pan. It sizzled in the oil, creating a fragrant scent that made her stomach compress with hunger. How long had it been since she'd eaten?

"Do you believe me, *mi alora?*" he asked, adding the meat to the garlic.

Brinna watched him stir, the muscles flexing as he did. There were moments when she needed to pinch herself because he was so beautiful. His golden eyes filled with copper bursts of light flashed up from his task to her and held, and though it wasn't very often, she saw the insecurity behind his gaze. Her Lucian. It seemed a strange realization. Hers. Slightly unbelievable.

"I do, and I love it," she said, reaching out to smooth a lock of his hair from over his eye. "Even if it makes me feel... overwhelmed."

His brows crashed against his eyes. "Overwhelmed?"

She'd known they needed to talk, and now, it seemed, they were having this conversation. Focusing on the carrots, she sliced carefully as she said, "Is that so surprising? I don't think I've wrapped my head around... everything. Around us. How I could be... your heart."

He stirred the pot next to her, then covered it and wiped his hands on the towel slung over his shoulder before moving to stand behind her. Reaching around, he removed the knife from her hand and set it down next to the chopped carrots, then turned her so she was facing him. With his hands pressed to the counter on either side of her hips, he leaned in, so his gaze was level with hers.

"Why is it surprising, Brinna? You are an amazing woman. You are kind and compassionate. You are fiercely loyal to your family and have a huge heart, even for a woman who drugged you all with a potion, I might add."

"Still my mother."

"Right. We can't choose our parents. I should know." He grinned. "But you choose to look for the best in people—even your mother—and your faith in them is inspiring. You're creative, you're smart, and you seem to like me, which is the true mystery."

Brinna reached up and pressed a hand against his chest. "Now that isn't much of a mystery to me, Lucian Uraiahs."

Luc

His innards were a chaotic mess of emotions and sensations that he didn't think he'd ever be able to untangle. The heat from Brinna's palm pressed over his heart seeped through his thin shirt. He wanted to lift her up on the counter and give her pleasure, to prove his devotion, because words didn't feel like enough. The sizzle of the meat cooking, her helping him in the kitchen, the smell of fresh bread and savory sauté, the domesticity of the moment, offered Luc a picture of their future.

He wanted it.

She continued speaking, tightening the joy inside him like a spring. Luc did his best to focus on her words when his gaze was lingering on her pink lips.

"When I was stuck and you arrived in my dreams, the relief I felt seeing you was transformative. I'd never felt safer, Lucian."

His eyes jumped up to hers.

"And when I was ready to give up, you encouraged me. You are strong and thoughtful and willing to make the difficult decision to see all of us out. There is no mystery for me as to why my heart races when you're near, or why I want you near when you're not."

His heart expanded in his chest, filled with all those emotions, her words providing sustenance. Moving closer, he needed to show her how he felt like he needed air, needed to feel her, taste her. Luc leaned in and pressed his nose to her neck, drawing in a deep breath, remembering the way she invigorated him with her sweet scent—spring flowers and sunshine—even *that* had been in the dream.

This was real.

She was his as much as he was hers.

Tilting her head, she allowed him access, her hands grabbing hold of his back. "We're not going to get the soup made this way."

"Who needs soup?" he asked against her skin, then bit, nipped, and kissed her.

She took an airy breath, then held it.

His hands roamed down her shoulders, her arms, skirted around to her waist, skimming her curves to her hips.

She whimpered and followed it with his name.

His lips made progress on the skin of her neck, her jaw,

and he crowded her backwards until they were both arched over the counter. Running a hand down her thigh to her knee, he lifted it, settling her leg over his hip so he could get closer. Then he finally met her lips with his, kissed her like he wanted to, with all that feeling wrapped up in the way he could show her instead of telling her.

"What is that amazing smell?" Nix asked as he walked into the room.

Luc groaned quietly. He pulled Brinna back up and dropped his forehead against her shoulder before turning to face his brother.

"Looks like you're doing a bit more than cooking." Nix grinned, looking decidedly less annoyed than he did earlier.

"Not anymore," Luc grumbled.

Nix's good nature seemed to have reemerged. "I can't remember the last time you made me a meal, Luc."

Luc lifted an eyebrow. "Can't remember?"

Nix scowled. "An expression, you ass. I remember what matters."

Luc heaved a sigh, refusing to comment, and instead considered how he might fix this mess as he returned to the pot.

"Nixus?" Brinna resumed her chopping. "Why is it you think your brother is lying to you? About your memories?"

Nix stopped at the end of the counter and tilted his head. "He's lied to me before."

"But what does Lucian have to gain by lying to you about this?" she asked, pushing her knife through the carrots with snap.

Luc watched Nix's dark gaze jump between Brinna and him, pondering her question. A dark panic mixed with a haze of anger overtook Nix's features. His shoulders tensed, his face paling. Luc could see his twin fighting to piece together the gaps Luc now knew existed between the spell and the present. He imaged the locks the oracle had placed on the doors inside Nix's mind.

Rather than consider Brinna's question, however, Nix slammed his hands down against the counter and glared at Luc. "You're jealous."

Shadows burst from Nix like a cloud of dark pollen, wreathing around his form, waiting.

"What?" Luc stared dumbfounded. His brother's anger—even if it was deserved—was formidable. Luc knew though they loved one another, they were often at odds. They were a study in contrasts, as was their nature, after all, day and night, darkness and light. Repelling one another was normal, but that push and pull was inspired by dominance. Not jealousy. "Of what?" Luc asked, unsure what Nix meant by the statement.

"Everything. That's why you trapped me in the first place."

"Over a milkmaid?" Luc laughed, shaking his head as he stirred.

Nix's eyes slid from Luc to Brinna. "And you're taking his side."

The tone was accusatory and set Luc's teeth on edge. His smile faded. "You better have a really good reason to speak to her like that, Nixus." He maneuvered between Brinna and his brother, grabbing hold of the light to soothe

the shadows, not that they ever had.

Their fights had always been fearsome, both walking away battered and bloody.

"I'm not lying to you, Nix," Luc said. "I haven't taken anything. I'm not jealous."

It was clear Nix either didn't believe him or was spoiling for a fight. His brother's shadows grew in strength, swirling like a swarm of dark creatures around him.

"But I swear to you, Nixus, if you ever disrespect my mate, I will fucking end you."

Brinna's hand curled around his. "It's okay, Luc. He's disoriented–"

"He doesn't get to talk to you like that."

Nix laughed, but it wasn't filled with the good humor of earlier. This laugh held rancor and ill intent. "Listen to your god-yoked mate, brother."

And Luc realized this wasn't Nix disbelieving him, but rather inciting a fight; he needed something to pummel to feel better. Rather than rise to his brother's need for violence, Luc released the light, disengaging, hoping that Nix would retreat as well.

Luc stepped away from Nix and his anger, still keeping Brinna behind him as he shook his head. "You're right baby brother. It's clear you're hungry."

"Don't you dare back down," Nix said, his voice too loud but carrying an eerie calm. The shadows reached toward Luc.

"I'm not fighting you," Luc said.

Brinna squeezed Luc's hand.

"Nix?"

Nix spun from the counter to face Aurielle, who stood at the skybridge opening, watching. She'd bathed, her brown hair loose around her shoulders. She was dressed in dark trousers and an overlarge shirt. Something borrowed.

That would need to be remedied, Luc realized, looking at Brinna in her borrowed garments.

"What's going on?" Aurielle asked. Her eyes jumped to Luc's, and he shook his head, wishing that things were different.

Nix's shadows dissipated like steam, until all that remained was Nix facing her. "Luc has been meddlesome," he said, casting an accusatory glance at Luc. "I'm angry at him."

"Why?"

For the first time since awakening, Luc could see the hope on Aurielle's face—hope he felt too even if he was also worried. This was the Nix he'd trapped, the Nix amidst the spell when the rage was so acute, he would have killed Luc rather than look at him. He wasn't sure Aurielle had ever seen that version of his brother.

But Nix didn't answer.

Instead of commenting on Nix's statement, Aurielle restarted her walk across the room and took a seat at the counter. "That smells good, Luc. You actually got Brinna to help in the kitchen?" she teased, her smile brightening her face. "She usually avoids it."

"I do not!" Brinna giggled and started her chopping once more. "I also haven't had such an agreeable chef to help."

Luc had to reset, breathing to release his own tension.

His eyes jumped between Aurielle and Nix, noting his brother's angry look at him. "Right. Yes. It took some convincing." He offered a tentative smile to Brinna with another glance at Nix, whose gaze slid to Aurielle.

"You're not going to try and convince me?" Nix asked Aurielle, his eyes narrowed on her, though less with malice and more with what appeared to be confusion.

Aurielle turned her head and regarded Nix with a look that Luc would have described as bored. It was a look he knew well. "Convince you of what?"

"That I've forgotten you?"

"Should I, Nixus? Have you forgotten me? Do you want me to convince you?" she countered, reaching for one of Brinna's chopped carrots before looking at him once more. "I thought you didn't forget anything. Besides, I figure if you wanted to remember," she said rather nonchalantly, "you would." She popped the carrot in her mouth and chewed. When she was finished, she stared at Nix. "I know my worth, and I don't feel like pushing you into remembering what you clearly believe isn't true."

Luc suppressed a smile and added the vegetables Brinna had cut to the pot while watching his brother process Aurielle's provocation. Nix looked flustered, and better yet, intrigued by her response. Wisdom indeed, Luc thought. The god-yoke might tie them together, but Aurielle definitely knew what his brother needed: a challenge.

"About thirty more minutes," Luc said.

"What about Tarley, Lachlan, and Mattias?" Brinna asked.

"Nix, will you retrieve Aurielle and Brinna's siblings?"

With a frustrated sound and dramatic flourish, Nix disappeared.

Aurielle's head dropped onto the counter. "What am I going to do?"

Brinna moved to her sister, a hand on her shoulder.

"Exactly what you're doing," Luc said, stirring the pot.

Aurielle looked up at him.

"Nix has always liked a challenge, and you've just dropped the gauntlet." He grinned. "How about a drink?"

Brinna's gaze followed Luc, drinks in hand, as he joined her and Auri in a cozy sitting area of the main living room. The windows were dark with deep night and stars sparkling beyond, their reflections casting a strange contrast against the darkness of the glass. Lantern orbs glowed around them, floating in the expanse, and filling the room with golden light. Lucian sat next to her, his warmth seeping into her skin. It was a comfort that she leaned into, her heart leaping as chills of anticipation raced across her skin. While she loved her family, she was ready for some time alone with Lucian.

"I summoned my brothers," Lucian was telling

Aurielle. "I'll meet with them tomorrow."

"Which brothers?"

"Eitan, Pax, and Lior."

"The Arguments?" Auri asked.

Brinna felt confused, never having heard of more siblings other than Nixus and Lexa. "The Arguments?"

Lucian laughed, however. "Yes."

"Why are they called that?" Brinna asked.

"It's what the triplets do," Lucian said, leaning a touch closer. "But they are master manipulators."

She appreciated the pressure of his weight, the reality of it against her body. Heat flared inside her at the thought of his weight in other ways. "And why would Mattias need to be with them?"

Auri frowned at the drink in her glass. "Nixus sent them to watch over Mattias when he was on his errand for the queen." Auri took a sip of her drink.

Brinna couldn't imagine how her sister was feeling but sobered considering the loss of Lucian. Though they barely knew one another, the dream realm made it very clear what it would feel like. Auri was technically still yoked to Nixus, so his not remembering her had to be excruciating. Brinna couldn't help but think about how strong her younger sister was.

"They were the ones who confirmed we had to look at time to find–"

"Mother," Brinna finished, glancing over her shoulder at Lucian.

He nodded. "They'd watched your brother manipulate his timeline."

"How can they help?"

Lucian shrugged. "I don't know if they can, but perhaps because they understand the art of manipulation, I thought maybe Mattias could learn something from them."

"And what will we be doing?"

"We'll be occupied trying to fix Nixus."

Brinna's stomach fluttered at the thought of being alone with Lucian but didn't say anything, aware of how difficult things were for Auri. So instead, she took another sip of her wine just as a flurry of sound and air cut the silence.

"Honey, I'm home! I brought guests." Nixus reappeared, Tarley, Lachlan, and Mattias with him.

"Good gods," Lachlan swore, bending slightly forward with his hand pressed against his gut. "I won't get used to that." He didn't look like a prince just then, but rather just a man with one hand curled around Tarley's.

They looked like hell warmed over. Tarley wasn't in her dress, wearing borrowed trousers and a shirt drooping on her frame. Mattias was dressed in a soldier's attire. The sheen of the spell still shone on their skin and hair.

Brinna stood. "Come. Let's find you a place to bathe."

After everyone's needs were tended to, they reassembled in the living room.

"There are drinks there." Luc indicated the filled glasses with his head. "Figured we all might need some."

"Thank the stars." Tarley grabbed one and drained it. "Maybe this will take away the urge to hurt Mother."

"Tarley," Brinna admonished.

"What?" Her older sister sat on a stark ivory couch across from her, smoothing her fresh clothes. "You can't say you aren't angry."

"We're all angry," Brinna said and stared at the liquid in her glass. It rippled as she trembled. She looked up. "I saw your dreams. All of you."

Lachlan sat next to Tarley taking up more space than he needed. A very princely thing to do, Brinna supposed.

Tarley touched him, her hand on his leg, as if it made her feel tethered. Brinna could understand.

"What was it like?" Tarley asked.

"Terrible," Brinna replied simply and took a sip of her drink. "Nightmares—the lot of you. There was a monster in yours, Auri."

Auri blanched. "Big? Ugly? Lots of eyes?" She fluttered her fingers around her face. "Boiled skin leaking disgusting fluid?"

Brinna grimaced. "Yes."

"Real. That monster was in the spell, fueled by a demon named Mange." Auri glanced at Nixus, who was staring morosely into his drink. "Do you remember that, Luc?"

Brinna noted Nixus's head snap up, his eyes narrowed on Lucian.

"I do," Lucian replied. "The smell." He groaned. "Putrid." He shuddered and took a sip of his drink. "But you saved us."

Brinna noticed Nixus stand and leave the space, just far enough away that he could still listen. He stood at the window. Nix's reflection was muted in the dark with his shadows at play around him.

"If you hadn't figured out the demon's endgame," Lucian continued, "we might all be in a different version of the Netherrealm."

"Wait? How was it real if you dreamed it?" Mattias asked. He took a sip of his drink, then coughed.

Lachlan clapped Mattias's back with a chuckle. "Don't worry. That's an acquired taste. Takes practice."

"Wait," Tarley said, her head tilting as she looked at Auri. "What are you talking about? How is it you saw a real monster and know Lucian? That doesn't make any sense."

"The Great Nap Escapade," Brinna clarified. "It wasn't a nap at all."

Nixus turned away from the window back toward them. "I don't think I've ever heard this story."

"I knew something was up," Tarley said, her eyes narrowed on Auri as she took a sip. "Knew you couldn't have met that one"–she pointed at Nixus with the hand holding the drink– "in the woods."

Nixus frowned.

"You met your husband in the woods," Auri chided.

"Totally different."

"Wait. Why?" Lachlan bristled.

Tarley ignored him.

"I want to know the story," Nixus demanded, moving into the room to rejoin their party.

Luc cleared his throat, glancing at Auri then at his brother. "I'd be happy to tell it to you–"

"No," Nixus said. "I want Aurielle to tell it to me."

She glanced at him as he sat on a couch near her once

more, a little closer this time.

"I think it's best that we hold off on that story for now," Auri said.

"Why?" Nixus demanded.

Auri tilted her head. "Well, because I don't feel like reliving it right now. I'm hungry, and we have darker things to ponder."

Nixus scowled at his drink. He pressed his teeth together, the skin over this jaw tensing. Then—when he seemed to find a space of control—he said, "You're right."

Lucian's hand wrapped around Brinna's arm and squeezed. "Dinner should be ready," he said and stood, helping Brinna to her feet.

After dishing out helpings of soup and fresh bread with butter, they sat casually around the dining table. Nixus's mood had dissipated into his usual sardonic wit, smiling once again, his shadows hidden once more. Auri and Tarley laughed with him as Lucian, Lachlan, and Mattias needled him, which made Brinna feel better that this was the way it could be even despite all that happened. She pondered her parents, worried about them, about Jessamine, and wished there was more that could be done. Wished they were there too. Worried that they would never be a part of this, and this was what she wanted more than anything.

"So what is the plan?" Tarley asked.

"Brinna and I will be going to the Library of the Oracles tomorrow. We'll also connect Mattias with the… Arguments."

"Arguments?" Nixus asked.

"Eitan, Pax, and Lior," Lucian clarified.

Nixus looked confused. "Why are you calling them the Arguments?"

"That's what Aurielle calls them." Lucian lifted his glass to Auri.

Nixus burst out laughing.

"You told me all they do is argue," she said and grinned.

Nixus's smile faded, as if he were trying to put together when he'd told her about them. Unable to, his scowl returned, except it wasn't directed at Auri but at the tabletop. "That's true." He swirled the spoon around the empty bowl.

"Why me?" Mattias asked.

"They have certain gifts that we think might be helpful for you," Luc said. "Since you manipulate time, I was thinking you might need some training with manipulation."

"They are rather adept," Nixus said and smirked.

"We should check in with Lexa tomorrow about finding someone to train you with your magic," Luc said.

"I can do that," Nixus volunteered.

"May I go with you?" Auri asked. "I would love to see Lexa."

Nixus frowned. "You know Lexa?"

"That's part of the story," Auri replied brightly.

"The dragon?" Lachlan asked.

"Yes."

"Why her?"

"As the god of the Netherrealm, she has access to demons," Lucian answered. "Since the magic each of you carry is demon-fueled, then it will take someone who understands that kind of magic to train you."

Lachlan nodded. "And so she'll know who to ask."

"How do you know it's demon-fueled?" Tarley asked.

"Since it was a spell gifted to your mother by the sorcerer, it isn't godlight, hence demon-fueled," Lucian explained.

"Well, each of you have a job. What about us, then?" Tarley looked at Lachlan.

"I have something for us," he told her cryptically, his eyes jumping to Lucian, which made Brinna curious.

But she didn't ask, sure Lucian would tell her later. "Was there any word about Jessamine?"

Tarley shook her head.

Silence descended until Auri stood as Brinna yawned, her heart picking up speed as she did, frightened by the exhaustion climbing through her. She jumped up to help Auri gather the dishes from the table, to stay awake.

"I'll help clean with Auri," Nixus said, standing with her. He took the dishes Brinna had begun to collect and followed Auri to the kitchen sink.

"You can't just use power?" Mattias asked.

"To what?" Lucian asked.

"Clean the dishes? Cook."

"That isn't really how godlight works," Lucian started.

Nixus returned to the table. "It's more like we have power over certain facets of things," he explained as he gathered more dishes. "Like me with the night and shadows. I can't control Luc's light."

"The kind of magic you're describing is more like the

spell."

Mattias shuddered.

Brinna offered Luc a smile, then suppressed another yawn, concerned she would need to sleep soon and knowing that was the last thing she wanted to do.

With his hand still on the Elsewhere-Door knob he'd just helped Lachlan take Tarley through, he turned and looked at Brinna.

"That's so kind, Lucian," Brinna said, stifling a yawn behind one of her hands—the one not touching him.

"They haven't really had time to celebrate their wedding. I thought a private, romantic place might be in order."

She smiled and yawned again.

"Ready?"

It was time for bed. Everyone else had retreated to their respective spaces, and it was time to escort Brinna to her room. He didn't want to be without her—was tentative about being separated from her after what they'd been through. But he also didn't want her to feel pressured to remain with him either. She would set the pace. Besides, he reasoned, they had their whole lives together, so patience, even if it wasn't one of his virtues, was an important skill to learn.

"I don't want to go to sleep," Brinna admitted as they walked over the skybridge toward their rooms.

Despite her words, he could see she was tired, her eyelids drooping. He knew it was her fear speaking, so he took her hand in his and pulled her closer. "You're safe here, Brin."

She pressed her shoulder into his side, then leaned her head on his shoulder. "I know…" Then she stopped in the hallway between their doors and turned to face him. "What if…"

"I'm not going anywhere." Luc skimmed his fingertips over her cheek, pushing a stray hair behind her ear. "What do you need?" He framed a side of her face with his palm.

She gave him a tired smile, leaning into his hand. "Maybe we can see if we can catch the piskies at their midnight work."

Luc chuckled. "Piskies are too stealthy."

She glanced at his lips. "Stay?"

He swallowed. "To sleep? Right." He nodded, giving himself the message. "To sleep."

"I don't want to be without you." She led him through her door, drawing him inside behind her, their hands still linked. "Wherever that takes us."

He glanced over his shoulder at the door as it shut behind him, then back at Brinna, understanding her sentiment. "Where is it going to take us?"

Brinna released his hand and pulled the shirt over her head, leaving her in a silky undershirt, her nipples pebbled underneath the thin fabric. "Wherever we want it to."

"Brinna," he breathed, his hands gliding over her now bare shoulders and down her arms, his eyes skimming her body.

She stepped closer and tucked a finger under his chin lifting his gaze to hers. "I want you," she said. "I want this. Us."

A growl rumbled in his chest as he leaned forward, pressing his lips to Brinna's. The kiss was like coming home, and the energy inside him surged, rushing from his heart outward like an exploding star so that their connection consumed him. He moaned.

She slid her hands up his chest and wrapped her arms around his neck, her body now fitted against his like a perfect puzzle piece.

"Brinna, baby," he said into her mouth, though he wasn't sure what he wanted. It was more of a prayer, an offering of worship.

Her tongue danced with his, her hands holding onto him tightly.

Luc tilted his head to deepen the kiss.

She matched him in the opposite direction, seeking more.

"Hurry," she said against his lips, and tugged on his shirt. Her words added kindling to the already raging inferno inside him. "I need you, Lucian."

He shrugged out of the shirt as she unbuttoned and pushed her trousers down her hips.

Stepping forward to help her, his growl deepened. "The woman of my dreams."

She smiled and closed the distance between them, her hands at his belt, fumbling with it. "Keep me awake, Lucian. I want this wide awake."

"Gladly," he said and grabbed the back of her head, pulling her lips to his, diving headlong into the desire he had for this woman. The kiss was glorious, lighting him up on the inside as her lips melded with his. Her tongue slipped suggestively with his into a rhythm he wanted to emulate with their bodies.

Their dreams had been beautiful, but this was something otherworldly.

He stepped from his pants and walked her backward until they were both lying on the bed, looking his fill at her laid out on the comforter. She wore nothing but her underclothes, her nipples tight peaks under her ivory silk top. Her red-gold hair fanned out around her head, and her lips were swollen with his kisses.

Wrapping a hand around her throat, he slid his palm down between her breasts. "You are mine," he said, his eyes jumping to hers. "You have been mine since the first time I ever saw you."

"Yes," she breathed and wrapped a leg around his hip, creating a space for him to sink closer. She mewled as his length slid along the path between her legs to her clit. "Yours." She moaned as his mouth slid down her neck.

Her hips lifted to find him, seeking friction, and undulated against his hard length still under the fabric of his underclothes.

"Stars," she breathed. "This is even better. So much." She whimpered, rolling her hips under him. "You feel so good."

"I need your skin against mine," he said against her lips and slid his hands under her silky shirt until her breasts were in his palms. "So soft," he said and pushed the shirt up, exposing her. He wrapped his lips around one of her nipples and drew the bead into his mouth with his tongue, groaning at her delectable taste.

Her hands sank into his hair, pulling as she arched against his mouth. "Wide awake, Lucian. I'm awake. This is a dream."

"I need to be in you, Brin."

"Yes," she panted, shifting to help him remove the remaining barriers between them. He yanked the panties from her body. "Yes." She shifted her hips to help him. "I want you in me. Now."

She tugged at the waistband of his briefs.

Luc moved onto his knees, cock in hand, and stared hard at Brinna lying open for him on the bed, her silk shirt pushed up over her breasts, her thighs spread, her sex glistening with her need.

"Fuck, Brin. You are a vision." He licked his lips, wanting to taste her.

Her hand slid along her belly up to her breasts, pinching her nipples as she moved her hips. "I'm so lonely without you. Please Lucian."

"Wait." Luc tugged on his cock once more before sliding down and settling his shoulders between her thighs, needing to please her. "This first." He cursed, spread her open with his fingers, and slid his tongue through her folds as she gasped and grabbed hold of his arms, her nails digging into his skin.

"Oh stars, Luc! That feels so good." She sucked in a breath as he swirled his tongue around her clit, pressed her hot thighs wider with his palms, and inserted his tongue inside her. "Gods," she cried out and grabbed the back of his head.

"There's only one god for you," he growled out between fucking her with his tongue and licking her clit. Her hips rocked, seeking the pleasure he was giving her.

"Yes! Luc!" she cried out.

"Exactly. Me," he demanded, his thumb skimming around her clit as he slid his tongue back inside her.

"Oh. Fuck!" She gasped and panted. "I'm going to come." She arched, her body pushing against his face. Her thighs tried to close around his head, but he pushed them open, holding her in place and continuing his attention as she moaned and jerked beneath him, crying out with her orgasm.

"Baby," she moaned over and over as her body deflated.

Luc eased off, still kissing and licking her, relishing the taste of her orgasm—clean and salty with a hint of citrus— content to know he'd given it to her and would be her only from here on out. He smiled and kissed his way up her body until he was hovering over her, his face aligned with hers. "Good?" he asked with a grin.

She smiled, her eyes closed, the fluttering open. "You know it was."

"Tired?"

"No."

"Liar."

"Fuck me," she said and reached between them to grip his hard cock. "I need that with you."

"How do you feel about babies, Brinna?"

She stilled, her eyes flashing up to his. "What?"

Luc laughed and slid a finger across her cheek, moving the hair stuck there. "I find I might have a kink with you."

"What does that mean?"

"It means I want to come so hard inside you and see you pregnant with my godlings."

Her blush and her smile increased the pace of his heart.

"Eventually, but not yet." She pressed a palm to his cheek. "I want time with you first, and to find Jessamine, and figure out all this family drama and figure out what being godblood means."

Luc kissed her cheek. "Yes. To all that."

Her hand slid up his shaft to his head, and he groaned. "Stars, Brin."

"I have herbs I can take," she whispered and slid her thumb over his slit. "Come in me."

Luc rose up onto an arm, grabbed hold of his cock and notched his head at her entrance. She gasped as he began to push in, her legs wrapping around his hips.

A sudden knock at the door startled them. "Brinna?"

Luc froze.

Brinna's eyes met his. "Auri."

"Right before the good part," he sighed and pressed his forehead into the mattress next to her head.

"Coming," she called out to her sister as she scurried off the bed to look for her clothes.

"You're not," Lucian replied as he searched for his own garments. He chuckled at his own joke, which made Brinna smile as she slid into her panties.

"You either, it would seem." She tugged on her shirt. "I'm so sorry."

He straightened, pulling his underwear into place, adjusting his still hard cock. Brinna wished this was different. Wanted to still be in bed with Lucian finding pleasure together.

"Your family needs you." He leaned into her and pressed his lips against hers. "They'll be time for coming later," he said, forming the words against her lips. "A lot of it." Then he faded from the room, effervescing to wherever he'd gone and leaving Brinna alone.

"Brinna?"

Auri's voice reminded Brinna her sister was still at the door. She grabbed hold of the handle on the tall, heavy door and pulled it open.

Auri was still dressed. "I'm sorry if I woke you," she said.

"You didn't."

"I can't sleep."

"Want to sleep with me?" Brinna asked.

Auri nodded and walked into the room, shedding her top layers. When it was clear that all either of them had to do was get into bed, neither Brinna nor Auri moved.

"I'm afraid," Auri whispered.

"Me too," Brinna admitted.

"What if we don't wake up?"

Brinna swallowed and took a step toward the bed, lifting the bed sheet and climbing under. "We don't have to sleep," she said, settling under the covers, her head resting against the pillow.

"You're right." Auri climbed in next to her. They settled into the large bed, though had they been in the cottage it would have been their usual place in their bed at home.

Auri's hand found Brinna's under the sheet and

grabbed hold.

"Do you think they are okay?" Brinna asked.

"Jessamine?"

"Yes. Mother and Father?"

"I think Mother is strong," Auri said. "Her force of will is enough to drag us through this latest crisis, probably. She'll only have to speak of Jessamine's return, and it will happen."

Brinna giggled, though it didn't have any force behind it.

"I'm worried about Father."

Brinna thought about the broken way their father had looked. "He was hurt."

"I think Mother lied to him too."

"About her secret?"

Auri hesitated as if she were thinking. "No. He knew about that. About the spell."

"We should go see them."

"I don't know if I can, Brin. I'm so angry."

Brinna understood, squeezing Auri's hand in hers. Their mother's choice had directly caused what was happening between Auri and Nix. "I'm sorry about Nixus," Brinna said.

Auri sighed and was silent for a time. "I have faith that he will return to me."

"You'll help him."

"I will." Auri rolled toward her. "So, Lucian?"

Brinna turned her head on the pillow to look at her sister. Though it was dark, the starlight shining through the window cast Auri's face in an ethereal glow. Brinna couldn't contain her smile. "Yes."

"Tell me everything," Auri whispered.

And for the moment, Brinna was transported back to their girlhood, of laying in their bed sharing stories and secrets where the only care they had was who would have to search the woods for herbs.

Brinna shared her story deep into the night, telling Auri about dreaming, about Lucian, until the words were harder to find and keeping her eyes open was difficult. "I don't want to sleep," she muttered.

"Me either," Auri replied, her voice muffled and stretched out like pulled taffy.

And somewhere between the sounds of words, Brinna lost her tether and fell into the darkness of sleep.

Awareness came in increments: warmth, light, a body curled up against her. When Brinna opened her eyes, she realized she'd slept, and she hadn't had a dream. She turned her head to look for Lucian, then remembered what had happened the night before when her gaze fell on Auri. Her sister was sleeping deeply, her face and mouth relaxed.

Brinna slipped from the bed, trying not to disturb her.

As she showered, she thought of Lucian and his kisses. As she dressed, she thought about cooking with him, their confessions, and how much she missed him. When she returned to the room, she wished he were asleep in her bed, that they were waking up together. As much as she loved her sister, Brinna knew that sleeping with Auri like they once did as girls wasn't what she wanted anymore. She was sure it was as much the same for Auri.

As if pushed awake by Brinna's thoughts, Auri groaned

in the bed, stretching.

"Time to get up," Brinna said. "You've got an errand to run with Nixus today."

Auri flipped the sheet off her head, her dark hair wild. "That's right. Lexa." She sat up, smiling. "I can't believe I fell asleep."

"I know. Me too."

Auri slid her hands over her head, smoothing her stray hairs. "I'm worried," she said. "What if Nix never remembers."

"Then you wouldn't be Scarlett Fareview's daughter." Brinna smiled. "You have a will of iron, just like her."

Auri frowned, and Brinna moved around to her sister's side of the bed. "You're too stubborn to allow it."

Auri offered a chagrined chuckle, then got out of the bed and helped Brinna make it.

"Besides, he knows there's something wrong," Brinna said. "We saw it yesterday."

Auri nodded. "Yes. That's true."

"You know what you need to do," Brinna added and pressed a finger to her chest before moving to the door to find Lucian. "In here."

When she opened the door to her room, Nixus stood outside in the hallway.

He froze, as if he'd been pacing, and cleared his throat as his eyes skittered past Brinna. "Aurielle wasn't in her room."

"You checked?" Brinna asked, wondering if he could see her sister just behind her, then decided he couldn't when his dark eyes returned to her.

"I knocked, and she didn't answer. So I peeked in."

Brinna's eyebrows rose. "You went into her room, Nixus? Uninvited?" she asked and suppressed a smile.

"Just to check to see if she was alright."

"And she wasn't there?"

"I checked with Lucian, who told me she was with you. But–" He leaned to look past Brinna once more.

"She is." Brinna moved, revealing Auri behind her, and noticed Nixus visibly relax, his shoulders returning to their normal position. His mind might not remember, but it was clear his body did.

"Good morning, Nix." Auri stepped into the hallway.

He scowled. "You weren't in your room." His tone was accusatory.

"Why does that matter?" Auri asked.

Nix's shadows drifted around him, his frustration apparent. His mouth opened, then closed, then opened. "It doesn't," he said. "But I wanted to leave for Lexa's and couldn't find you."

"Where is Lucian?" Brinna asked, closing the door behind her.

"The kitchen."

"I still have to get ready," Auri was saying as Brinna left them behind, moving through the massive spaces of Sol to find Lucian.

When she reached the kitchen, Lucian was there with Mattias pouring coffee into a cup. Her brother smiled at something Lucian had said, then laughed.

Brinna loved that sound. It had been some time since she'd heard it.

"There she is," Lucian said, his heated gaze sweeping over her and rising to her eyes, warming her insides so they began to melt.

Her chest squeezed, recalling the feel of his body pushing into hers before they were interrupted. Her skin heated.

"I had a horrible dream last night," Lucian said, only he was smiling.

She glanced at her brother, who was eating voraciously, then stepped closer to Lucian, worried. "What?"

Lucian leaned forward and whispered in her ear, "You know those dreams where you get to the good part and then wake up just before–"

Brinna drew back and gave him a playful slap, recalling when she'd confessed her sex dreams to him. "You fiend."

"For you I am." He laughed and handed her a coffee with cream. After she took it, he slid a heavy hand from her waist, curving around her hip to her backside to give her a playful squeeze. "Drink up. We've got stuff to do today."

A quick breakfast and the flurry of being portalled away from Sol a little later, Brinna, Lucian, and Mattias stood in an expansive marble hallway of a huge structure. The white stone laced with amber and gold, hues of gray, and even threads of green lined the floors, the walls, the columns, and the huge stairway before them.

Brinna turned in place. "Where are we?" Her voice echoed in the massive corridor.

"My family home, Alabastrine."

"How many cottages do you think could fit in this

hallway, Brin?" Mattias asked as he spun in place, taking it in.

Brinna glanced at Lucian, who was blushing. She grabbed onto his arm. "What is it?"

"I'm ashamed to think I've never spent much time considering those who don't have what I do."

She slid her hand down to his. "And now you are." She smiled. "Growth."

Lucian squeezed her hand. "Let's find the triplets."

The three of them walked through the hallway, up sets of stairs, and down new wide hallways. It was a maze, and Brinna was sure she'd never find her way out without Lucian. She noticed how sterile the environment was. Nothing that said a family lived there. This space might have been gigantic, but she adored the coziness of the cottage.

"Where is everyone?" she asked.

"Around. My mother isn't often in residence here. She prefers the country. She probably has several of my siblings with her there."

"And your father?"

"He's here and there and everywhere." Luc grinned. "God of the Vasmost and all that."

Brinna frowned.

"Does that bother you?"

Her eyes flashed to him. "I couldn't do that, Lucian."

He grinned and took her hand. "Good thing. I couldn't either." He pressed a kiss to her check before leading them into a large sitting room, where three young men— triplets—sat.

"Luc," one of them said and stood, turning to face them as they crossed the expanse.

They were dressed in similar garments, trousers and button up shirts, the cut of which always surprised her even though she was wearing attire—a fluttering dress with pockets that offered ease of movement and no apron—that she could never have imagined in Sevens. The fabric of their clothing was fitted in a way that showed off their forms. All three had brown hair threaded with auburn highlights that shimmered in the light. Whereas Lucian's skin was golden, theirs was a shade lighter, and their eyes were a brilliant blue. The only thing setting them apart at first glance was the way they wore their hair.

"And this is?" The standing triplet tilted his head. His hair was neat, his face freshly shaved. He grinned at her, and inexplicably, her stomach fluttered.

"Eitan," Lucian warned. "I will end you if you mess with my girl."

The man laughed. "Yours, huh? Does she agree?"

Brinna felt warm suddenly, and it rushed up into her cheeks. "I'm Brinna."

Lucian's hand pressed against the small of her back as he leaned in and said into her ear, "His gift is charm. He can manipulate you right out of that dress."

Brinna shifted to look into Lucian's golden eyes, twinkling with delight. She smiled at him, shy suddenly, knowing the only one she wanted to get her out of this dress was him.

"But then you'd end me," Eitan said. "And with your new, upcoming role–"

Brinna looked at Lucian, "New role?"

"He didn't tell you?" Another triplet walked around the sofa. His hair was longer and wavy, drifting like a gentle sea over his forehead. He swung the longer locks out of his face and pinned his bright gaze on her. Then his eye drifted to Lucian as he leaned against the back of a couch, his legs crossed in front of him. "She's surprised."

"Don't, Pax."

"What?"

"What's his power?" Mattias asked, folding his arms over his chest.

"Emotions," Pax said, his eyes raking Mattias from head to toe. "This is the kid. The time jumper?"

Mattias straightened, his arms dropping back to his sides. "What?"

"Nixus sent us to check on you," Eitan said.

"When?"

"When you took the message for the queen," Lucian said.

"I didn't see you—"

"We won't be seen unless we will it," the third man said from his seat. "I'm Lior." His hair was a combination of Eitan's clean cut and Pax's longer locks, but whereas the other two were clean shaven, Lior's jaw was dusted with the hint of stubble.

"And your power?" Brinna asked. "Do I have to worry about my dress coming off?"

Lucian's irritation grumbled in his chest, and a possessive hand gripped her hip.

She loved it.

The triplets laughed.

Mattias groaned.

Lior, still grinning, said, "I can manipulate the way you think. So, maybe."

Lucian growled.

Brinna's gaze jumped between the three men. They were beautiful, which she supposed was obvious given their mythos as gods, but she found herself longing for Lucian, for his time, his touch. She laid a hand over his still gripping her hip.

"How's Nixus?" Pax asked.

"Lexa told you?" Lucian asked.

He nodded.

"Not happy."

"Is that why you summoned us?" Lior asked, running a hand down his thigh before recrossing his legs where he sat in his chair.

"Not directly. I was hoping you might work with Mattias here, teach him the art of manipulation."

"He dabbles with time," Pax said, his eyes jumping to Mattias. "Not really the same as our kind of manipulation."

"I'm right here," Mattias snapped. "And I don't dabble."

"Do you know how to control it?" Pax asked and frowned.

"Not yet."

Pax made an impatient sound, and Brinna thought for someone who could manipulate feelings, he sure seemed openly volatile with his own.

"We're working on it," Lucian said. "Lexa will help

with that. And manipulation of any kind is an artform, whether it's people or magic. Learning the art of wielding, the choices we make, when, where, and how. Who better to work with him than master manipulators."

"So flattering, Lucian," Eitan replied with a frown.

"Leave him," Lior added. "We'll help."

The sun had crossed its zenith and was starting its descent by the time Luc portalled to the library. Beside him, Brinna sucked in a breath as she looked up. He watched her face as she took in the building before them, rising high above with pillars and arches, the hint of a dome, spires, stairs, and stained glass. It was the largest building in the city.

"It looks like a church," she said.

"Perhaps that is the point, in Elcadia," Luc replied. "What do gods worship?"

She looked at him then, her eyes searching his face. "Knowledge."

He leaned forward and pressed a chaste kiss to her lips, needing to ground himself. "Among other things, I suppose." He thought of worshiping her later. Of offering her his supplication, his prayer.

"What is your new role?" she asked, searching his face.

Luc sighed and looked away, focusing on the building. The alabaster lightning cut through the facade of the building's face. He knew the dome was coated in gold, and atop that a spire rose toward the sky—toward the Vasmost. He was hesitant to tell her, but also cognizant that she would need to know, given their god-yoke. She was his eternity, and he didn't want the sort of partnership he'd grown up resenting.

"I agreed to take my father's place."

"I don't understand," she said.

Luc started toward the portal door of the library, pulling her up the stairs after him. "The plan for succession is always for one of his progenies to take his place when he's ready to fade."

"I thought gods lived forever."

"Yes. We do, except under circumstances where our godlight is affected."

"Like with a god-yoke?"

Luc stopped before entering the building and turned to look at her. "Yes. That's one. But succession exists so that a god's power and influence remain dynamic and fluid. If there isn't a line of succession, the power is returned to the Cistern, and the power sits until it is claimed for an ascension."

"So, a fading?"

"A stepping back of sorts. A passing of the torch of one's power. When I take my father's place, I will have to fade as the god of light and day to take up his power."

"So your father wants you to be the god of the Vasmost? Over everything?"

Luc wrapped his free hand around the back of his neck and looked down at the ground between them. "I had to agree, to save Nix." He was nervous to look at Brinna's face, worried to see the disbelief written there. She knew him at his worst, and certainly his prior choices would cast aspersions on his ability to hold that kind of power.

But when he glanced at her, she didn't look doubtful. She was beaming as though… proud.

She touched him, her gentle hands offering some of the same devotion he'd just imagined. "I can think of no one more deserving, Lucian," she said quietly.

His heart knocked against the inside of his chest, an untamed rhythm that made him antsy with need. He grabbed her hand. "Let's do this so I can take you home."

When they walked into the vestibule, an acolyte greeted them and led them through the library.

"We were here," Brinna whispered. "In the dream."

He grinned at her and squeezed her hand.

"You insisted we look at all the naked art."

He chuckled. "I think you're remembering that wrong. You insisted."

She laughed and bumped him with her shoulder as they followed the acolyte up a spiral walkway into the cosmos. Varied planes of time dotted with planets and stars floated around them in the expanse of dark sky inside the building.

"It's so beautiful," Brinna said.

Eventually, the acolyte led them into a room where the oracle who had helped with Nix stood waiting. A stained-glass window behind him framed him in dark relief, so Luc cast his light out to brighten the room around the man.

"Brother Rom," the acolyte said. "I have brought you the god of light."

The man dipped his chin to his chest. "Thank you for your service," he intoned as the acolyte bowed and left, his keys jangling.

When he was gone, Brother Rom gestured to seats. "God of light." His eyes drifted to Brinna. "And your guest."

Luc turned to introduce her. "Brinna Fareview—"

"Godblood," Brother Rom interrupted, his eyes interested, unnerving Luc. While the oracles were celibate, Brother Rom's gaze sparked Luc's possessive streak.

"You know?" Brinna asked.

The oracle's dark eyes found Luc's. "I can see the godlight, but that is all. Your family?"

Brinna turned her head, looking at Luc as if seeking his guidance. Her confidence in him grabbed hold, making him feel somehow bigger, worthier. He gave her hand a reassuring squeeze and said, "Maximora—Alea Maximora was her grandmother."

"But that line disappeared—"

"Yes," Luc nodded, finally looking at Brother Rom, noting the deep crease between the oracle's brows. "In the 5th era."

"Prudence suggested this was true… a disowned godblood."

"My mother–" Brinna cleared her throat then added, "Azleah was her daughter."

"And she time walked," Luc said, filling in the gaps.

The oracle hummed and nodded. "Intriguing. I would like to interview her. Your family. For our records."

Brinna's mouth dropped open.

"We'll look into it," Luc said, interrupting. "But that isn't why we're here. "We are–"

"God-yoked," Brother Rom interrupted and tilted his head, his gaze unnerving as most oracles tended to be. "This is curious."

"Yes, but that isn't why–"

"Does that matter?" Brinna asked, glancing at Luc.

"God-yokes are rare. My brothers and sisters back and back thought the god-yoke had passed into lore. It has been so long since the last documented occurrence. Until the god of darkness, and now the god of light," Brother Rom said as he sat, his plethora of keys rattled as he did. He perched on the edge of the chair, his back ramrod straight. Paired with his narrow features, the whole image gave him a severe quality. He hummed, then added, "Two sides of the same coin. Same two families." He paused. "Curious." His eyes shifted between them before resting on Luc.

Luc wasn't sure how to reply, and instead switched to the reason they were there. "I wanted to see if there was a way to reverse the oblitorium, now that it had served its purpose."

"How is the god of darkness? Is he thriving?" Brother Rom asked.

"Thriving is an overstatement. Surviving, yes. But…" Luc stopped, unsure how to describe Nix's state. His panic, his volatility. While he'd been impetuous before the spell, Luc wouldn't have associated his brother with the unsteadiness. Guilt crawled into Luc, knowing that it was because of the choice he'd made.

"But?" Brother Rom prompted.

Luc settled on, "He's angry."

"Understandable," Brother Rom said. "Considering he now can't account for a block of his experience that he probably recognizes exists. It would be upsetting at the lowest end of an emotional spectrum, yes? The god of darkness, however, who functions by adhering to his baser urges, is perhaps a bit more dangerous."

"Can it be fixed?" Brinna asked.

The oracle stood and took a few steps away to face the stained glass, his hands clutched behind his back. "I'm not sure." He stood silent for some time, then turned back. "The oblitorium has never been done as you and I performed it. We are, should I say, in an experimental phase of things." He turned his head to focus on Luc. "In the past, it has been irreversible, and while it might be feasible to attempt a reversal, I'm not confident that we could avoid inflicting more damage on your brother's mind with our tampering. It could do irrevocable damage. It is unknown."

Luc stood, heart hammering in his chest with anger. "I have my answers." He turned to Brinna.

"God of light," Brother Rom said.

Luc turned back to the small man.

"Your intervention saved him. Do not regret the choice, for it was an impossible one regardless."

Luc swallowed, grateful to feel Brinna's warmth at his side. Unable to speak, he instead offered Brother Rom a nod.

Once outside, the golden lights of the city glowed against the darkening blue of the sky.

"How long were we in there?" Brinna asked.

"Longer than we thought," he said and faced Brinna. "I had hoped there would be a way."

"There is always hope," Brinna said, stepping closer. "You freed me and my family from the spell. That seemed rather hopeless." She reached up and touched his face, sliding a lock of hair back, then laid a palm against his cheek. "Don't underestimate Auri. She'll figure out how to reach Nixus."

Luc appreciated her positivity. "All this power, and no way to fix what's broken."

"Perhaps it isn't in the immediacy of fixing things where the lessons are learned, but rather in the time and effort it takes to discover the remedy where the difference is made." Brinna rose to press a kiss to his lips. "Take me home?"

"I know exactly where I'm taking you," he said as Elcadia drained away and Sol—his bedroom—appeared around them. "Somewhere we can be alone." The sun cast the room in golden relief.

He wrapped his arms around her back and lifted her so

she was even with him, then pressed his lips against hers once more. Brinna tilted her head to the side, her tongue asking for entrance, and he complied. When she wrapped her legs around his waist, he walked her to his bed.

"I haven't stopped thinking about last night. Stars, Brinna, I want you so badly."

She leaned back and smiled. "What are we waiting for?"

A loud clamor of voices carried through from the other side of the closed door, startling him. Brinna released him, sliding down his front so her feet were once more securely on the floor.

With a frustrated sigh, Luc said, "What now?" then dropped his forehead against Brinna's shoulder.

"Should we check?"

"No. Let's not." He turned and pressed his lips against Brinna's neck. "Let's stay here." She tilted her head to give him more room, and he nipped and sucked at the tender skin. "Let's just exist in this room and pretend there's nothing else."

Brinna held his shoulders and sighed.

The din beyond the door grew louder.

Luc huffed a breath, "Fine." He straightened. "We'll check."

With Brinna's hand in his, he led her out into the hallway and over the skybridge to the atrium, where they found Nix bursting with shadows, facing off with the demon Ozland. Lexa and Auri standing between them.

"Fuck," Luc muttered.

"What's going on here?" Lucian demanded as Brinna followed him into the atrium.

The light faded above them, casting the room in the shadows of the coming night. Though the glowing, golden orbs and sconces offered some light, they couldn't compete with Nixus and his shadows. He was also pulling darkness from outside, streams of it drifting down from the arched skylight above them and flowing like waterfalls toward his outstretched hands, to the flames of shadow dancing there.

Lucian held out an arm to keep her sheltered behind him, warming her insides with his protective side.

She cataloged Auri standing with Lexa, in her human form. Brinna hadn't yet met Lucian and Nixus's sister, but she knew exactly who she was. She looked like Nixus. Her black hair was sleek and bluntly cut to the top of her bare shoulders, her torso, wrapped in a crimson… corset, or something like it, though the whole contraption was smooth and silky—no ribbing, or ribbons, or ties. She wore matching trousers that fit her slim hips with a giant crimson bow tied at one hip. Only her eyes were different from Nix—more like Lucian, golden and bright.

It was hard to fathom that this tiny woman could shift into a dragon. Though the atrium was huge, Brinna wasn't sure how Lexa's dragon would fit. Was it small like the woman? She didn't think so, not based on what she'd been told by her siblings.

Lexa smirked at Nixus. "This is interesting."

"Why?" Nix growled.

Brinna would have smiled if it weren't such an intimidating sight, thinking about her own relationship with her siblings.

"For someone who says he doesn't care"–Lexa flipped one of her hands for emphasis as she said it– "you sure are doing a lot of possessive growling."

"I don't want your mate," a feral man—though Brinna wasn't exactly sure it was a man—said from behind Lexa and Auri. He was tall, lean, and muscular. His skin was dark, perhaps gray covered with a layer of dark smoke though the light made it difficult to see. He had dark hair pulled into a bun, though the sides were shorn with swirling designs to reveal pointy ears. His green eyes flashed with anger, fangs on display with his unfriendly smile. "I was being polite."

"She's not my mate!" Nixus's shadows swelled around him.

"As you can see, Luc, Nix is misbehaving." Lexa crossed her arms over her chest and looked over at them, her golden eyes flashing with mirth.

"You've brought the demon into Sol," Lucian accused Lexa. "Ozland."

Brinna glanced at Lucian, shocked that was what he'd chosen to say at a time like this, then snapped her gaze back to the other man. A demon!

"Reformed," the fanged man said. "God of light."

"You all asked for help, so yes, I brought Ozland because I trust him."

"You do?" Ozland looked wonderstruck, his fanged grimace turning into a satisfied smile.

Lexa ignored him. "Is there a way to fix it?"

"No," Lucian replied. "The oracle said it could obliterate more than just the memories. We could lose his mind."

"Don't talk about me like I'm not here," Nixus snapped.

"Then act like you want to hear it," Lexa snapped back. "You haven't wanted to hear what either of us had to say regardless. I was there. I watched you die."

Auri sucked in a breath.

Brinna moved to go to her sister, but Lucian blocked her with his arm, then pulled her into his side.

"She's okay," he murmured.

"I know what happened," Lexa continued. "And you"–she pointed at Nix and swirled a finger at his shadows– "would rather believe that we're lying to you. Have I ever lied to you, Nix?"

He paused, his shadows tempering, receding, then flaring back. "This isn't about that. It's about him."

Lexa looked over her shoulder, then back at Nix. "Ozland?" She chuckled. "I have him in hand."

"I wish you did," Ozland said flippantly.

Brinna giggled and blushed.

"What do you care, anyway?" Auri moved past Lexa to face Nix. Fearless. "You aren't interested, remember? You don't care."

Lucian leaned into Brinna, his lips tickling her ear. "This is nearly as good as what we were just about to do."

She turned to him and smirked. "Really?"

"Okay. Maybe not, but I do love watching Lexa—and now Auri—hand Nix his ass."

They laughed together quietly.

Nix's shadows dissipated as if they were steam in a boiling pot removed from the heat. "I care," he said quietly.

"You have a very odd way of showing it," Auri said.

"He touched you," he whispered to Auri, but the sentiment was loud enough that everyone heard it.

"And so?" Auri replied, a hand on her hip. "You don't want me, but no one else can have me. Is that it?"

"I–" But he stopped, glancing around at them.

Brinna stifled a yawn and leaned a little more against Lucian.

"Are you and Ozland staying?" Lucian asked, then turned and lifted Brinna into his arms. "You know where the rooms are," he called as he carried her back over the skybridge.

"Aren't you worried?"

Lucian shook his head. "They'll be fine, and you're nearly asleep on your feet, my love. I want to take care of you."

Her heart expanded, and she rested her head against his chest. "I don't need to sleep."

"I beg to differ.

"I don't want to sleep."

"I'll be with you."

She nestled closer, realizing just how exhausted she felt even as afraid as she was to allow sleep to take her. When she was settled into his bed, she turned to face Lucian, to kiss him.

"Just sleep," he said, turning her and curling around her from behind. "We have time."

She hummed, disappointed but unable to do any more. Settling deeper against him, she let the heat and comfort of his body lull her until her eyes drifted shut and her mind went dark.

Luc

Luc listened to Brinna's breathing as it evened out, worried for her. He understood why she was fighting sleep but knew it wasn't healthy. The sooner she could control her ability, the better. He tightened his arms around her, wishing they could be closer and knowing there was time for that later. Rest was more important just then.

He held Brinna and pondered his brother, everything they'd seen and heard, the inability to reverse what he'd done to Nix. Eventually, he too succumbed to sleep.

When he became aware, he stood at a small wooden door, the copper metalwork dulled with a heavy patina. There was nothing around him, nothing but the door—the only way forward. He pushed it open and stepped through.

The main room of the library coalesced into being. The glowing orbs of light floated around him, the books, the dark blue sky, the cosmos. But it was empty—no oracles or acolytes. When he turned, Brinna stood there across the space, waiting.

She looked like a vision. Her hair was down, the spun sunshine of it glowing in the light as if flowing in waves over her bare shoulders. She held nothing but a slip of sheet in front of her, her arm crossed over her chest to keep it there, and he realized she was naked before him. Ready.

She smiled, and it was brilliant. "You're here."

"You seem surprised."

"I wasn't sure we would be able to dream together beyond the spell," she replied.

"We did before. On the first night."

She smiled, remembering. "We did."

"Stars, you are so beautiful," Luc said, the truth of the statement grabbing hold of his insides and squeezing. He stalked toward her, needing to touch her. "I love that we can."

She smiled. "It has been difficult to find time alone."

He tugged at the buttons on his shirt. "It has."

"We're alone now."

He grunted his response, because he'd reached her and instead of talking, he let his body say what he needed to. Grabbing hold of her hips, he tugged her closer and kissed her with ferocious need, his tongue taking and giving, tangling with hers. "Brinna," he chanted between kisses. "I need you so badly."

Her hands tightened in his hair, the sheet falling between them to their feet. "Yes. Lucian. We might be asleep, but what a gift to meet you in my dreams."

Sliding his hands down over her hips to her thighs, he lifted her, and she wrapped her legs around his waist, moaning into his mouth. They bumped against a low shelf, knocking a stack of books to the floor.

"We should be careful," Brinna said.

"Why? We're dreaming," Luc replied.

She smiled against his mouth. "I forgot."

He chuckled and resumed kissing her as he walked between the shelves, the sheet caught on his feet, trailing him.

"Stars, I can't wait," he groused, taking them to the floor. His elbows on either side of her, he touched her face. "You're so beautiful."

"Lucian?"

He searched her face, falling into her blue-gray eyes. "Yes."

She rose up to meet his mouth. "Let's get to the good part."

He smiled, and somewhere between thinking about taking his clothes off, they were gone, and he was notching his cock at her entrance, sliding his head through the slick between her legs to her clit. "You're so wet."

"So ready," she hummed, moving her hips. Her hands slid down his back to his ass where she grabbed hold. "Please, Luc."

"Oh baby. I'm here." He slowly pushed into her, a

tentative invasion, and she gasped.

"More," she said, her feet sliding up his legs. "More, Luc."

He pulled his hips back. "Are you sure, baby? I'm not holding back."

She nodded. "Yes. Fuck me," she said. "I need you."

He drove into her all the way, his hips grinding against the inside of her thighs.

She cried out, "Yes! Lucian. More," she gasped.

So he gave it, pounding into her. "Stars, Brin. You feel so fucking good," he grunted out, driving into her again and again. "Touch your clit, baby. I want to feel you come on my cock."

Making those addicting mewling noises he'd come to love, she reached between them to touch herself. The sight drove him crazy, whipped up a hot frenzy of need so powerful he was sweating to contain it. He watched her fingers in her curls, felt the tip of one find the slick of his cock as he slid into her. Caught the sound of her cries straight in his chest as her cunt tightened around him.

"Baby. Baby," he repeated in a rhythm with each of his thrusts. "Baby. I'm close."

"I'm there!" she cried out. "Fuck, Luc, I'm coming," she gasped, her hips rising to meet his as she arched with the intensity of her orgasm.

Her body tightened around his cock, the sheath constricting and pulsing until his own body burst, his orgasm arriving on the shout of a curse, a harried gasp, and a groan of her name. Every ounce of energy left him, and he moved to the side to avoid crushing her, but she rolled with him, snuggling in against his side.

"That was–" Brinna breathed.

"–so good," he finished, his fingers drifting across her skin, needing to touch her, to feel her to remind himself this was true.

"Why the library?" she asked eventually.

"We were sitting there with Brother Rom, and all I could think about was fucking you." He turned his head to look at her. He grinned. "Maybe that's why."

She smiled and pressed closer, her thigh draped over his. "What if this is all we'll have?"

His hand stilled, and he met her gaze when she tilted her head to look at him. "Why would you say that?"

"I just mean, things have been…"

"Chaotic?"

She nodded.

"We'll have this, and more," he said, an oath.

"You promise?" she asked.

Luc tightened his hold on her as an answer. "I promise. And we'll find her," he said. "And things will return to normal." He rolled to face her. "And you and I will make a life together."

"I want that," she said, leaning forward to kiss him. "And more. Is that bad?"

"We'll have it all," he promised, and kissed her back before the dream faded away.

The sun warmed Brinna's skin so that when she realized she was waking, she smiled and stretched. The slide of the sheets felt sensual, and she recalled she'd had an amazing dream. Her body bumped up against a barrier, and her eyes flew open. She jerked away, turning her head.

Lucian.

She'd dreamt of him. They'd dream shared.

Stars, he was gorgeous. His eyes were closed, his blond hair unruly against his tanned skin, a beautiful contrast against the white sheets. A dusting of dark hair on his face and his chest drew her gaze to the slim trail down his abdomen that disappeared under the sheet draped across his hips. The muscles of one arm bunched, tucked under the pillow where his head rested. The other's sinew was stretched out on the bed between them.

He smiled, his eyes still closed, then struck out like lightning, to grab her.

She squealed with surprise.

"Good morning," he said, gathering her into his arms and pulling her back against him. "I was enjoying that." His hands grabbed hold of her hips, and he pushed his hard cock against her backside, then moaned as if relishing a tasty meal. "We're awake, my love, and here I am feeling your body in the full light of day."

"We shared a dream."

He hummed his "yes."

She moved, to sit up and pulled the clothing from her body with haste. "Let's not waste it." Pushing him onto his back, she straddled him.

"Good gods, woman." His hands slid up from her hips to grab hold of her breasts, to kneaded them with gentle fingers. "What's the rush?"

She arched into his touch. His cock offered the friction she wanted, so she rocked her hips against him, seeking relief. "I need you, Lucian. Here and now, with your light shining on us. Where it's real."

He groaned and gasped, his eyes greedily watching where she rubbed against his shaft. "I wanted to take it slow. To pleasure you with my tongue."

"For something to interrupt us?"

"We have time."

"Slow after. Hard and fast right now." She grabbed his

cock and adjusted so that the strength of him was aligned with her soft entrance, then started to sink down onto him, groaning as his girth stretched her perfectly. "I need you."

He hissed and sat up, his hands on her hips holding her still.

She rose to her knees, now framing his hips.

"Wait," he said. His golden gaze searched her face. "Brin?"

Caught in his grip, Brinna panted, desperate for the feel of him moving inside her. "I need to feel you, Lucian. Awake. The first time."

He groaned. "Who am I to argue?" he asked and kissed her hard, one hand wrapped around the base of his cock. "Use me, baby."

She lined them up again and lowered herself on him, forgetting that this was truly her first time. "Oh, fuck, Luc," she gasped as he stretched and filled her, grabbing hold of his sturdy shoulders for support.

He froze. "Are you okay?"

She nodded, then tested the sensation, and though there was a twinge of pain, the pleasure overtook it as she began to rock in earnest. "So good."

Lucian grabbed hold of her hips and moved her up, thrusting as she sank down once more. "You take me so well."

Brinna moaned simultaneously with Lucian, who wrapped his arms around her.

She moved then, chasing the climax she wanted.

"Stars, you're so fucking beautiful," he grunted, his eyes greedy as he took her in. "You fuck me so good."

Brinna grabbed her breasts, pinching her nipples, throwing her head back as she used his cock for her pleasure.

"Oh baby," he groaned and reached between them, his fingers finding her clit.

Brinna's eyes flew open. "Yes, Luc. That feels–"

"–good," he growled and ground his hips up against her before bending his knees to keep her still. "I want to feel you come. I want to see it. Eyes on me, baby."

He held her still, his cock stretching her as his fingers slicked around the bundle of nerves that made her feel so good. She tried to rock her hips, still impaled by his cock, but was trapped between his touch and his legs holding her still.

"Eyes on me."

Brinna opened her eyes again, unaware she'd closed them, and connected with Lucian's. She moaned, laying back against his thighs, opening her legs wider. "Please, Luc. Please," she begged, her eyes connecting with his.

He licked his lips. "Yes, baby. I'm here. I'm going to make you come." He lifted his fingers and inserted them in his mouth, humming as if he relished the taste. Once he slicked them with his spit, he touched her once more, sliding his fingers over and around her.

She cried out at the pleasure sparking through her. "So close, Luc."

"I fucking love your sounds, Brin. I love the way you look when you get close. Beautiful."

Her body tensed. "Oh gods," she panted.

"Only one," he said, leaning toward her and slicking

his tongue over nipple before leaning back and looking at her. "Come, baby."

"I'm there. Oh stars, Luc. I'm there."

"Yes, you are," he growled, shifting so that she was on her back, and he was finally pounding into her. "Yes, Brin. Fuck yes. You're so tight."

She cried out as she fell over the precipice of her orgasm, Lucian's invasion an onslaught on her senses. The orgasm continued as he fucked her, her body wrapped up the sensation of lightning zipping through her at their connection. "I love you," she gasped, grabbing hold of his shoulders. "I love you so much."

"There, baby," he gasped. "I'm there." He swore as he pushed into her once more, completely buried to the base, and stilled, grunting as he came. And he was beautiful, his brows drawn together over his eyes, squeezed shut, and his lips parted as gasped through his own orgasm.

When it passed, his eyes opened, and he released his weight onto her. "Brinna." He said her name like a prayer. His hands framed her face, and he kissed her.

She held onto him, kissing him back.

He drew back, his eyes searching her face. "I love you," he said.

Tears filled her eyes, and she buried her face in that wondrous space between his neck and his shoulder. She couldn't help but smile as perfect peace slid through her. Though things around them felt as if they were falling apart, this—she and Lucian—wasn't one of them. They were coming together, and it was real. This gave her life and strength to face the darkness and wasn't something to be guilty about. She had Lucian and his love.

"Brinna?" Lucian asked, rolling to the side and taking her with him, still connected. His hands skimmed her hair, and he lifted her head to search her face.

She offered him a teary smile. "You make me happy," she said. "And we finally got to the good part."

He laughed. "We did, didn't we?" He pressed a kiss to her smiling mouth. "Let's do it again."

In the Shadow of a Memory

Aurielle & Nixus

By Maci Aurora

Nixus Uraiahs, god of night and darkness, could tell there was a gaping hole in his memory even if he wouldn't admit that was the case. How could he, having insisted that wasn't true, that he never forgot anything? The more everyone brought it up, the more he wanted to dig in his heels and say it wasn't so. His pride wouldn't allow him to acquiesce.

There he was, however, seething like an idiot because the demon Ozland—who was actually a rather rational fellow that Nix enjoyed being around when visiting Lazuli with Lexa—had put his hands on Aurielle Fareview, the woman he was supposedly god-yoked to. Sure, the touch had been innocent. But Nix's rational brain had ceased working. What remained was the desire to end Ozland.

And for what? Touching a woman Nix didn't even remember, even though everyone insisted he should.

She's mine, the shadows slithering through him whispered.

But she wasn't because he couldn't remember her.

Mine, the shadows reiterated.

His brother and sister claimed he was madly in love with her. In love and god-yoked!

His shadows agreed as they spread across the floor, rose up around him, sucking darkness from the sky beyond and drawing power to cut the demon in half. Even as Nix tried to scoff at the preposterous notion, a swirly feeling of unease collected around his heart and squeezed with ferocity. He should remember that because it was a nightmare! And what was left behind in the spaces inside him was a doubtful, maddening refrain that something had been stolen, locking in on the insecurity he should remember.

"Forget it." Aurielle shook her head. "I'm done." She glanced at Nix, and even in the darkness of the solarium of Sol, his twin brother's godseat, her gray eyes hinted at her exhaustion.

Given she'd slept for so long under a sleeping spell, he wasn't exactly sure why.

"I'm done," she repeated and shook her head, then looked at his sister. "Thank you, Lexa, Ozland, for coming to help us."

Nix gritted his teeth at her acknowledgement of the demon.

"Anything for you, Aurielle." Lexa smiled, and Nix

scowled at his sister's predatory gaze. When Lexa swung her smile his way, the part of his brain that was still rational recognized she was purposefully pushing his buttons.

Aurielle moved past him, being extra careful not to touch him by turning her body as she passed, then disappeared through the glass corridor enshrouded by darkening sky.

"Good night, Aurielle," he called after her.

But she ignored him, saying nothing, the first time she'd done so since waking up from the spell. He wasn't sure how to take that. It had been what he wanted—or so he'd been saying, because he insisted he didn't know her— except her silence, the loss of her hope felt wrong somehow. Perhaps it hadn't been what he wanted at all.

"Nix," his sister quietly admonished when Aurielle was gone.

Nix had the feeling he'd messed something up, maybe something irreparable, and though he didn't know what, panic hit him squarely in the chest.

"What?" he asked, pressing his fingers against his heart, then glanced at Ozland and glared.

"She is the best thing that ever happened to you," Lexa said.

"I don't–" He'd been about to say remember but refused to say it again.

"Don't let her go," Lexa said, nodding at the empty space behind him.

"Why?" he asked, trying to ignore the fact that every muscle, nerve, and bone in his body urged him to follow Aurielle.

Lexa moved closer and grabbed hold of his face. It was a surprising move on her part—surprising to Nix, at least. His sister, goddess of the Netherrealm, wasn't the most affectionate of gods. Yet here she was, her dark eyes diffused with her normally hidden gentility. "We aren't lying to you," she repeated, softly. "I wouldn't lie to you."

"What are you doing?" he asked, jerking out of her touch.

She sighed. "Your pride is going to cost you everything, Nixus. And believe me when I tell you that everything to you just disappeared down that hallway."

When he was finally alone—Lexa and Ozland disappearing down another of the glass hallways toward a different wing of Sol—he walked through the same hallway Aurielle Fareview had, annoyed now at his confusion.

Maybe he could trust Lexa, but Lucian had lied to him before. Tricked him, though the particulars were hazy. He pressed his fingers against his chest, willing the rising panic to recede like his shadows. What he knew was that he couldn't continue like this. Unsettled. Indecisive. Emotional beyond reason.

He was a mess.

Drawn to the room where he knew Aurielle was sleeping, he stopped outside the door and pressed his palm to the smooth surface, wishing he could be who she thought he was. Clearly, he wasn't. He was disappointing her, disappointing everyone, and while normally he wouldn't care, the look on Aurielle's face haunted him.

He closed his eyes and imagined her. In his mind, he could see her with her arms thrown around her sister—

Brinna—after she'd woken from the spell, her dark hair in a haphazard braid exploding with escaped strands. He hadn't known what to expect, having found Lucian's declaration to Brinna, a woman Nix had never met, strange. But then Aurielle had turned her head to look at him, and the emotion in her gray eyes had been a gut-punch. His shadows had wreathed inside of him, responding to her—a stranger—his power surging with heat.

But he hadn't known her.

She'd seemed to know him, however, which was more of a truth than the words of his brother and sister. She'd thrown her arms around him and kissed him. That kiss had told truths he couldn't grasp, but that moment, seared in his memory, screamed for him to pay attention. His body had responded as if he was the one to have been awoken.

But she was a stranger.

Except he dreamed of her. One dream resurfaced over and over: Aurielle standing in a jungle, rain dripping through her hair and staining her white linen shirt with water droplets, her skin showing through, her eyes loaded with desire.

It hurt to think that he had a great love story and couldn't remember a single thing about it. That he was supposed to look upon this woman and feel it even if the story was missing.

He sighed and pressed his forehead to the door.

That's when he heard the muted sob, followed by a succession of ragged breaths filled with sadness. Aurielle was crying.

He knocked on the door.

The crying stopped and after several beats she called out, "Who is it?"

"Nix."

"Go away," she said, sniffing.

"Please open the door." He might have listened to her request the day before, but now with his sister's words lingering in his mind and his heart, he didn't think he could.

"No," she said, her voice muted.

"If you don't open the door, I'll come inside anyway."

Silence swelled until the sound of footsteps thumped against the floor. The door snapped open, but only enough so that a slice of her face was visible. "What?"

He swallowed, suddenly unsteady in his course as if a strong wind was tossing him about on an angry sea. He felt… something. Something warm and inviting and desirous kicking up inside his chest. "You promised me the story," he stammered, annoyed with himself for stammering at all.

Fucking hell, he was a god, and this woman reduced him to his boyhood insecurities.

"You want the story?"

"Yes. I mean, not now, as in just this moment, but yes."

"Are you admitting that you've forgotten something?"

He cleared his throat and equivocated, not quite ready to acquiesce to the idea he had forgotten a whole love story. That seemed preposterous. "I admit that I feel as if I don't have the whole picture."

She snorted and shut the door on his face.

With her back pressed against the closed door, Auri swiped at her eyes, wishing she didn't feel the need to cry. But everything had fallen apart, and she couldn't seem to find her compass. With Jessamine missing, her parents—her mother, specifically—liars, and Nix unable to remember her, Auri closed her eyes and slid down the door until she was sitting on the floor, wrapping her arms around her knees, as she let the tears take control.

"Aurielle?"

Her eyes flew open as her head snapped up to find Nix crouched in front of her.

"What are you doing?" She scrambled to her feet.

"You shut the door on me."

His words from so long ago drifted through her mind: *Don't shut me out. I don't like it.* Oh! What she wouldn't give to have him back. Her Nix. To feel his arms around her and know that in the storm of what was happening she, at least, had him. While this man was her Nix, he was a shadow of the man she'd come to know and love.

"Get out."

But he didn't budge. Instead, he stood there frowning at her.

"You don't want to remember," she snapped. "Why should I waste my time sharing a story that means something to me?"

She tried to step around him, but he grabbed hold of her arm, stopping her. "I don't want to be stuck here."

"We're all stuck!" she yelled.

He leaned forward until her back pressed against the door once more. Only now, Nix was taking up her space, so close she could feel his heat, his hands pressed on either side of her head.

"You said you would," he insisted.

She wanted to reach out and touch him, slide her hands up his chest, wrap her arms around the back of his neck and kiss him, remind him what they were. She wanted to rage fuck him, but she was a stranger to him.

Would that be so bad, she wondered, longing for the release of the physical chemistry they'd shared. That, at least, had still been obvious when she'd kissed him after waking from the spell.

His eyes dipped to her lips, then back up. "Help me?"

His tongue slid over his bottom lip, his gaze dropping to her mouth once more.

He still wanted her, even if he didn't remember, she realized. But the idea that he might want her just because she was any woman instead of his broke her heart. The yoke existed between them—that much was true—but he wasn't admitting it.

What if it helps him remember?

"Why?" she asked, an idea forming in her mind.

I locked up his memories, Luc had said. Which meant they were still in there, needing a little prodding to unlock them. The question was how?

Auri knew Nix was stubborn. He couldn't be prevailed upon to do anyone's bidding, but he loved the chase. Loved to win. That, she could use, she supposed.

He glanced at her mouth once more and remained where he was, refusing to give her any room. She wasn't complaining, but it irritated her.

"I don't like feeling stuck," he said.

She hummed a note in reply. "So you do feel like something's missing?"

"I didn't say that."

She suppressed a tired smile at his predictability.

"I meant that until we figure this out, neither of us can move forward."

"And how, exactly, do you expect me to help when you've insisted there's nothing amiss?"

He took a step back, his arms returning to his sides. "I agree to listen to the story openly."

"And what do I get out of telling it?"

He grinned. "Me."

She groaned and ducked around him. "Look what that's gotten me." She walked to her bed and climbed under the sheet, feigning boredom, knowing the only way to invest this Nix was to appeal to his hunter instincts, his competitive nature.

He followed, making a surprised sound. "Okay, then. What do you want?" He sat near her feet.

She pulled her feet up and leaned back, pretending to think but knowing full well that what she wanted was her Nix back. Her Nix had spent a lifetime in the spell learning what it meant to be kind and compassionate, learning what it meant to be selfless, learning what it meant to love her.

This Nix was who he'd been before the spell had changed him. He was arrogant and self-centered, just like he'd told her. This was the Nix who'd followed a milkmaid into a spell because he'd believed himself in love with her, just to spite his brother. His pride was too grandiose for his own good. This was the Nix she had to coerce into remembering her.

But telling him that wouldn't get her the Nix she wanted. So she said, "For you to leave me alone. I want my freedom."

He leaned back as if she'd slapped him, his brows arching, as if he hadn't expected that. Of course he wouldn't. He believed himself to be quite a catch at this stage in his life. Couldn't fathom that someone wouldn't choose him. It had taken a hundred years trapped in the spell for someone to choose him. It had taken her. Truth be told, she wouldn't have chosen this Nix either. She chose him now because she knew who he'd become.

And she loved him. Adored him. Missed him.

His mouth opened, then shut, then opened again. "Wait. You want me to leave you be?"

"Yes."

He tilted his head. "Why? I thought–"

"Because I'm done," she said and laid her head back against the headboard, still studying Nix a few feet away. "I shouldn't have to convince you, Nix. I have no intention of coercing you into some relationship that perhaps you don't even want. Besides, I think I'm ready to move on."

"Move on?" he asked, his eyebrows furrowed. "To what?"

"Someone else." She raised her head and shrugged, deciding it was time to institute the physical part of her plan. "Since waking up, I don't think our... connection is the same."

"Connection?"

"Physically," she said, waving a hand between them. "It used to be... powerful."

He hummed, plucking at something on his knee, then stood suddenly and walked to the window before whipping back toward her. "Perhaps we should test it."

"Why?" she asked and suppressed a smile.

"Well, things have been awkward, considering. Perhaps a single kiss isn't enough to base this premise that our physical connection has dissipated."

"You don't want me."

"I wouldn't say that."

She ignored his hollow flirtation. "There isn't a reason

to test the theory. My better option is to go out and meet others. Kiss as many as possible until I find that…" She snapped her fingers as she finished the thought with the word "spark."

His shadows shimmered around him as he frowned, then returned to the bed, sitting closer this time. Clearly, his shadows remembered.

"Are you opposed to the test?" he asked. "To check for a spark."

"And why would you like to test for it?" she asked, pushing his buttons. "This is what you want. Your freedom."

"We're god-yoked—or so I've been told—which means–"

"I know what it means." She waved a hand with nonchalance. "We can figure that out when I finish telling you the story." She watched him work over the idea, his dark eyes searching her face. "Do we have a deal?"

She watched emotions play over his features. "We have a deal, after we test the connection."

"You aren't going to let that go?" she asked but knew full well he wouldn't. She pictured his panic after learning she loved him and had left him sleeping alone. His dramatic flare. She wanted to grin, but didn't, holding onto it instead to keep her Nix close.

"I just think we should exhaust all possibilities before we come to an agreement."

"Fine," she said. "How shall we test it?"

He couldn't believe what he was hearing. The ridiculous notion that they didn't have a physical connection grated against his nerves, his pride. Not that he recalled their prior chemistry, but that kiss she'd given him upon waking had been mind-blowing. And he had every intention of proving it to her. Why, he wasn't sure, because she was right, he just wanted to move on.

"You want to do this now?" she asked from her place in bed.

Stars, she looked good, sitting there.

He'd noticed the second he'd portalled into the room. She'd stood, and he couldn't help but notice her pebbled nipples under the thin shirt and the bare skin of her thighs, her hair free and flowing over her shoulders, her eyes flashing with anger. Her appeal hit him squarely in the chest making hard to draw a steady breath.

He could imagine kissing her now, but timing was everything, and that felt all wrong. He stood. "No. I would like to reserve the right to run the test at a point during your story at a time of my choosing."

"And when the connection fails?"

"It won't. What do you have to lose?"

She shook her head and sighed, taking time to answer. "I don't understand you, but fine. I agree."

"We'll get started with the story–"

"After training. Tomorrow."

Nix frowned, imagining Ozland's hands on her, but didn't argue. He'd have to find a way to keep an eye on things. So he nodded and portalled into his bedroom. There was no sense in wasting words on a goodbye when he'd see her in a few hours.

He stripped out of his clothes and collapsed into bed, but sleep evaded him. Try as he might, each time he closed his eyes he saw her. Just now sitting in her bed. Earlier that night facing off with him in the atrium. Her smile. Her laughter with her siblings. He saw her in the woods, her back in the loam, his body housed between her legs as he moved over her.

"Please, Nix. I need you."

His eyes flew open, heart racing as the morning light revealed he'd slept restlessly, the last thing he'd experienced in his sleep more like a memory than a dream.

When he walked into Sol's kitchen, he was the first one up. He made coffee and stood at the window watching the storm clouds unleash their anger. Though the sun shone on Sol, warming the living room through the glass, lightning flashed with bright fervor below them.

"You're up early," Luc said, catching Nix off guard. He hummed a pleasant sound. "Coffee. Thank you!"

"Father must be angry."

"A storm? He must have goaded Drisstol to attack the sky."

Nix didn't reply. The contrast in the sky felt prophetic somehow. As if he, himself, were torn in two. He turned his back to it and met his brother in the kitchen. "Probably mother."

"She does have a way of riling him."

"I've wondered," Nix said, "how those two can care so much about what the other does and still choose to hurt one another."

Luc sipped his coffee. "I don't want what they have."

"If the last few days are any indication, you won't," Nix replied.

Luc smiled into his coffee cup, a grin that kicked up jealousy inside Nix. "Brinna is pretty amazing."

They were quiet together in Sol's kitchen, sitting near one another as Nix's thoughts drifted to Aurielle and the night before. The way she looked in that nightshirt. Her legs. Her lips. Her wary gaze. The resignation on her face. His heart slipped its rhythm considering her sadness, and he pressed his fingertips against it to put it back into place.

"So what happened last night, baby brother?" Luc asked.

Nix turned his head to regard his brother. "Four

measly minutes, Luci," he said and noticed Luc's gaze slide from the fingertips against Nix's heart up to his face.

"Four minutes is still four minutes, Nixi, and stop deflecting. You were ready to eviscerate Ozland, and the piskies would have been cleaning up demon blood in the atrium if Lexa hadn't stepped in. What did Oz do?"

Nix didn't want to own up to the truth since it felt more revealing than he wanted, especially with Luc's chorus that he'd forgotten Aurielle. Only he needed to talk to someone, and Luc had been the most helpful recently. They had their challenges, of course, but Luc was his twin and closest to him. "He put his hands on Aurielle."

He suddenly imagined putting his hands on Aurielle the night before. Of sliding his hand up her bare thigh under that nightshirt–

Luc set his mug down with an indignant thud, startling Nix out of his reverie. "He tried to hurt her?"

"No."

"Oh." Luc's eyebrows rose over his eyes. "Oh," and he hummed a soft noise as he recognized what that meant.

"I asked Aurielle to tell me the story. She agreed."

"That's good. Are you ready to hear it?"

"Ready?" Nix scoffed. "I don't think it will matter since I haven't forgotten anything–"

"Nix. Don't–"

Nix held up his hand stopping his brother. "I have no intention of hurting her," he said.

"Then why go through with it at all?"

He wanted to fuck her.

And maybe figure out what was missing, but he had no

intention of revealing either of those things to Luc. Not and have him say he was right. Nix had too much pride for that nonsense. But Aurielle seemed opposed to sex in order to avoid the added complication of attaining her freedom. He was a god, however, so he could probably find a way to turn her toward his favor. Compelling her was an option, but there was something that didn't quite feel right about that option, so he decided to avoid it. He wanted her hungry and willing. In fact, he wanted her to beg.

He grinned.

Luc cleared his throat. "Be careful there," he warned.

Nix was saved from having to say anything because Aurielle walked into the room with Brinna, both wearing form fitting attire leaving very little to the imagination. While Brinna was a beautiful woman, the sight of Aurielle did things to his insides, and his shadows flared at the sight of her. Her dark hair was pulled back into a ponytail, her face clean and bright, her cheeks rosy. She had a constellation of freckles on her cheeks and nose— seventeen of them. He'd counted. She was smiling at something Brinna had whispered, then raised her eyes to meet his gaze. Her smile dimmed, and it gutted Nix, though he didn't understand why. His shadows, on the other hand, hated it and grew, reaching toward her, as if they had a mind of their own. Nix reined them in.

"Good morning," she said, her eyes drifting away from him to Luc.

Nix gritted his teeth, hating that it made him feel ridiculously jealous.

"Good morning," his brother replied and reached for Brinna, pulling her into him, his nose pressed into her hair. Brinna gripped Luc's shirt and hummed against his chest.

The sight did something strange to Nix's heart, leaving it hanging in his expansive chest cavity without a tether, waiting for the impending free fall.

"Nix." Auri's voice grabbed his attention. "Stop."

His shadows were curled around her legs and waist, and she was doing an odd dance inside of them as if trying to avoid their touch. "Are they cold?"

"No. They tickle. And this goes against our deal," she said.

With a grin, he pulled them back once more, enclosing them inside himself.

"Deal?" Brinna asked.

"She's agreed to tell me the story," Nix said. "And I've agreed to listen."

"Well, isn't that magnanimous of you." Brinna rolled her eyes. "When will this be?"

"We'll start after this morning's training session with Ozland," Aurielle replied.

"I think I'll attend that too," Nix said, not wanting to let her out of his sight for some inexplicable reason.

"No," Aurielle replied. "I'll be doing my sessions without you."

Nix narrowed his eyes and tilted his head. Did she like the demon? The thought annoyed him.

"And that is why," she said with a wave of her finger at his exploding shadows. "We don't need a repeat of last night's atrium fiasco."

He crossed his arms, wrangling his shadows back. "Fine."

287

Each room at Sol amazed Auri. The training room where she was with Brinna, Tarley, Mattias, and Ozland was no exception. In the same wing as the massive pool complex, this room was situated at one end with an outside wall of glass open to the sky beyond, offering brilliant natural light. Black mats with a touch of give to soften a fall stretched across most of the room. There were mirrors and contraptions with pulleys and weights and systems for moving in place at one end. The whole of the room had been made for strength, endurance, and flexibility of the body.

It was a bit perplexing.

Having grown up in Sevens where they worked from sunup to sundown without any time in between for things that didn't require survival, the idea of a place just for exercising the body was nearly unfathomable. Yet here they were.

"Are we going to use this one?' Mattias asked from across the room, catching Auri's attention. He was holding a bar with bulky bulbs at either end, his face glowing like a kid in the sweets section of the mercantile.

"Not this second," Ozland said with a smile, his fangs on display. "But I can show you after."

Initially, meeting Ozland had been a shock, though perhaps no more than when she'd first met Lexa as a dragon. Ozland, she'd learned, was a reformed demon, which meant he'd left the ruling tether of the Netherrealm to accept mortality. While seeing the demon had been unnerving at first, the more she was in his company, the less his charcoal skin, green eyes, fangs, and pointy ears surprised her. Currently, his lean, lengthy body was encased in form-fitting material—the same kind they were all wearing—and Auri admired the way he looked. It made her think of Nixus and his outburst the night before, and she couldn't help but grin at it now.

"Come sit." Ozland beckoned to Mattias with a nod of his head and took a seat on the mat. "We're going to start simple."

Ozland waited for each of them to take a place on the mat in a circle with him. "Lexa has filled me in on the particulars of your magic, and Brinna has offered me a few more details to fill in the rest. The first thing I think we need to do is help you connect to the magic inside you."

"Connect?" Tarley asked.

Ozland nodded. "Think of the spell like this." He held up a hand, his palm perpendicular to the floor. "This is you. And this"–he held up his other hand– "is the spell." He pressed his palms together. "Your energy runs parallel to the magic, but not together. Our work will hopefully help you connect it." He interlaced his fingers.

Over the next hour, Ozland led them through several breathing and visualization exercises.

"As you take this next breath," he said, the gentle rumble of his voice a comforting waterfall over river rocks, "imagine your magic like a light."

In her mind's eyes, Auri imagined a dark green glow effervescent with golden bursts.

"The most important element of connecting to the magic," Ozland continued, "is to understand that it is a part of you. That your instincts are the magic, and the magic is your instincts. Breathe it in."

Auri imagined the lights moving in time with her breathing, pulsing like her lungs, in and out. The longer she breathed, the deeper and less brilliant the light shone, as if with each breath she took, she drew more of it inside to become a part of her.

"Trusting yourself and the magic within you," Ozland said, "is the hardest part of the process."

By the time Auri pulled open the door of her bedroom after the training session, she expected to have to wait for Nix to meet her. Except there he was, leaning against the wall opposite her door, his hands in his pockets and an irritated look on his face. His dark hair was as unruly as always, a mass of dark curls she absolutely loved to run her fingers through. Or had. The rest of him was perfectly coiled tension ready to strike, which made her think about the spell. About him once stalking her through the library.

She stalled in the doorway, suddenly insecure that she'd taken very little care in her appearance, though everything in her indicated it was the right move where Nix was concerned. Her nonchalance with respect to him would drive him to distraction. He needed the chase. She was as sure of that as she was of the air filling her lungs. Just as she'd learned from Ozland earlier in their first lesson, understanding her magic was about feeling its thrum and trusting her instincts.

Nix's dark eyes sparkling with night-sky stars, traveled her body from head to toe, then back up again, catching on her damp hair.

He frowned.

Unable to interpret his response, she narrowed her eyes. "What? Do I not meet your approval?" She added as much bite as she could to her tone.

He straightened, looked away, and tugged at the cuffs of his black shirt. "You look fine."

Auri closed the door to her room as she stepped into the hallway.

"Where are we going?" he asked, still avoiding her gaze.

"Your mother's rose garden," she said, remembering his replica of it inside the spell. Though she couldn't remember everything they'd spoken about, she remembered feeling something shift between them there.

"How do you–" But Nix stopped when Auri raised her eyebrows at him. "Right. Because we know each other." He held out his arm and Auri took it, the magic between them sparking so that Nix shuddered, his gaze caught on their link.

"Does that prove to you we know one another?"

His dark eyes leapt up to hers.

"How come you keep denying it?"

"I don't like admitting any weakness."

Auri frowned at him, trying to piece together the Nix she knew with this version of him, wondering how to reach him.

"I can't remember," he said, finally admitting it. "And I should, I think, remember you. Remember what we supposedly shared."

As much as she wanted to be annoyed at him, she couldn't. "Well, I owe you a story because we have a deal," she said instead.

"A deal," he repeated.

"And I think your mother's rose garden is the place to begin."

"Fine," he replied as Sol faded around them, replaced by darkness and the sensation of moving while standing still, her body tugged and upended until a vibrant green garden coalesced, to fill in the space with hedges, fountains, roses, and sunlight.

"Wow," she breathed and turned in a circle, taking in the hedge, the autumn blooms, the marble fountains, the meandering pathways. "It's nearly identical. And yet, so much more."

"To what?"

"What you conjured in the spell."

"And that is how we met?" he asked.

"In the rose garden? No." She turned to face him. "In a meadow of the Whitling Woods."

"That's where you found the key?"

"You remember the spell?"

He sighed, disconnecting from her, to run a hand through his hair. Then, as if he realized it didn't make sense to fight it further, he said, "I have a gap. I remember the spell and several keepers, then it's blank. The next thing I remember is waking up in my father's office surrounded by Luc, Lexa, my father, and an oracle."

Frustrated by his stubbornness but unwilling to tread that path for this current one, she said instead, "Well, the meadow is the first time we met."

"Why not take me there?"

"It isn't time," she said.

"Because?"

She paused, recognizing that magic inside her that inexplicably informed her that saving that moment felt important, pivotal. That if she took him there too early, it wouldn't have the impact she needed it to have. Instead, she needed to work around it until her instincts told her the timing was right. "There are other places to go and see first, I think."

"Like here." He glanced around and walked under a trellis along the trail.

"This was the first conjuring you made for me," she said, following a few steps behind him. "I'd asked for something to do within the spell."

He turned to watch her, and she had that familiar sensation of him being out of place once more, there amidst the green of a garden dressed in his black attire.

Reminding herself of the goal, she told him her version of the story up to the moment they'd walked through the garden together. "You didn't tell me why you conjured this garden, but I had the sense that you missed your family."

"Did I tell you that?"

Auri shook her head. "No. You were a closed book." She gave him a slight smile and continued down the pathway. "You asked me about mine, however, and we spoke at length about them."

When she glanced at him, he was frowning at his feet as they walked, his shadows growing around him.

She laid a hand on his forearm. "It's okay, Nix."

He stopped, turning toward her but looking elsewhere.

She could see his teeth pressed together in frustration, his jaw working under his skin.

"It doesn't have to come all at once," she said softly. "Do you remember anything here?"

His eyes dipped to hers, and he swallowed, then moved a step closer. "No," he said, his eyebrows lowering over his dark eyes. "But I wish I did.

He reached out to touch a lock of her hair that had worked itself from her loose braid, then skimmed the skin of her ear as he pushed it back. Energy flared to life under her skin, racing through her to grip her muscles in a vice of desire and need. She missed him, her body reminding her as much as her heart.

She swallowed.

Resisting anything physical with him was going to be so much harder than she'd bargained.

Being this close to her was wreaking havoc on his insides. She smelled so good, like rain and roses. And fuck him, the moment she'd appeared in her doorway, her hair damp, her face bright from either her time training or her warm shower, he'd imagined exerting her with a solid fucking. Looking at her had been impossible.

Now, this close, he was running the risk of breaking their deal. Or rather, he was running the risk of using his one-time allotment to test their connection right at the beginning.

He pushed them from his mother's rose garden to Ombra, needing to know how she felt about his godseat, though he didn't want to think about why that suddenly seemed so important. The garden faded as the darkness rose like a thick fog, encasing them in its protective embrace.

"What are you doing?" she asked.

"I need a drink, and my mother's rose garden doesn't offer refreshment."

Ombra—or rather, the living room—fused together around them. The comfort of the dark walls, the tall, wide windows offering the vista of the remote, emerald moors beyond, the wooden accents, the dim lighting wrapped him like a hug. It was still daytime, and the sun lit the mossy green of the moor along with the black crags and crevices of the rocky cliffs, creating the sense they'd been hemmed in. The light didn't diffuse the remoteness, however.

Ombra, like Sol, was set apart. But unlike Lucian's godseat, or even Lexa's Netherrelm, Nixus's godseat wasn't on the true Elcadian plane of time, but between it. It existed in a space he'd made, so remote, he could disappear there unmoored and untethered in between the Circles of Vasmost.

"Where are we?" she asked on a breath as she turned in place.

"Ombra. You've been here?"

She shook her head and walked away from him to stand at the window. "You told me about it. I–" But she stopped, bit down on whatever she'd been about to say, and he found himself, wanting her to finish the thought.

"And?"

She turned, the breezy linen of her shapeless gray and

white dress sliding around her body as she did. "This is the first time I've been here." Her eyes jumped around as she took in the details, and he knew that wasn't what she'd stopped herself from saying.

Nix didn't push her, however, understanding that she couldn't be pushed without wanting to be, and just then, she didn't want to be. "Would you like a drink?" he asked.

"Yes. Whiskey?"

When he carried over their drinks, she was looking at the books on the shelf that lined one wall of the room.

"Find something you'd like to read?" he asked, holding out a glass to her.

She straightened and glanced at his offering. "I was looking for the book you gave me in the spell."

"What book was that?"

She shrugged as she took the glass, her fingers brushing his and sending sparks racing up his arm, colliding with the beat of his heart so it stuttered in his chest. He swallowed and watched her turn away with a smug smile on her face. He suppressed the urge to kiss it from her lips.

"Perhaps you might try and recall it." She laughed to herself, walking away as she took a sip.

That grated on him.

"So tell me, is every god of night and darkness seated here. At Ombra?"

"Ombra, yes. Here, no."

"What does that mean?" She sat on a couch, and Nix had the impression she belonged there.

"The name of the seat is the same, but the location is dependent on the god."

"Sol isn't like that?"

"No. Sol is always a fixture in the sky above the god city."

She hummed a sound, then took another sip of her drink. The sound hit him in the groin, and fuck him, he knew he wasn't going to be able to withstand being with her. He'd known how attracted he was to her the moment she'd kissed him after waking from the spell. He'd known there was something more between them when every brush of skin created energy that arced like lightning straight to his heart. He knew he hated the idea of her with Ozland more than anything, of her seeking her freedom to find someone else after this was all said and done, even if it had nothing to do with love and everything to do with whatever chemistry was informing his pride when it came to her.

He took a sip to fix his thoughts. "What was the book?"

She set down her drink with a thud and stood, walking back to the window to gaze outside. "You'll remember in time. Don't need to give you too much all at once," she said cryptically.

Nix set his glass down on the table and effervesced behind her simultaneously, leaning heavily against her back so that her hands came up to brace herself against the window. "You're playing a dangerous game," he said into her ear.

"Am I?" she asked and arched, her backside pressed into his groin.

Nix groaned, and with one hand, reached over her

shoulder to brace himself against the window, his palm flat next to hers. With the other, he grabbed hold of one of her hips. Then he pulled her against the swell of his cock, feeling the cleft of her ass through the thin fabric. "Yes," he breathed.

She arched her back deeper, using the glass for leverage, her hips driving against him. "And what are you going to do about it?" she challenged.

He fucking loved it.

"Are you going to use your test now?"

At that, he blinked, his mind sliding to a moment that felt new: Auri on all fours in front of him as he entered her from behind, her head turned so she could look at him over her shoulder, her eyes closed, her mouth open as she moaned with pleasure. *"Auri, look at me,"* he'd said, and her eyes had opened. Then she'd smiled, and his had heart exploded in his chest with brilliant light.

"What?" she asked, stilling in front of him, her head turned to look over her shoulder just as she had in his mind. "What did you just say?"

"Did I say something?" he asked, rolling his hips against her, trying to recapture the heat before whatever had invaded him upended the moment. But he was unsettled by what he'd seen. A memory? A vision?

"You said to look at you." She remained still.

Nix stopped, hating that the moment was gone, wanting to lose himself in whatever had just transpired between them. "Fuck," he muttered and swallowed his frustration, stepping back. He turned away from her, adjusted his hard cock in his pants, and said, "Yes. Why?"

She stared at him, measured his features with that knowing gaze, then straightened and looked away. "Nothing. I think you should take me back to Sol."

Annoyed, he did what she asked, and Ombra disappeared only for the hallway of Sol just outside her bedroom to replace it. "What now?" he asked.

She swallowed and wouldn't look at him.

Until she did, her eyes bright with tears. "Tomorrow," she said. "I'll tell you more tomorrow." Then she disappeared into her room.

Nix stepped back, reaching to find the wall across the hall from her door for support and leaned against it. His heart pounded out an unsettled rhythm, his body aching from the loss of the physical connection they'd created. A touch. A suggestion. A vision.

What had just happened to him?

Pressing his fingertips to his chest, he tried to calm to storm in his heart.

He swallowed down the worry forming in his gut that perhaps Lexa had been right. That perhaps he could lose something very important to him if he didn't remember what was missing. And soon.

"I'm not sure how to recreate it," Auri told Brinna, still reeling from the sound of Nix's need echoing in her ears and body. *Look at me, Auri.*

After the previous night, after Ombra and the feel of his hands on her, she'd struggled to find sleep, struggled to find a place where her mind found peace. Even after making herself come, hoping that release of tension would help her to relax, she hadn't succumbed to sleep, afraid. Time had passed since the spell, but sleeping was difficult. And interrupting Brinna wasn't an option anymore, not now.

"What? The green dress you mentioned?" Brinna met her gaze in the mirror.

They'd already worked with Ozland that morning. His

lesson for the day had consisted of finding the thrum of energy and letting go to let it build. Auri had spent the time imagining the light, holding it in her center and watching it build and recede like a deluge of water.

Auri nodded at Brinna and added another lock to the braid she was doing for her sister. Brinna looked beautiful, dressed in a silky blue dress nothing like the dresses they'd grown up wearing, while Auri had taken to wearing the comfortable pants she found in the closet. "I mean, at the time I was trying to be dramatic—"

"You? No. I don't believe it." Brinna smiled.

Auri grinned at her sister and finished the braid, tying it off. "That dress—well, the whole situation—was rather scandalous."

"Lucian has been everywhere." Brinna hummed a note as she thought about it. She stood and smoothed the fabric of her dress. "We could ask him where to go to find a dress unfit for the public."

Auri swatted at her sister with a giggle. "Don't tease." She sobered. "I will do anything to get my Nix back, even if it means resorting to appealing to his attraction for me." She hadn't told Brinna about what had happened physically between them the day before. Just recalling it, she felt the tingle between her thighs. The words he'd said so frequently within the confines of the spell.

Look at me, Auri. I want to see you come.

"I would too, Auri," her sister said, gathering Auri into her embrace. "I'm sorry this is happening."

Auri relaxed into Brinna's embrace and closed her eyes. "Do you think there's any news about Jessamine?"

"We could visit home and see."

Auri nodded. "We should. Then I can see Father."

"Don't be so hard on Mother."

"How can you say that?"

"Her story, Auri. You'd have to be heartless not to feel some compassion for what she went through."

"Yes, except Nix almost died and now he doesn't remember me. So forgive me if my compassion is a little lacking," she snapped.

Sympathy stirred Brinna's features. "I'm sorry," she said, nodding. "You're right." She crossed to the door. "Come on. Let's go find Lucian and ask about finding you a dress."

A few minutes later, Lucian looked up at them from the chair he was sitting in near a window, the expanse of sky brilliant with light. A book lay face down in his lap as he listened intently to the problem she and Brinna presented, minus the sex part, of course.

"So let me get this straight, you need a green dress to seduce my brother."

"Lucian!" Brinna gasped.

He grinned at her.

Leave it to Luc to get to the heart of it.

"Yes," Auri admitted.

Brinna's head twisted to look at Auri.

"That wasn't the intention," Auri clarified, "when I wore it. But if I'm retelling Nix the story with the intention of trying to help him remember, that dress was important. To him."

Lucian nodded, closed the book, and set it on a side

table before standing. "I know a place we could go."

"Where are we going?" Nixus interrupted from the doorway to the skybridge.

Auri nearly groaned, he looked so good. His hair was damp, and instead of his usual attire, he'd dressed down. He wore a black short-sleeved shirt that hugged his torso, leaving little to her imagination, and his pants hung perfectly on his hips, blue rather than black. Jeans, she'd heard Lucian tell Brinna.

She liked the way Nix looked in them. A lot.

"To look for a dress," Lucian said. "You're welcome to join us."

"A dress?" Nix's nose wrinkled.

"Yes. Auri wants to find a dress."

Nix straightened, his gaze colliding with hers. "Why?"

"Doesn't that defeat the point?" Brinna whispered a little too loudly to be incognito, not that Auri thought they should be.

She felt Nix's gaze on her and the burn of his curiosity. "You're welcome to join us."

Sol faded from view, replaced with a busy street, beautiful people moving around them as if they hadn't just appeared out of thin air. They stood in front of a storefront that read *Marzelle's Ready-to-Wear and Custom Tailoring* on the window. A white and black striped awning hung over the shop's pink door. When Lucian pushed open the door, a little bell announced their arrival.

With Nix behind her, Auri followed Lucian and Brinna into the shop.

"Marzelle," Lucian said. "We're looking for a dress."

He turned toward Auri.

Auri nodded. "An emerald-green dress."

The woman asked a series of questions which Auri answered as best she could, then said, "I might have something."

"Why do you need a dress?" Nix asked. "Are you going somewhere?"

Auri suppressed a smile at his fishing expedition. "Perhaps," she said. "Maybe I'll wear it for a date."

"With who?" he demanded.

"Why?"

He bristled, his dark eyes flashing with annoyance as he opened his mouth to say something.

"Oh!" Brinna interrupted. "I… um… forgot. I have… something," she said, tugging on Lucian's elbow. "Will you take me back to Sol?"

Auri could see the confusion on Luc's face, but then he glanced at Brinna, and awareness lit his features along with a grin. "Oh! Yes. Right…" Luc grabbed hold of her greedily. "That. Can't be late."

Auri could see the lie, her sister probably hoping for some alone time with Luc, maybe even to leave her and Nix alone.

"I'll be okay here," Auri told them.

"Can't leave you alone," Luc said. "You can't summon us. Nix?"

"I'll stay," he replied, his eyes never wavering from Auri's.

Then Luc and Brinna disappeared, leaving Auri alone with Nix.

"Glad we'll be free of Sol for a bit," Nix said grumpily, then focused on her once more. "Who are you going on a date with? We have a deal."

"That had nothing to do with whether I was going to date anyone else."

"It was so you could be free to find someone else, not that you'd date while you were sharing this story," he said.

"You're being rather petulant." She paused after she said it, her thoughts transported to a time inside the spell when she'd asked him once: *Is this the arrogant hubris or the self-centered petulanc*e?

She bit down on her lips to keep from smiling at the memory that knocked her heart into an enjoyable rhythm. They'd had sex after that. She squeezed her thighs together remembering. Missing that physical connection with him.

When she looked at Nix, his gaze was distant as if drifting with his thoughts. When he came back to himself, he blinked.

"Are you okay?" she asked.

He frowned, his shadows whipping up like a dark aura around him. "Yes, and yes. I don't want you to see anyone else while we're going through this together."

She spun away from him, "Well first, you have no right to ask that of me." Of course she had no intention of dating anyone else. She only wanted him. But so far, this challenge to his pride had been the only thing to motivate him to admit he was missing his memory. So be it. She'd use it if necessary to keep him curious. "And second, you're being rather demanding and heavy handed."

"I have set up a dressing space for you," Marzelle

interrupted from the back of the store.

With a nod, Auri left Nix where he was in the small shop and moved past the woman into a small chamber partitioned with a heavy black curtain. As Auri unhooked the pink rope and tassel for privacy, Nix's hand stopped her.

"Do you need any help?" he asked.

Auri gave him an incredulous look. "No. I'm quite capable on my own."

He leaned forward and said into her ear, "Were you capable last night with your own hands, Auri?"

Her breath caught, and she leaned back to look at him. Had he spied on her? "What?"

"Mine were. I couldn't stop thinking about your sweet ass pressed up against my cock as I finished myself off."

Her skin heated, the warmth traveling down from her cheeks until it ripened between her thighs, her sex clenching with the memory of him inside her. As she imagined it, it took everything in her not to grab hold of him and kiss him with all the pent-up energy flowing through her body. But she couldn't. Not yet. She swallowed and hummed, drawing on that power Ozland had taught her to lean into. She knew Nix wanted her reaction. Old Nix expected her capitulation, but this Nix needed her challenge.

Instead of giving into his desire to know if she acknowledged their chemistry, she stepped back. "I would like your opinion," she said. "But you have to wait to see." She nodded at a chair.

His gaze dipped to her lips, and she could see the war

on his features as he fought with his desire of wanting her and his pride at forcing her to make the first move.

"As you wish," he finally said, his pride obviously winning.

The curtain swished shut between them.

Auri took a deep breath, her heart hammering that addictive rhythm of want inside of her. To keep herself from calling out to him, she tried on the first dress. While the color was good, the fit wasn't even close. The sleeves were too long, the neckline too demure, the slit too conservative. She sighed and looked at the dresses Marzelle had gathered. Too short. Too loose. The wrong color. Too many glittery baubles. None of them were right, and she didn't bother trying them on.

But then, hanging between one that was too full and another that was too layered, she found a dress that pushed the pace of her heart.

She slipped out of the one she was wearing, the fabric sliding into a puddle at her feet.

"What's taking you so long?" Nix called.

"Just want to make sure it's the right fit." She hung the discarded dress on a hook and took out the one she hoped would work.

"You should let me be the judge of that," Nix said from the other side of the curtain.

She worked herself into the dress. It was tight, compressing her like a hug, and while it wasn't like *the* dress in any way, not really, there was something familiar about the way it fit. The dress from the spell had been a plunging V, but for some reason the sweetheart neckline of this one barely concealed her nipples spoke a common language. The fabric crisscrossed around her waist, as if woven to cinch it tightly. She recalled the dress from the spell, its intricate folds and layers of fabric pulled taught around her body. While those strips of fabric had fallen to leave her hips and thighs exposed, this dress's skirt draped around her hips, cascading around her legs but for a single slit that rose to her hip. She'd known she wasn't going to find *the* dress, but this gave her the same feeling.

Light pulsed inside her, an awareness that tugged on her insides with knowing.

"Well?" he asked.

"I need your help," she said, meeting her own gaze in the mirror.

She heard him move, the rustle of fabric. "Oh, now you need it," he groused, and the curtain parted.

She held her breath.

He froze.

His mind conjured another time, another dress with the echo of the words *I felt empowered* running through his thoughts. The dress from his mind didn't look like this one, but it was her, laid out on a bed in emerald silk pooled around her body as he thrust between her thighs.

Another fantasy just like the night before at Ombra, but no less enticing.

He released his breath. "Fuck me," escaped with his exhale.

Auri smiled, twisting and running her hands over the fabric. "You like it?"

He didn't answer. The only thing he could do was look at her. She was mind blowing, standing there in this green dress that looked like a second skin, the swell of her breasts bursting over the bodice. Her bare hip peeked through the slit. No underclothes.

She turned, offering him her back. The bodice plunged low revealing skin, skin, and more skin.

He licked his dry lips.

"I can't fasten it," she said, glancing at him over her shoulder.

The elegant lines of her neck made him want to taste her there. To bite. To claim.

Stars, he wanted her, and he wasn't of the mind to be patient about it just then. Not after what had happened at Ombra. He didn't want to fasten it. He wanted to bend her forward and fuck her in it.

He stepped into the small room, the curtain swinging closed behind him, to shut out what was beyond the tiny room. Moving closer, he slid his fingers along the edge of the bodice over the skin of her back until his fingers met at the fastener. Her skin erupted with chills, and she shivered.

"Are you cold?" he asked, his voice low. He worked through his memories, trying to remember a moment he was more physically aware of someone, and couldn't think of one.

She shook her head, her breath moving through her quickly.

Seeing her affected by him did something to his control.

He'd nearly lost it the night before at Ombra, and he was on the cusp of losing it again. Leaning forward so his mouth was near her ear, he asked, "Did you?"

"Did I what?" She breathed the words.

"Did you make yourself come last night?" Done with the fastening, he ran his fingers along the edge once more, following the trail he'd taken, then over and down the bare skin of her arm before wrapping his hands around her waist, spreading his fingers wide so his fingertips rested just on the underside of her breasts, his pinky teasing the sliver of skin bared by the slit at her hip.

"Yes," she sighed.

He groaned, his cock swelling thinking about it. "Did you think about me?"

She didn't answer, her lips thinning as the words remained locked behind her teeth.

"I thought about you," he admitted and pressed his lips against the skin of her neck.

She sucked in a breath, tipping her head to give him more room.

He slid one of his hands between the fabric at her hip and her bare skin, teasing the joint of her leg, wanting to surge forward to touch her but holding back. "Are you wet right now?"

She nodded.

"How wet?"

"So wet," she answered. "Dripping."

He growled, wanting nothing more than to check, to slide his fingers into her, to play with her clit and have her gasping his name, only he didn't like where they were. He didn't like that she was buying a dress that could be for someone else. He didn't like that she'd asked for her freedom.

And that was what, he realized, he couldn't give her. He might not be able to remember their grand love story, but he could feel the attraction was one of a kind. And that, he refused to let go of.

Grabbing hold of his control, he stepped back, releasing her, then met her gaze in the mirror. "The deal's off."

She turned toward him, her cheeks bright. "What? No."

He grabbed hold of her face and held her gaze. "Who are you buying the dress for?"

Her eyes narrowed. "That's why the deal's off? You don't want me, but you don't want anyone else to have me either?"

"Whoever said I didn't want you?" He crowded her, pressing against the wall. With a gentle hand, he reached for her knee and lifted it, the slit of the dress falling open, as he wrapped her leg around his hip. "Feel that?" he asked, rocking his hardness against her center.

She grabbed his shoulders and mewled a bright, quiet sound as her head leaned back against the wall.

"Feel it?"

"Yes."

"What about that says I don't want you?" He thrust against her, wanting so much more than to be dry humping her against the wall in Madam Marzelle's boutique.

She gasped and rolled her hips against his, finding her own pleasure.

Fuck him, he loved that. "Take it, Auri," he whispered.

"Use me."

And she did, grinding against his length as he met her movement with his own, needing to see her release as much as he wanted his.

She drew in a quick breath and released a sigh. "Oh," she whispered. "Oh, Nix."

"We don't need a test," he said, just as breathless watching pleasure take over her features. "This tells me all I need to know."

His mind slid from the room into another fantasy, their bodies speaking to one another as they were just then in the middle of a dressing room, her words driving warm spikes into his heart. *I love you,* she'd said. *I wish to stay here with you.*

He blinked.

"Look at me, Auri," he commanded. "I want to see you come."

She gasped, her eyes flying open as her body tightened, the grip of her orgasm holding tight.

Nix lifted a finger to her lips and leaned forward. "Can you be quiet?"

Tears flooded her eyes, the gray iris swallowed by the darkness of her pupil. Her mouth was open, her tongue touching his fingers as she panted with her release.

Stars, she was everything.

And then she relaxed, her body unfurling like the petals of a flower opening, but she didn't smile like he'd hoped. She frowned, a tear sliding down her cheek as her gaze met his.

"The deal is off," he replied, stepping back.

"No. It isn't." She wiped the tears away.

It was his turn to frown. "Yes. It is. I just made you come in this dress, and I'm not going to allow you to wear it going out with someone else."

"Allow?" She surged forward, challenge in her eyes.

He adjusted his hard cock in his jeans. "Yes. Allow."

She poked his chest with a fingertip, high color on her cheeks. Gods, she was beautiful.

"I choose for myself, Nixus. You don't get to tell me what I can and can't do."

Choose. That word rang like a loud bell in his mind.

"You have always tried to choose for me, and I don't appreciate or accept it."

"Who is the dress for, Auri? Who are you going out with?" he demanded, his hands framing her face. He expected her to tell him Ozland. What he didn't expect was what she said.

"You, you ass. It's part of the story."

"What?" He took a step back, releasing her face, realizing he'd already known that. He'd seen it. "Tell me."

So she told him. Told him about him ignoring her, about the first wish, about the green dress.

"I wore it after making my first wish."

"And–"

"You made love to me for the first time while I wore it."

Nix sucked in a breath and pressed his hand to his heart.

He'd seen it. The memory. Which meant last night at Ombra had been memory. *Look at me Auri. I want to see you come.* His eyes jumped up to hers. "I think I'm remembering."

317

In the Shadow of a Memory

come. His eyes jumped up to hers. "I think I'm remembering."

"May we keep talking, please?" Nix asked.

He was shaken. She could see it in his pallor, in the way he wilted, shoulders curled slightly, his hands shoved into his pockets as they stood outside Marzelle's shop, with her new dress in hand.

"Anywhere you want," he amended. "We can go back to Sol."

"Take me to Ombra," she said, knowing that was the place he felt the safest. Clearly, his reality had been shaken.

He looked surprised by her choice, but the Elcadian street faded, and Ombra took its place. Unlike the day before, however, this time night was coming, the dimness of twilight casting shadows through the room and filling the glass walls with gray-blue relief. A fire burst forth in the hearth offering warmth and golden light at the same time the lamps around the room brightened. The room—the same from the night before—was still dark, dressed in dark paint, leather, wood, and metal, but it was Nix far more than any other place she'd ever been with him.

"Are you hungry?"

She turned and looked at him. He stood with his hands in the front pockets of his jeans, his head tilted to look down at his feet. The contrast between Nix several days ago and the present was glaring. His pride, his bluster, his arrogance had been stripped away. And while he wasn't exactly her Nix, this was a closer version.

"I could eat," she told him.

His head came up, and he offered her a tentative smile. "Wait here. Make yourself comfortable."

She tracked him across the room where he disappeared behind a counter and busied himself in the kitchen. Cupboards opened. Things clacked, but she moved deeper into the living room to sit near the fire.

He returned with an assorted platter of things. "I don't have much on hand. I'll need to summon some piskies."

"The secret workers?" Brinna had mentioned wanting to see them.

He nodded, setting the platter on a nearby table, then left once more. There was fruit and cheese, nuts and unleavened bread. When he returned, he set two glasses on the table and opened a bottle of wine.

"You have wine." She grinned.

He poured them both a glass, and after setting it on the

table near the platter, sat down on the floor, his back to the couch where she was sitting, his legs stretched out in front of him and crossed at the ankle.

She sipped the wine and waited, unsure how to proceed and feeling as if it wasn't up to her to do so.

Her patience was rewarded because Nix said, "There are these moments I see in my head."

"Oh?"

He swirled the wine glass, the burgundy liquid whirlpooling inside. "Words. Images. You." He took a sip of the wine.

"You've fought it valiantly," she joked.

He huffed a laugh, but there wasn't any joy in it.

Silence descended between them again, broken only by the crackle of the fire. The gray of twilight turned darker, and stars began to twinkle in the sky.

"All I've known is that Luc tricked me, you know, before." He glanced over his shoulder at her.

She nodded and sipped her wine, waiting.

"I remembered that, so when he claimed he'd locked away memories, I didn't believe him. Couldn't. He's my brother, and I know he loves me, but I was afraid to believe him."

Auri moved off the couch to sit next to him on the floor. "That's understandable," she said. "When he told me what he'd done, my first thought was to kill him."

He turned his head and smiled at her, but it didn't quite reach his eyes. "Luc inspires that feeling in many, excluding Brinna, it would seem."

"Oh, I'm sure there were times she wanted to throttle

him." Auri laughed quietly, recalling how angry Brinna had been after a recent dance in Sevens.

"Will you tell me the rest?"

"Of our story?"

He nodded.

"There's a lifetime of memories," she said but did her best to tell him the whole of it as she remembered.

She told him about the spell, the wishes, and the obligations, about her being the last key keeper. She told him of the demon-monster and shared how they'd discovered it was Poe who had double-crossed Lucian. She told him of the final wish, the sacrifice, and how the spell ended. "Through it all, you always told me that words matter." She paused, taking a sip of her wine. "I'm not surprised you remember words."

"I wish I remembered it," he said, his eyes finding hers. He twisted to face her. "All of it."

"What are you remembering?"

"I keep seeing you," he said and smoothed her hair behind her ear. "I thought they were fantasies, but then your words lately have matched what's in my head. I knew it couldn't just be my imagination."

"Fantasies?" she asked, knowing what he'd meant but wanting to hear it from him anyway. Needing to hear it.

He set his wine glass on the table, hers beside it, then took her face in his hands. "Yes. Fantasies… visions of making love to you." He leaned forward and kissed her cheek, then lingered. "I want to remember our story, but not just the words of it. The feelings too."

While she'd planned to withhold herself from him, she

hadn't planned that he'd be so upfront about it. And now, it felt more like a punishment than a wise choice. So she said, "Maybe having sex will help you remember."

He leaned back and searched her face, then shook his head. "I won't use you that way."

She grinned and pushed him backward, straddling his hips as he lay on his back. Then she bent over him, her hair falling around them like a cocoon. "Perhaps you are the one who is being used." She searched his face.

His hands squeezed her hips, his breath moving quickly. "Auri. I can't agree that I'll honor the agreement… let you go after," he said. "You understand? You want your freedom, and if this god-yoke is true, the way I'm feeling right now…"

"How are you feeling?" she whispered and pressed her lips to his cheek.

His grip tightened, and he shifted his hips under her. She could feel the length of him nudge her center perfectly.

She sucked in a breath.

"Like there's no way I would ever agree to let you go."

"That's good," she murmured and kissed his opposite cheek. "I could never let you go either."

"But the agreement?"

She pulled away so she could see his face, tilting her hips so she pressed tighter against him. He groaned with her movement, her name a sigh.

"I was willing to say whatever I needed to get you to want to remember, Nix," she admitted. "Never doubt that I will do whatever I need to for what I want."

He grabbed the back of her neck with one hand, the other pressed against her back, holding her firmly against him. "Spoken like a queen of the shadows. What is it you want?"

"You."

Nix rose to meet her mouth with a forceful kiss full of angst and want and need. Their lips, their teeth, their tongues spoke all the words that needed to be said. He sat up, one arm banded around her hips, tugging her tighter against him. With a rock of his hips, the hardness of him creating friction was delicious. Auri moaned.

With a twist and a flare of his shadows, Nixus rolled her over, his creatures pushing the table out of the way as he settled between her thighs and found her mouth once more. He bit at her bottom lip, then invaded as if he was a conquering hero.

"This," he said. "I knew it would be like this."

With frantic motion, Auri pulled at the hem of his shirt, pushing it up over his torso. "I need you," she gasped as his lips and tongue trailed from her mouth down her neck. "I've needed you."

He ducked out of the shirt and pulled back, his eyes locked on hers.

"Are you stopping?" she asked, panicked that he was going to change his mind.

"I'm savoring," he said and rested on his elbows, his hands caressing her face as his mouth followed the trail his fingertips made.

"As much as I want savoring, Nix–"

He silenced her with a kiss and adjusted his weight to

the side so he could lift her shirt.

Auri helped him, shrugging out of it and her undergarment.

His eyes greedily consumed her as he popped the fastening of her pants. His lips and tongue made a trail over her neck. "Is this okay, Auri?"

"Yes," she breathed, grabbing hold of the back of his head. "Savoring is nice." She sucked in a breath as his mouth closed over one of her nipples. "So good."

He chuckled, the vibration creating an addictive sensation inside her. His hand slid between her legs, testing her with his fingers. "So wet, Auri."

"For you," she admitted. "All for you."

He groaned and moved to his knees, giving her more room. "Take them off," he ordered, the helped her.

Now bared before him, Auri shivered under his gaze. He lifted her leg, kissing the arch of her foot, then her ankle, then her calf, his eyes focused on her core as if it were the prize.

Auri shivered again.

"Are you cold?"

"No. I'm overflowing with awareness of what your touch does to me. I've missed you so much."

He growled, then kissed, then bit, and licked her inner thigh as his shadows swirled around him. They covered and wrapped around her like extra arms and hands. The whisper of their touch heightened everything, and she moaned. It was as if he was everywhere.

So when his tongue swept her cleft to her clit, swirling, suckling, she moaned his name, arching into his mouth, wrapping one of her legs around his back, her knees falling open.

"Oh, yes," she cried.

His tongue swirled, his hand holding her apart so he could lavish attention exactly where she needed it. "I. Want. You. Screaming. Auri," he said between licks, then inserted a finger inside her.

She gasped at the welcome invasion. "Nix. Yes, please."

Between his hands and his tongue, he devoured her to complete devastation as she came apart beneath him, rolling her hips so he had to hold her down. Every part of her was open to receive him, his shadows drifting over her skin like gentle touches, teasing her as his mouth and hands worked their magic.

"I'm coming," she whimpered. "Nix. Oh. I'm coming," and she gasped, crying out as if her life had reached the pinnacle of all that there was and all it would ever be.

When Auri went limp with a sigh, he grinned against her depleted body, the sounds of her orgasm feeding him contentment. But that wasn't all—a connection of light swirled between them so he could feel her pleasure pulse inside his own body. God-fucking-yoked. Fuck him, it was beautiful. He needed to feel her body wrapped around his cock. Needed it like he needed to hear her come again.

He kissed up her belly, wrought with a sense of having done that before, and wishing he could recall the moment, or moments. He was sure there were many, considering how addicted he felt to her.

"I'm not done with you," he said when he reached her

gorgeous breasts, then spent time sucking and nuzzling her.

She smiled and grabbed hold of his hair. "I hope not." She pulled him up until their faces were aligned. "Take your pants off," she ordered, then kissed him before releasing him.

Nix rose to his knees, and she followed, sitting up to help him remove his jeans, before stopping at his erection. He groaned under her touch. She shifted, bending down to kiss the head of his cock, swiping his slit with her tongue.

"Auri," he warned. "I won't last."

"Just let me. Just a moment," she begged and swirled her tongue around his head.

He grabbed hold of her hair. "Stars," he groaned as she took him in her mouth and teased, dropping lower, the warmth of her mouth addicting. "Fuck."

She slid lower, then back up, her hand wrapped around the base, sliding her tight fingers with her hot mouth simultaneously. He moaned, relishing in the pleasure she offered, but as much as he wanted to let go with her sucking him, he wanted more with her. He wanted her with him.

"Auri," he groaned. "Stop, or I'm going to lose it."

She looked up, then withdrew, his cock smacking against his stomach.

"I want to be inside you."

She pushed him backward. "I'm taking what I want, Nixus."

There was nothing graceful about his journey to the floor. Auri climbed up his body, straddling him, her knees on either side of his hips, his legs still in his pants. He worked them off.

"I've been thinking about this—"

"You have?" he asked, holding his cock for her, sliding it through her wet seam to her clit.

"Stars!" She gasped, her mouth dropping open and her eyes slipping shut. "Yes." She grinned and covered his hand with hers, sliding him down to align the puzzle pieces of their bodies, notching his head into her opening. "Earlier, you asked me if I fingered myself thinking of you." She slowly worked her body down his length. "Oh, Nix. Yes," she said, moaning with him as he hissed at the feel of her greedily taking him in. "I did."

"Fuck me." Nix grabbed hold of Auri's hips the moment she bottomed out, her body flush against his pelvis. He groaned. "You are everything."

"You told me that before," she gasped, rising and sliding back down his length.

"Baby, you are." Nix helped her move, sucking in a breath. "You feel so fucking good."

As Auri rode him, he held her hips, thrusting into her, both fighting for control. Her moans, her breath, her body, her movement became his reason. His shadows swirled around them, locking them together. *Remember,* they whispered.

But he didn't. Couldn't. He wanted to, and while there was a distant echo offering him more, he couldn't grab hold to discern what it was telling him.

"My turn," he said, moving and getting Auri onto her back. He grabbed her legs, using them for leverage as he slammed into her.

She cried out. "Again."

He did. "Touch yourself."

Her fingers found her pleasure point, and it wasn't much longer before the sound of her screaming, crying out his name as she came undid him. Golden threads wove together with his shadows, bursting from them both.

If he'd ever doubted the god-yoke, he couldn't any longer. He'd never experienced anything like it before. Her cunt convulsed around his cock, tightening to milk him, and Nix followed her into the pleasurable abyss.

"Auri," he groaned. "Fuck, Auri. You own me."

Weakened by the most amazing orgasm he could remember, he collapsed, rolling to the side so he didn't crush her, his cock sliding from her body. He missed her warmth but loved that she was grinning.

She turned her head to him. "Remember anything?"

He wished he could tell her yes, but he couldn't, and his eyes dropped to her mouth. He shook his head.

Her grin faltered, and she looked up at the ceiling.

"Do you regret it?"

"No," she said quickly, decisively, but tears shone in her eyes.

"Auri?"

She closed her eyes, and a tear slipped from the corner. It gutted him.

I miss you.

Words drifted through his thoughts, her quiet refrain in his head. He wondered if it were another memory.

"Auri."

She turned toward him, eyes still closed, and grabbed hold, burying her face in his chest as she cried. All he could do was hold her as she did, hating himself for not remembering.

Trying to comfort her with his touch, he rubbed her back. Moved her hair. Kissed her tears, her neck, her jaw. He whispered words he hoped might bring comfort but knew that the only thing that would solve this was doing the work to remember.

And that, he knew he needed to at least try.

After she stopped crying, after they got up and sat in front of the fire wrapped together in a blanket, after they'd talked as if getting to know one another better—though Nix knew it was for his benefit rather than hers—he said, "I think we should go to the shack."

"The shack?

"Where the spell began."

"Oh." She looked down at her hands. "Right." She looked at him. "That's a good idea."

"I want to remember," he told her.

She offered him a small smile, a smile that grabbed hold of his heart, yanked, and twisted. Because for the first time since she'd woken, it was the first he'd seen Auri look as if she'd truly lost hope.

The shack looked exactly like he remembered, which brought forth the reassurance that his memory wasn't faulty. A quick look at Auri, though, reminded him that something was missing.

"I had to hide the memories," Lucian had told him.

Because of the god-yoke, which Nix couldn't argue against any longer. Besides the heightened pleasure between them, there was light and the pulsing sensation of warmth in his chest.

"Here?" she asked.

Nix focused once more on the small, dilapidated building and nodded. It was unassuming, sitting at the edge of the Fathma Forest as if it were once a sentinel to the now overgrown passageway.

Auri made a sound.

"Luc had asked me to come with him, so I had."

"Because of the milkmaid."

Nix glanced at her and tilted his head. "You know about her."

"You told me the story."

It was his turn to make that noise, a soft hum of awareness moving through his head. "So, then you know the rest."

She nodded. "You were locked inside the shack to wait, while Poe–"

"–lured the woman. She was shown the key."

"And when she touched it, the labyrinth of the spell began."

Nix nodded, stepping up to the doorway, tentative suddenly to touch the doorknob. It wasn't as if that was how the spell had happened, but it worried him, nonetheless.

"The spell's broken," Auri said quietly behind him, placing a comforting hand on his shoulder.

"Right. Yes." He took a deep breath, then glanced at her over his shoulder, wanting so much to remember. Just in the time since she'd kissed him, after the spell had broken, before she'd realized she was a stranger to him, he was different. He couldn't lie to himself about that anymore. She *was* everything.

Resolved to rediscover his great love story with her, he grabbed hold of the doorknob and turned. The door—a warped mess of aged wood covered with lichen—scraped along the floor as he pushed. With a glance to make sure Auri was still with him, to make sure he was still in the Elcadian countryside, he released a sigh, then stepped into the darkness of the interior. But he ruled the darkness and gathered it like a blanket, rolled it into a ball inside his hands, and held it as Auri made her way inside.

The remnants of the spell were still there—candles, one of which Auri plucked from the floor before searching for something to light it with. Lines of chalk on the floor, stray items set about, implements a woodcutter might use, the detritus of time, a thick layer of dust.

Light flared.

Auri held a flickering candle, her beautiful face the focal point in its golden light, as if the candle, too, only wanted to look upon her face.

"Is it how you remember it?"

"No," he said. "Seemed a bit cleaner last time I was here. Someone's let the place go."

Auri chuckled, then went quiet—waiting for him, he knew, to follow his lead, but he wasn't sure why he'd wanted to come there.

"Why are we here?" she asked, echoing his thoughts.

"Luc told me they locked the memories. I thought…" He paused, turning away to take in the room again before turning back to her. "I thought being here might inspire the memory."

"But it hasn't?"

He shook his head. "It just makes me remember how angry I was at Luc."

"Justifiably."

Nix cleared his throat. "But I don't feel that anger with him anymore." A memory of sitting in a wooded meadow caught his mind's eyes. Luc supporting him, a worried look on his brother's face. "I think I told him recently that I was grateful for the spell."

Auri took a step toward him and tilted her head waiting. "Why?"

"The recollection is hazy," he replied.

"When was this?"

Nix closed his eyes, trying to see the memory, but it wasn't clear. "The woods, somewhere. I think."

Nix opened his eyes, the depth of his emotions bright, and hope hit her hard in the chest. He wanted to know. He wanted to remember. Everything inside her said it was time. "I need you take us back to the Whitling Woods," she said.

"Why?"

"I need to finish the story."

He nodded. "Okay. Anywhere specifically?"

She knew he wouldn't remember the meadow, but she could walk him there from the cottage. Except, she wondered if the edge of the memory on his mind was the place they needed to go.

The light inside her surged.

Please remember, she wished.

His brows bunched, a frown on his mouth as she blew out the candle, then dropped it with a thud and stepped closer. "Follow your instincts and take us there," she said.

"But–"

"I trust you, Nix. Do you trust me?"

He hesitated a moment, and though she might have considered that it was because he didn't, she didn't feel that at all. Instead, it reminded her of the spell, of when she'd asked him to trust her with his power and he'd gifted it to her, a quiet resolution to accept it wholeheartedly.

"What if I get it wrong?" he asked in the dark.

"But what if you get it right?" she asked and grabbed hold of his shirt at his stomach. "It doesn't matter, does it, if we're together doing it?"

The darkness of the shack dissolved as twilight of the forest appeared in shadows and dim light until that's where they stood, huddled together. Auri turned her head and looked. Then smiled. They were in the meadow, the basalt rocks covered in snow. She shivered.

"Well?"

"It was winter when we met here," she said and searched his features. "Like now."

"I took us to the right place?"

She smiled and nodded. "Exactly. Your memories are there, Nix." She pressed a hand to his heart. "Luc wasn't lying to you."

He took a breath.

"After the spell ended, I woke up here," she started.

"Much like this, night falling for the first time in years."

"Why?"

"Because the spell was broken, and you were okay somewhere in the cosmos. I didn't know it at the time–"

"What? Why?"

"I didn't remember."

"What?"

"But you did. And when you were able, you came to find me. Here."

"In this meadow?"

"And you told me a story about a woman and her three wishes. So let me tell you about a god," she said.

And she did. She told him of a bitter god trapped in the confines of a spell by his brother, and though he could have been an evil tyrant, instead he tried to protect the woman. He guided her with her wishes, and when she was afraid, he was there, waiting, wanting to protect her, willing to sacrifice himself to the spell for eternity to help her be free.

"But you sacrificed yourself for me," Nix said.

She took his hand in hers. "That's love, Nixus. True love. And I truly love you. We once fought because I was afraid that the god-yoke was forcing you to love me. I sent you away."

His palm pressed against her cheek.

"But while we were apart, I realized it didn't matter, because I would choose you regardless. I love you with everything I am," she said. "I don't want anyone else. I just want you."

She rose up on her toes and kissed him.

Despite the cold and the darkness, Auri's kiss was filled with warmth and light. Like her touch, the memory of Luc in this meadow solidified, becoming as real as her hand pressed against his chest. "It brought me Auri," Nix had said.

His mind moved backward, unlocking memories as they kissed.

The pain of their separation.

Standing outside a monstrous hedge.

Of kissing her.

Of stolen moments.

Of finding her there, helping her remember.

Of the story she'd told him of their time trapped together in the spell.

Of meeting her in this meadow.

He kissed her with all the love swirling through him, and warmth cascaded around them like the beginning of a fire. When he opened his eyes, golden light swirled around them like his shadows, a part of their love.

Her eyes opened, and she gasped.

"I remember," he said, grasping hold of her face.

Tears filled her eyes.

"Auri. You helped me remember."

She shook her head, and tears slipped down her cheeks. "You did that. I just told you a story." She smiled.

Words matter.

He gathered her in his arms, holding her against him. "I'm so sorry I forgot."

She shook her head. "No. Luc saved you. Saved us."

He knew she was right and pressed a kiss to the top of her head. "But I think we need to figure out a way to get back at him."

She offered a teary laugh. "Maybe after we save Jessamine."

He nodded and hugged her tighter.

"Take me home," she whispered.

"To the cottage?" he asked.

She leaned back to look at him.

Never without you again.

"Auri?" he asked.

She hummed.

"Why am I hearing you in my head?"

She stilled. *What are you hearing?*

Nix drew back and grabbed hold of her face. "Am I hearing you in my head?"

Tears filled her eyes once more as she smiled, tears—this time of joy—drifting down her cheeks. She nodded. "Like in the spell."

We spoke in the spell? he asked without using his voice.

"I think it's part of my magic," she said, pressing her cheek against his chest. "We haven't been able to do it."

"Communicate without speaking."

Not since the spell, her voice drifted in his head. He smiled.

Take me home.

To the cottage.

No. To Ombra.

Nix leaned back, grinning, to look at her. Then he bent and kissed the woman of his dreams before whisking them home. "Be prepared," he said between kisses. "I'm about to ruin you."

She grinned. "I'm looking forward to experiencing your efforts."

"Oh," he said. *I remembered the title of the book.*

She grinned. "You did?"

"Yes. We're about to reenact chapter fourteen."

Auri laughed, and Nix decided it was the most glorious sound.

The Cast

in alphabetical order

Aurielle (Auri) Fairview: The fourth daughter of Scarlett and Tomas Fareview. She found an enchanted key in the Whitling Woods that trapped her in the spelled labyrinth of Nixus Uraiahs, where she was given three wishes. She fell in love with Nix and to her bewilderment, discovered they were god-yoked.

Brinna Fareview: The third daughter of Scarlett and Tomas Fareview. She is inherently good-natured and the nurturer of the family. A romantic dreamer, sometimes her dreams have seemed to come true.

Credence Crendell: Owner of the Copper Pot Inn.

Horance Forte: Brother to Credence, he helps her run the Copper Pot Inn.

Gemma Barnwell: The cook at The Copper Pot Inn.

Jessamine Fareview: The oldest daughter of Scarlett and Tomas Fareview. She is a typical oldest. A dependable and responsible daughter, she is her mother's right hand as a gifted healer in Sevens, and rarely leaves Scarlett's sight.

Johesha Malinor: The captain of the guard for the Crown Prince of Jast, Lachlan Nikolas. He is loyal, brave, and heroic. He was instrumental in saving Tarley Fareview from marauding assassins.

Keyanna Hollis: The crowned Queen of Kaloma rose to power in the male-dominated land of Kaloma. Her advisory counsel and the church of Kaloma —the Rayoran—were against her ascension and she narrowly escaped an assassination attempt on her way to negotiate a treaty with Jast—her late mother's family—for military support.

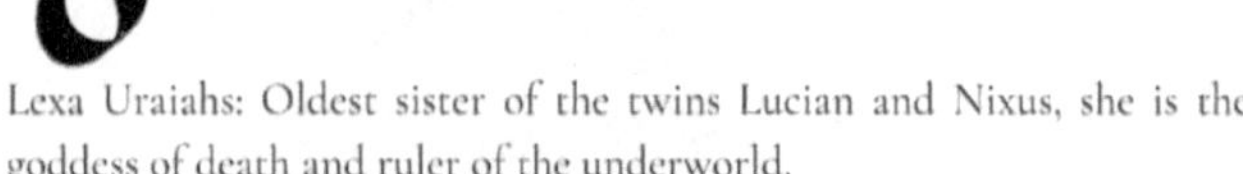

Lexa Uraiahs: Oldest sister of the twins Lucian and Nixus, she is the goddess of death and ruler of the underworld.

Lachlan Nikolas: The crown prince of Jast, he recently married Tarley Fareview. He has been tasked with remaining in Kaloma with his new wife in the capital city of New Taras to support Queen Keyanna's transition of power, a stipulation of their treaty.

Lucian (Luc) Uraiahs: Elder twin brother of Nixus Uraiahs. He is the god of light and day, but due to his meddling in his twin's life and inadvertently trapping Nix in a spell, he's been sequestered at his sky-home, Sol, until his father decides his punishment. He is the reason Auri found the enchanted key.

Mattias Fareview: The youngest child and only son of Scarlett and Tomas Fareview. At twenty, he's ready to make his way in the world.

Meera Hollis: Sister to Queen Keyanna, a Princess of Kaloma.

Nixus Uraiahs: The younger twin brother of Lucian Uraiahs, he is the god of dark and night. He fell in love with Auri Fareview when she saved him from a spell where he'd been trapped. Her sacrifice saved him and inadvertently changed the world. During their entrapment, Nix discovered he and Auri were god-yoked.

Olliander Berkman: The King of Jast's prime advisor has been sent to New Taras, Kaloma, to support Queen Keyanna's transition to power.

Ozland Aeluros: The owner of the night club Lazuli in the Lower City of Elcadia.

Poe Demertitus: Goddess of chaos and cousin to Lexa, Lucian, and Nixus, she was instrumental in trapping Nix and keeping him trapped,

making a deal with a demon to sacrifice Lucian and Nixus for power. She was spared by Auri's sacrifice, but has been imprisoned for her trickery.

Scarlett Fareview: Mother of the five Fareview children and wife to Tomas, she is a healer and extremely protective of her family. She has promised her family to share secrets she's been keeping from them.

Tarley Fareview: The second daughter of Scarlett and Tomas Fareview is fiercely independent. Considered the rebellious daughter, she is often at odds with her mother. She saved Lachlan, was asked to marry him by Queen Keyanna for the treaty with Jast, but fell in love with him. Now his wife, she is finally going to leave Sevens.

Tomas Fareview: Father of the five Fareview children and husband to Scarlett, he is the voice of reason with his wife, but also unfailingly keeps her trust by maintaining her secrets.

The Darkling: a magical creature with the ability to shapeshift, it lives on blood and will imprint on its victims, choosing either to kill immediately or satiate (turn them). A darkling has the ability to see magic spells, even those that have been designed to be concealed.

Trevis: The stable boy at the Copper Pot Inn.

The Wizard: A dark sorcerer who is looking for someone named Azleah. When he appeared at the end of In the Shadow of a Hoax, he recognized Tomas—calling him Tom—when they came face-to-face. The wizard controls the darkling.

VOW

White Lies	Sultan + Shepard, The Cut
Birdcage	Novo Amor
Sad Tune	*AK*
I See My Evil	Owsey
Autumn is Here	*AK*
Worthy	St. Finnikin
don't leave me	Desolent
STAY	Franciys
Into the Woods	Second Light
just for the night	yaeow, Rnla

KISS

Dreams in Bloom	*Sol Rising*
We Are in this Together	Ah. BLOOM, Ben Laver
Take Me Higher	yaeow, Rnla
Tender	*Aether*
Free With You	Rnla, yaeow
We Could Have it All	Emmit Fenn
Shelter	Broken Elegance

MEMORY

Trouble in Your Eyes	Yoste
Lost	Forester
Wish I Was Better	Kina, yaeow
Where I Find You	Gray North
Medicine	Boundary Run
everything to me	yaeow
Home	*Kazukii*

denotes instrumental music

AKNOWLEDGEMENTS

Well this book was a f*cking surprise! The colorful language is to denote how surprised I was. I've said from the beginning that this series was going to be four books: Aurielle, Tarley, Brinna, and Jessamine. Then all the sudden, Scarlett had to go and trap her family in a spell, Lucian and Brinna had to have their entire love story happen in a dream, and Nixus had to go and lose his memory. (What in the blazes are you doing, Maci?!?!)

As I sat down to think about Jessamine's story, I knew that I wasn't going to be able to wrap up her story without addressing some major plot points: Scarlett's past, Brinna and Lucian IRL, the magical powers, and Nixus's memory loss. These bits couldn't be done in the final book and have it about Jessamine's love story. That is when the idea of a series of novellas took shape, were written, and came to be (I wrote one for Tarley and Lachlan as well as one for Mattias, but they didn't make the cut for this publication. Maybe they'll drop in a newsletter as an extra soon).

I need to thank some fabulous people. First, Beth, who always helps me see the light when I'm lost in the dark. She is Lucian to my Nixus. Next, Stephanie, who was so supportive as a beta reader! Thank you for your feedback and help in refining these stories. Another critical person is Kate, my amazing editor. This is book number seven together and I am so grateful for your critical eye. Finally, Sara—cover artist extraordinaire—thank you so much for creating such a beautiful doorway to the stories. Your artistic vision has been perfect. I'm so grateful.

Thank you, always, to the readers who mean so much to this series. Readers like Lindsey, Joanna, Willow, Leisa, Maggie, and Mae to name a few of the original supporters when *In the Shadow of a Wish* was a new-born story. You have been champions of this series, and I'm so very grateful. Thank you to everyone who has purchased pre-orders, bought multiple copies in various formats, left a review, shared a post, made a reel, told a friend, bought a book as a gift. I'm so grateful.

Thank you to my husband, who is represented on the page in each story in some way. I love you.

Finally, my faith drives me: I am so thankful that my God, my Lord and Savior, Jesus Christ, and the Holy Spirit are my guides on this wild journey.

The Conclusion to *the* Fareview Fairytales

Publishing 2025

In the Shadow of an Obsession

By Maci Aurora

Jessamine

Jessamine Fareview, first daughter of Scarlett and Tomas Fareview, was in between, trapped like a specter in her own body. For all intents and purposes, she could sense everyone believed her to be asleep, except her mind was actively awake, locked in the silent space of her body. She could hear, smell, think, and feel despite being as blind to the world as the world had been to her.

Before.

Growing up in Sevens, she'd known something was different about her, about them all, though she couldn't identify it, couldn't put words to her thoughts. To put it mildly, her mother wasn't just overprotective but overbearing. Strangely so, and more so with Jessamine than the rest of her siblings. Rarely out of her mother's sight,

Jessamine had learned the healing arts and remedies as her mother's apprentice. And she had a knack for it which had given her a sense of pride.

But there was something strange about the way others interacted with her when she went on a call. It was the way they would look at her, then look away, their eyes skimming past as if they understood she was there, but then would immediately forget.

Jessamine herself struggled to identify what made her unique, made her… well, her. She existed. She felt and loved. She interacted with her family, her sisters, others, only nothing remained to fill her and flesh her out into a wholly unique being. It was as though she were a living, breathing vessel, no more filled than that of an empty vase waiting for flowers.

She suspected it had something to do with the ribbons. Hers had always been different. Her siblings wore red ribbons at their wrists, as did she, but her crimson ribbon was twisted up with a second ribbon, a deep shimmering pink, like that of a pearl, entwined with violet threads. Beautiful, yes, but different. Just like her.

When Auri had returned from the *Great Nap Escapade* without her ribbon, and then Tarley, both with new loves, Jessamine suspected. When her mother refused to answer questions, Jessamine suspected magic was at work. But her suspicions felt locked inside her throat and even if she'd wanted to voice them, she couldn't. As if even when she'd once been awake, she'd been asleep. A living, breathing doll no more or less than the assignments she'd been given by her master—her mother.

Only something had changed—besides being imprisoned in the in-between—because the voices weren't those of her sisters or her parents.

They were strangers. Men.

All but one voice, though she couldn't place him.

Each day—she assumed, because time was strange in this in-between where she existed, moving like both the rush of a river's current but also the slow meander of a viscous, muddy mixture—he would open the box that housed her and take her hand. She couldn't see the box, of course, but she'd come to believe that to be the case, because she could hear the muted voices, hear the creak and groan of something being opened, then feel the gentle warmth of his calloused hand on hers.

Then he would whisper, "I'm here, Jessamine. I'll figure it out. I promise." In the beginning, he would tell her where they were—a manor house—in the home of a sorcerer without a name known as Master. The man with the voice that shimmered with recognition gave her the facts as he understood them. He told her she'd been taken by the sorcerer and told her he'd followed. He would tell her of the sleeping spell, the witch, the broken hedge. He would remind her of her family and that they were waiting. "I'm going to get us out of here," he'd say. "I'll get you home."

She listened to his voice, unsure who he was, only that there was something vaguely familiar about him. As he spoke, she thought of horses and the forest, of the time she'd gone after Tarley. Of the sensation of strong arms encircling her and a sturdy chest against her back. The feel of her heart's pitter patter with the movement of a horse beneath her, of a soft exhale against her neck. Of dancing and dark eyes curled slightly at the corner. She could smell leather and pine, the crispness of an outdoor chill. But time passed, somehow, and the scent of him changed to a springtime forest layered with petrichor, to the summer woods and wildflowers, to the fall forest and the depth of earthen pine, until the crispness of winter cool was on him once more.

Time was passing. She remained locked in. And the voice she longed to hear, whose touch she longed to feel never wavered, but she could hear the weariness in his sigh.

"There's a spell on the manor," he said. "Every time I leave, I forget. It is only when I return from the hunt that I remember. I don't know how to get past it."

She felt his thumb on her wrist, moving back and forth over her skin, felt a keen heat that had begun to intensify each time he touched her.

"I am failing you."

She wished she could comfort him. Wished she could lift her arm, place her hand on his, feel him with her own fingertips. Wished she could thank him for being with her. And if she could, she would assure him they'd figure it out together.

Except she couldn't. She was useless. Locked in the prison of her own body and this spell.

But she could feel his thumb, back and forth across her wrist. And suddenly it hit her.

Her ribbon was gone.

ONE

Atlas

I straighten at the sound at the door of the garage. Being sure to avoid the car hood above me, I grab the blue mechanic's rag to wipe my hands and turn to watch two of my four brothers walk into the shop, their steps echoing against the concrete floor. I wait to hear how the hunt went, watching as they unbuckle and remove their leather harnesses, the weapons clanking as the metal of their knives, daggers, and other assorted weapons clash. Rome is silent but Samson hums. They're both clean, not a drop of gore anywhere.

Rome, the oldest of my brothers, hangs his harness in the cabinet, glances at me. "All good?" His intense, dark eyes bore holes into everything, including mine. His dark brows shift slightly, and that's about as much emotion as he'll offer. Fucking dipshit. But it's nearly impossible to deny Rome a thing due to that damn intensity. Fucker doesn't back down.

"Not really."

"Why not? Something happen?" I hear the concern in his voice, which sounds more like he's pissed. He might be emotionally bankrupt, but he isn't without emotions. They display in two ways: anger and angrier.

"All clear here. Chill out," I say and turn back to the car, releasing the hood so it slams back into place. "It's just being stuck here instead of hunting." My grumbling makes it seem like I'm pouting. Perhaps I am. I hate being left behind.

"Didn't miss much," Samson says as he flops onto an old red couch marred with grease stains, his gear strewn over the cushions next to him instead of put away. He leans his head back on the couch and rolls it to look at me. "A lot of nothing actually. Didn't need four of us. Didn't need two of us."

"And you're getting over an injury," Rome snaps again, over my bitterness. "You're too good a fighter. And if what the Grays have said is right, we need you healthy."

Samson makes a noise from his nose that sounds like he's annoyed. My middle brother is itching for a fight, like always.

"How did it go?" I lean against the car that occupied my hands while they are gone. I'd rather have had a bow at the ready. My four brothers might drive me crazy, but I love them. Being left behind isn't only about me, but because I worry when they're out on a job without me.

"Sammy's right. Nothing. Not a demon in sight." Rome crosses his arms over his chest and scowls, making a huffy noise of disbelief. "The question is where they're hiding. With the summer solstice coming, they're around and will show up, surely." He walks across the shop to a counter where I know he'll find something to keep himself busy. He's always busy. "Luka and Tate back?" he asks.

"Not yet," I reply. "Tate wasn't happy you didn't take him with you."

"Is Tate ever happy with any assignment?" Samson asks with a snicker.

"You're always giving Tate the shit jobs—"

"Being the youngest sucks," Samson quips.

"Checking Grams' property isn't a shit job," Rome snaps, glancing over his shoulder.

Incredulous, I tilt my head and cross my arms over my chest, "Grams could kill a demon with that razor-sharp tongue alone."

Samson laughs. "Isn't that the truth."

Rome looks annoyed—as usual. "But she'd need help if multiples show up." He pulls his phone from his pocket and glances at it. "Bus coming into the Hollow."

Samson and I groan. Buses mean tourists. Obnoxious tourists drag in the demon riffraff hiding among them, and they aren't usually the organized kind, but rather the fledgling demons or the deserters attached to the *taedae*, unsighted humans.

"Not it," Samson says.

"How's that injury?" Rome asks me.

"Not an injury," I repeat. "How many times do I have to say it?"

Rome looks me over, eyes narrowed, as if he can see beyond my skin and bones. "Fine," he relents. "You go into town. Wait for the bus to roll in, see if any demons have hitched a ride." He points at me. "But don't engage, not without backup."

I'm already walking over to the cabinet,

pulling on my harness, sliding a sharpened dagger into a sheath, along with another into my boot. "Me? Engage?" I glance at my bow but leave it, knowing I probably won't need it. Those off the bus are rarely difficult to dispatch. I glance at Rome with a smile. "Never."

Samson laughs.

I shrug into my black leather jacket and grab my helmet before I'm out the door, headed for the heart of town. After driving past Lowry's Gas and Sundries, where the bus stops, and seeing the hulking, metal can is already empty, I ride down Main. I park my bike, cross to the other side, and duck into The Hole in the Wall, a small bar sandwiched between a diner called The Getaway, and a witchy souvenir shop that sells Carran Hollow guidebooks. One of these three establishments is often the first stop for tourists, and thereby their parasitic demons, when they reach town.

My eyes adjust to the dark. There's an older guy playing guitar near the door. The shiny wooden bar is on the left and runs the length of the room. There are a few people lined up along the counter, atop barstools. Booths—mostly empty—line the right wall, and in between is a stretch of space big enough to walk between the two. I've been here before. I have been in every single shop in Carran Hollow, every single home—though the owners haven't known I was there. The Hollow is my town.

The locals glance at me then look away, giving me a wide berth. They might know me. They might know I'm a Black. If they don't, they feel it—that sensation skittering across their skin telling them danger is near. That's all that's needed.

The bartender, Gus, an older guy with a huge mustache, tops off a beer before handing it to a patron. "What can I get you, Black?"

"A shot of whiskey."

He turns to the wall of bottles behind him, selecting one and a shot glass as the bell rings, indicating someone has walked in. I glance at the newcomer since it's never a good idea to be caught unawares. Walking across the room is a woman—twenties—with a duffle slung over her shoulder. She's dressed mostly in black: black jeans with tears at the knees, and a white shirt hidden under a black V-neck sweater, also sporting holes from wear and tear. Her silver hair is shoulder-length and wavy. She's pretty— gorgeous, actually. She's got one of those heart- shaped faces with giant eyes, a pert nose, and full lips, the bottom just a touch fuller than the top. It's too dark to see the color of her eyes, but I've got a pretty good suspicion they're green, because this girl's got an aura gleaming bright green, as bright as if I were standing in front of a flashing neon sign.

My body tenses as she passes, and power hits me—the raw magnetism of it slams into mine, grips my balls before sliding up to my pelvis then racing white-hot up my spine until it hits the back of my head. I blink and grab hold of the counter to keep on my feet.

What the fuck was that?

I was born a Sentinel, have fought with all manner of creatures, fucked a few more, and I've never experienced that reaction in all my twenty-seven years.

But I have an idea.

My calix has finally arrived.

TWO

Ivy

I drop the duffle into the booth of the seedy little bar in the godforsaken fucking town where I'm stuck. I feel strange, like a bright light has erupted on my insides and filled all of them with brilliant light, then cranked up the amps so it's super loud. What the fuck? I follow my bag into the booth and rub my head, taking a deep breath, waiting for the strange sensation to wane.

It doesn't, and I don't have time to fixate on it.

I need to get the fuck out of this town.

I need a fucking map. The stupid bus broke down, and now I need to figure out a way to get another thousand miles to Onyx City. No back- up bus for another week. No rental cars. No ride shares. No train stations—unless I can figure out how to get a ride to one. The closest airport is farther than that.

Fuck.

Ignoring the tingles racing through my body, I dig my phone out of my back pocket and slide it open, pulling up the map of Murrus Province. Carran Hollow is the town where I'm fucking stuck. If I don't fucking get to Onyx—I swallow, trying not to think about it, and start looking for options.

My body heats. I can't afford to suddenly be coming down with something. I need to get to my sister.

"Hey."

I look up from my phone at the shadowy figure at the end of the table. I sigh. "Fuck off."

He—because that's a dude's voice—chuckles. "Figures," he says.

Annoyed, I use my body to deter him, but the energy pulses inside me. I shiver. Dammit. I can't be getting sick.

Fucker doesn't take a hint and slides into the

booth across from me. Only now I can see him, and I fucking hate that my breath stops up for a moment. Dear fucking fuck. He's… fuck. Not only is his voice nice, deep, with a butter-smooth accent, but he's gorgeous. His face is perfect if a bit intense and dark. Dark brows frame dark eyes with thick lashes. His nose is a touch wide and a touch crooked, from fighting, perhaps, and there's a scar across the bridge. His lips are perfectly shaped, proportional to everything on his face. There's ink sliding up his neck from under the collar of his t-shirt. All that rugged beauty is framed by wavy dark hair, short on the sides but longer on top, so strands of it fall across his face.

Fuck me, I think, but say, "What part of *fuck off* wasn't clear?" I look back at my phone but struggle to concentrate between hot as fuck dude across from me and the weird pulsing energy ripping under my skin. As much as I could sit there admiring this asshole's good looks, I don't have the time or the energy, even if I have the inclination.

He has the nerve to laugh again. "You're not from around here."

"Oh. What gave me away?"

"You look like you could use some help."

"Are these your go-to lines?" I scoff and toggle back and forth between schedules, but I blink. I can't seem to concentrate. What the fuck is wrong with me? "I suggest you return to whatever cave you crawled from and find an idiot who will fall for it."

Silence greets me. I'm used to silence, even if I hate it. It's when the voices are the loudest. The longer the silence stretches, I wonder if my words have chased him away. Disappointment slides through me considering that might be the case, because I would have liked him to work a bit harder—which is a stupid thing to think. When I look up, expecting to be disappointed, I'm not. He hasn't left. He's just sitting there in that black leather jacket with those intense dark eyes watching me, as if waiting for something.

I give him a questioning look. "What the fuck do you want?"

"Probably shouldn't say." He smirks, and fuck if that doesn't work for him. Fuck if it doesn't work for me.

Surprised by his audacity and in need of some distance, I sit back so I'm pressed up against the vinyl back of the booth. "Wow."

His grin deepens, and that fucking smile hits me right between my legs so that I have to squeeze my thighs together and adjust in my seat. That tingling sensation slams right into me, right there, as if I were touched, and I'm sure I've got a weird look. His smile widens, and it's one of those smiles that makes promises. I make a frustrated noise, which I swallow because I don't want him knowing he's got something that's working for me.

"Yeah. I mean, I should be a bit more modest, but I've heard that a few times." He leans forward, arms on the table.

I scoff and glance back at my phone, flipping between the map and the next town's schedule. "Unbelievable," I mutter.

"That too."

I can't help but look up at him again, shocked, but I want to laugh for some reason. That's even more off-putting. He's a fucking stranger in a Podunk town who could charm the pants right off me. And it's only been ten fucking minutes. In the course of my twenty-five years, I've come across my share of guys. Smart ones, dumb ones, charmers, alpha assholes, comedians, and pushovers. Some have been kind, most have not, so dealing with dudes is usually the same. But the brass on this one is something else along with... that fucking feeling that has me wanting to... I'm not sure. Moan? Vomit? Strip? Flick my clit? It's maddening.

I clamp down on my reaction, worried now as the sensation shifts, grabbing hold of the back of my neck, sending a message to the rest of me that I might need to run. Only... I don't want to run away. My impulse and the idiotic thought in my head are to run toward smirking, audacious, hottie. Which is stupid and dangerous.

It's me. I'm the stupid idiot from his cave!

"I could help." He looks at my phone.

"Did I ask?" I snap.

He leans back, and it's as if maybe I've finally pushed him off whatever track he'd been taking. He shakes his head. "Fucking hell," he mutters, "it totally fucking figures," and moves as if to leave the booth.

His words are hooks that sink in. *What the fuck does that mean,* I wonder. "I don't know you," I say.

The bell on the door jingles.

He glances at the door and tenses. "Fuck," he says under his breath, having caught sight of something that he obviously doesn't want to see. Then he glances at me, then shrugs. "Don't worry. You will." He stands, and fuck, his form is as gorgeous as the rest of him. He's long and lean. Tall in a way that isn't too much, but just fucking right. I glance at his ass as he leans toward the bar to grab something. His backside is rounded so nicely in those blue jeans that hug his hips perfectly. Not too tight but fitted enough to know that what's underneath is going to be good.

I bite my bottom lip then skim my tongue over the treatment I've given my skin.

He straightens, a helmet in his hands.

A vehicle!

"Hey," I say, scurrying from the booth before he can leave. "You've got a motorcycle." I stand, blocking him from the door.

He isn't looking at me. He's looking at

something over my shoulder. "Yeah," he says, his face tense, his demeanor completely different now.

Fuck. I might have fucked up, I think.

I glance over my shoulder at a couple of guys standing near the entrance. They look feral, red-faced, and sweaty, as if they need a fix and quick. I ignore them and turn back to hottie.

"You're right. I could use some help. The bus I was on broke down and I really need to get... somewhere else. And there's no way out of this town for another week. I need to find a ride to the nearest bus depot." I don't know what I'm doing. This is a fucking stranger, and what exactly am I suggesting? Stupid. I shake my head.

The door rings again.

I turn and glance over my shoulder. Where there were two feral, red-faced men, now there are four, and weirdly, they all kind of look the same. The second two are an amalgamation of the first two, with their ruddy features and hungry gazes.

"I'd love to talk about that ride," he says, pushing me behind him. "But maybe we can do it somewhere else."

"My bag!" I exclaim.

He leans into the booth, grabs the strap, and pulls it from the seat, hoisting it over his head and settling it on his shoulder, all the while keeping his eyes glued to the front of the room.

I want to yank my bag away from him so it's

safely back in my possession, but what was four men at the front of the bar is now eight. "What the hell?" I say, though it comes out like a whisper.

The hottie takes a step back into me, pushing me backward. "Out the back."

The mass of men at the front of the bar follows. "We'll take the calix," they all say in unison, which is creepy as fuck.

"Sorry. No can do," the audacious hottie says. "She's mine."

"What the fuck?" I snap. My first impulse is to duck around this guy for his presumptuous statement, but there's a pack of frightening- looking men between him and the door talking gibberish, and I have a horrible feeling that it has something to do with me.

Out the back.

Only he has my duffle and I need that.

"Go," he says. "As much as I would like to think I can take eight of them. It's going to be sixteen soon, and I don't like those odds."

"You have my bag. I can't leave my bag."

"I'll give it to you outside," he says between clenched teeth. "Now go."

"Listen. I don't like being told—"

"I don't give a fuck what you like right now. Get the fuck out the back," he snaps. The domineering edge of his voice snaps at my spine with something altogether pleasurable, despite the situation, and while normally I'd be telling him where he can take his bullshit, I listen, hurrying out the back of the bar. I burst through the metal door out into the alleyway, where I stumble through the door and catch myself against the pavement. When I look up, I freeze.

"What the fuck?" The words expel on a breath. I'm surrounded by a group of giant men, except they only have one eye. Then I scream.

Publishing in June 2024

ABOUT THE AUTHOR

Maci Aurora has been writing stories since she was a child. At eleven, she fell in love with reading Sunfire Historical Romances about girls who made a difference in their lives while falling in love. When she discovered Lavyrle Spencer and Judith McNaught, their novels cemented her own journey to tell stories about love. Since then, she's been forever lost between the pages of a book as both a reader and a writer. While the Fareview Fairytales series is the first published under her pen name, she's written several contemporary books as CL Walters. Currently, she's busy writing the conclusion to the Fareview Fairytales series and working on some new ideas for the future. For the most up-to-date news about Maci's upcoming releases, fun extras, and behind-the-scenes bits, sign up for her newsletter on her website www.maciaurora.com.